'*Snare* is a smart, ambitious, and hugely satisfying thriller, striking in its originality and written with all the style and poise of an old hand. Lilja is destined for Scandi super stardom' Eva Dolan

'Clear your diary. As soon as you begin reading *Snare*, you won't be able to stop until the final page' Michael Wood

'An emotional suspense rollercoaster on a par with *The Firm*, as desperate, resourceful, profoundly lovable characters scheme against impossible odds' Alexandra Sokoloff

'For a small island, Iceland produces some extraordinary writers, and Lilja is one of the best. *Snare* is an enthralling tale of love and crime that stays with you long after you have turned the last page' Michael Ridpath

'Zips along, with tension building and building ... thoroughly recommended' James Oswald

'Crisp, assured and nail-bitingly tense, *Snare* is an exceptional read, cementing Lilja's place as one of Iceland's most outstanding crime writers' Yrsa Sigurðardóttir

'Sleek and taut, *Snare* delivers a breathtaking blend of Nordic Noir and high-stakes thriller. Not to be missed!' Crime by the Book

'*Snare* will ensnare you' *Marie Claire*

'Lilja Sigurdardottir delivers a diabolically efficient thriller with an ultrarealistic plot ... We cannot wait for Sonja's next adventure' *L'Express*

'The suspense is gripping' *Avantages*

Snare

ABOUT THE AUTHOR

Icelandic crime writer Lilja Sigurðardóttir was born in the town of Akranes in 1972 and was raised in Mexico, Sweden, Spain and Iceland. An award-winning playwright, Lilja has written four crime novels, with *Snare*, the first in a new series, hitting bestseller lists worldwide. The film rights have been bought by Palomar Pictures in California. Lilja has a background in education and in recent years has worked in evaluation and quality control for preschools. She lives in Reykjavík with her partner. Follow Lilja on Twitter @lilja1972 and on her website: www.liljawriter.com.

ABOUT THE TRANSLATOR

Quentin Bates escaped English suburbia as a teenager, jumping at the chance of a gap year working in Iceland. For a variety of reasons, the gap year stretched to become a gap decade, during which time he went native in the north of Iceland, acquiring a new language, a new profession as a seaman and a family, before decamping en masse for England. He worked as a truck driver, teacher, netmaker and trawlerman at various times before falling into journalism largely by accident. He is the author of a series of crime novels set in present-day Iceland (*Frozen Out, Cold Steal, Chilled to the Bone, Winterlude, Cold Comfort* and *Thin Ice*), which have been published worldwide. He is the translator of Ragnar Jónasson's Dark Iceland series, available from Orenda Books. Visit him at www.graskeggur.com or on Twitter @graskeggur.

Snare

Lilja Sigurðardóttir

Translated by Quentin Bates

**ORENDA
BOOKS**

Orenda Books
16 Carson Road
West Dulwich
London SE21 8HU
www.orendabooks.co.uk

First published in Icelandic as *Gildran* by Forlagid in 2015
First published in English by Orenda Books in 2017
Copyright © Lilja Sigurðardóttir, 2015
English translation copyright © Quentin Bates, 2017
Map copyright © Martin Lubikowski

ISBN 978-1-910633-80-9
eISBN 978-1-910633-81-6

The publication of this translation has been made possible through the financial support of

🗹 ICELANDIC LITERATURE CENTER

Typeset in Garamond by MacGuru Ltd

Printed and bound by CPI Group (UK) Ltd, Croydon CR0 4YY

SALES & DISTRIBUTION

In the UK and elsewhere in Europe:
Turnaround Publisher Services
Unit 3, Olympia Trading Estate
Coburg Road,
Wood Green
London
N22 6TZ
www.turnaround-uk.com

In the USA and Canada:
Trafalgar Square Publishing
Independent Publishers Group
814 North Franklin Street
Chicago, IL 60610
USA
www.ipgbook.com

In Australia and New Zealand:
Affirm Press
28 Thistlethwaite Street
South Melbourne VIC 3205
Australia
www.affirmpress.com.au

For details of other territories, please contact *info@orendabooks.co.uk*

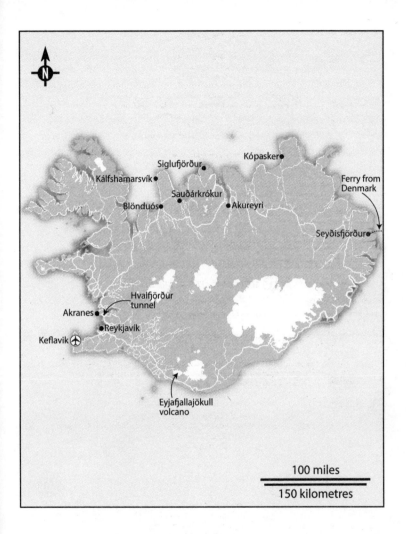

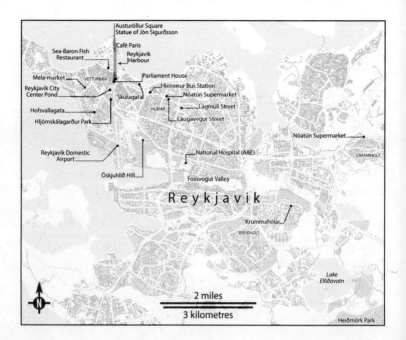

Austuröllur Square
Statue of Jón Sigurðsson
Café París
Reykjavik Harbour
Sea-Baron Fish Restaurant
Parliament House
Mela-market
VESTURBÆR
Hlemmur Bus Station
Reykjavík City Center Pond
Skúlagata
Nóatún Supermarket
Lágmúli Street
HLÍÐAR
Hofsvallagata
Laugavegur Street
Hljómskálagarður Park
Nóatún Supermarket
Reykjavík Domestic Airport
GRAFARHOLT
National Hospital (A&E)
Öskjuhlíð Hill
Fossvogur Valley
R e y k j a v i k
Krummahólar
BREIÐHOLT
Lake Elliðavatn
N
2 miles
3 kilometres
Heiðmörk Park

Pronunciation guide

Atli Þór – Atli Thor
Austurvöllur
  – Oyst-uur-voet-luur
Breiðholt – Breith-holt
Davíð – Dav-ith
Dísa – Die-sa
Eyjafjallajökull
  – Ey-ya-fyat-la-jeok-utl
Glerártorg – Gler-owr-tirg
Guðrún – Guth-ruun
Gunnarsdóttir
  – Gunnar-s-dottir
Hallgrímur – Hatl-griem-oor
Hljómskálagarður – Hl-yowm-
  scowl-a gar-thur
Húni Þór Gunnarsson – Hueni
  Thor Gunnar-son
Iðnó – Ith-no
Jói – Yo-ee
Jón Jónsson – Joen Joen-son
Jón Sigurðsson – Joen
  Sig-urth-son

José – As in Spanish
Kauphöllin – Koyp-hoet-lin
Keflavík – Kepla- viek
Kópasker – Keop-a-sker
Krummahólar
  – Krumma-hoel-ar
Lágmúli – Low-muel-ee
Libbý – Libb-ee
Listhús – List-huus
Margeirsdóttir – Mar-gayr-s-
  dottir
María – Maria
Mjódd – Mjow-dd
Ólafur – Ow-laf-oor
Öskjuhlíð – Usk-yu-hlith
Reykjavík – Reyk-ya-viek
Ríkharður Rúnarsson – Riek-
  harth-uur Ruenar-son
Smáíbúðir – Smow-ieb-uuth-ir
Tómas – Teo-mas
Valdís – Val-dees

Icelandic has a couple of letters that don't exist in other European languages and which are not always easy to replicate. The letter ð is generally replaced with a d in English, but we have decided to use the Icelandic letter to remain closer to the original names. Its sound is closest to the hard *th* in English, as found in *th*us and ba*th*e.

Icelandic's letter *þ* is reproduced as *th*, as in *Th*orgeir, and is equivalent to a soft *th* in English, as in *th*ing or *th*ump.

The letter *r* is generally rolled hard with the tongue against the roof of the mouth.

In pronouncing Icelandic personal and place names, the emphasis is placed on the first syllable.

November to December 2010

1

There was no coffee left in her paper cup. Sonja stood still by the circular table and pretended to sip through the hole in the plastic lid, watching the check-in line for the flight to Iceland. Kåstrup Airport was quiet at this late hour with only a few airlines still having flights scheduled, so the sound of 'Jingle Bells' sung in Danish could be heard, tinkling from the café's loudspeakers. The Samsonite suitcase brochure was on the table in front of her and she turned the pages occasionally, although there was no need. She knew it off by heart by now and clearly recalled those pictures she had marked the last time she had been through this airport.

There were still two hours until her flight departed, but Sonja was already mentally preparing herself to postpone travelling and use the seat she had booked for the next morning instead. That was plan B. It made no difference whether she travelled that night or the next morning, anyway; all the preparations remained in place. She always had a fallback position and often postponed travelling, or took another route when things didn't work out, or if she had a hunch that something was wrong. There was never anybody waiting for her at the other end and she had become accustomed to staying at airport hotels.

She was just coming to terms with having to put plan B in action, when she saw the woman come into the terminal building. She was walking fast, but slowed her pace as she took in how short the line for check-in was. Sonja could almost hear her sigh of relief. The woman was tall, with typical Icelandic mousy-blonde hair, and as Sonja joined the line behind her, she felt a stab of guilt in her belly about what she had planned for her. This complete stranger had never done her any harm. Under other circumstances Sonja would have happily killed an hour chatting to her while they waited at the airport. But this was no time for guilt. The woman was exactly right. No need for plan B now. It was her silver Samsonite case that made her so perfect, and the fact she had a smaller bag on her shoulder, which meant she would be checking in the case as hold luggage. It was just as well that Icelanders were so style conscious, even when it came to suitcases.

The line inched forward and Sonja watched the woman as a reminder not to leave luggage unattended echoed through the airport's loudspeakers. The woman appeared to have her mind on other things, as she seemed either to have not heard the announcement or thought it didn't apply to her. She didn't even glance to one side to check on her case, as most people did instinctively in response to the announcement. Just as well she wasn't the worrying type; it only made Sonja's job easier.

Sonja smiled as a family joined the line behind her. This was going to be almost too easy.

'Go in front if you like,' she offered.

'You're sure?' the man asked, already manoeuvring a pushchair containing a child in front of Sonja.

'People with kids ought to go first,' she replied amiably. 'How old are they?'

'Two and seven,' said the man, and his answer was accompanied by the fond smile that fathers invariably have when they mention their children. Sonja had often tried to analyse this smile and always came to the conclusion that its main ingredient was pride. She wondered if Adam still smiled that way when he spoke about Tómas. It was two years since she had last seen Adam, other than by chance. These days their only communications were short text messages concerning what time Tómas could be collected and when he should be returned.

She watched the family shift their baggage and children forwards as the line moved along. It felt like decades since she and Adam had travelled abroad with Tómas as a small child, loaded down with luggage, and constantly concerned about finding somewhere with changing facilities or being the victim of some sharp-eyed pickpocket. Back then they had often been stressed by what now seemed trivial details;

they'd had no idea how precious it was to have nothing serious to worry about. The petty things they had allowed to worry them now seemed so unimportant – ever since Sonja had been caught in the snare.

She was struck by how these past regrets were still so painful. Seeing children often sent her on a downward spiral like this. The older boy was seven, but was easily as big as Tómas – or the size he was when she had last seen him. He must have grown since. He seemed to add a few inches every month at the moment.

The blonde with the Samsonite case had reached the check-in desk. Having the family in front of her gave Sonja the chance to make sure that the woman's silver case was checked in and slid onto the conveyor belt without a hitch. It was soon Sonja's turn at the desk and she felt her heart begin to pound. When she had first been caught in the snare, she had felt guilty about how much she enjoyed the fluttering heartbeat, the tension, and then the feeling of well-being that followed, but now she knew there was no other way to do this than by riding the excitement, harnessing the adrenaline rush and using it as a means to an end. It was those who couldn't take the pressure who trembled, their eyes flashing from side to side, and this was what got them caught. Those who stayed the distance were the ones like Sonja: quiet people with middle-class looks and a high stress threshold. And it didn't do any harm to be smart and cautious. Being cautious paid off.

'No baggage?' the check-in attendant asked.

Sonja shook her head and smiled. She handed over her passport and once she had it back in her hand with her boarding pass, she could almost hear her own heartbeat in her ears, like the regular beat of a drum.

2

Tómas folded two T-shirts and put them in his bag. Then he decided to take the orange pullover his mother had given him as well. His father said it was a girly colour, but Tómas and his mother didn't agree as they both knew it was the colour that the Dutch football team always played in. Dad knew nothing about football, he was only interested in golf. Tómas was actually relieved about this, because the few times his father had come to football practice, right after his mother had moved to Reykjavík, he had stood on the touchline yelling ridiculous instructions: tackle this defender or that one; stop kicking like a cripple; and not to run like an old woman. So Tómas preferred to go on his own. Sometimes, when there was a tournament, he would see his mother among the spectators, waving and giving him a thumbs-up. He could see from her smile that she was proud of him and that she loved to see him running about the pitch, even though he never scored a goal. He hoped that one day Dad would let Mum go with him to football tournaments so she wouldn't have to sneak in and watch him from a distance. She could be like all the other mums, with a snack in a box, and giving him a hug at half-time.

Tómas took his Yahtzee set and put it in his bag. He had asked his mother last month if she wanted to play, but she said that she didn't have a set. Now he was going to fix that – he was going to leave it with her. Nobody at Dad's house ever played it, anyway.

'You're not packing already?' His father's voice was irritable, as it always was when it was anything to do with his mother or weekends with her.

'I just wanted to be ready,' Tómas said, closing his case so that his father wouldn't see the game or the orange pullover. Every time his father took an interest in the contents of his case, there was a problem. Tómas found it was easier to pack early, so that when his mother came to collect him, he could give Dad a quick kiss, say 'I'm ready,' and run for the car.

3

At the security gate Sonja took off her belt and coiled it into the tray with her overcoat and shoes. The belt buckle was the only piece of metal in her clothing. She had already taken off her earrings and pulled off her rings and stowed them in the pocket of her overcoat. She knew there was no need for this but she wanted to avoid any risk of a body search, even though the packet was secured between her legs, and the security staff would never go as far as her crotch in a search. Being cautious paid off; no harm in being a hundred per cent certain. She held her breath as she went through the metal detector even though she knew it wouldn't squeal. She gave the security staff a quick smile and then took her bag off the conveyor belt. There was nothing suspicious in there, just passport, boarding pass, lip salve, a powder compact, a comb, an open packet of chewing gum, a creased, dog-eared paperback, and the Samsonite brochure.

Sonja watched the family in front disappear into the departure lounge then hurried in the opposite direction, towards the luggage shop. The row of shops was quiet, and she had a moment's panic as she saw that many of them were already closed. She knew that airport shops opened at odd times, depending on the number of travellers, but plan A was in motion now and there was no way back. This had to go smoothly. She walked as fast as the packet in her crotch would let her, taking a deep breath of relief and feeling an almost narcotic high sweep through her as she saw the luggage shop was still open. She said 'good evening' to the sales girl and looked quickly over the shelves. There it was, in a corner at the bottom: the titanium Samsonite cabin case. Sonja lifted it from the shelf and shook her head as the sales girl pointed out that there was a newer model available at a better price. This case was the right one.

Once she'd paid for the case, Sonja took it to the ladies' toilets and locked herself into a large cubicle intended for mothers and babies. She opened the case, scratched off the price sticker and put her handbag in the case, leaving everything inside it but her passport and boarding pass, the paperback and her wallet. That meant there was nothing in the case that could be linked to her. Then she pulled up her narrow skirt, rolled down her tights and pants, and retrieved the packet from between her legs. It was damp with sweat, so she wiped it off with a tissue before putting it into the case's zipped side pocket. Now she just needed to fill it with junk.

Leaving the toilet, she headed back to the shops and walked along the row, looking out for bulky items to fill the case with. As usual, she thought of Tómas. There was always something Christmassy about Denmark, maybe because many Icelandic Christmas traditions came from there, but she wasn't in the mood for the festivities yet, so she passed the decorations and special gifts by. Instead, she bought Tómas a teddy bear emblazoned with a Danish flag, a big tin of biscuits decorated with pictures of the Danish royal family and a giant bag of little chocolates that he could give out to his friends at his birthday party. At the till she added a striped T-shirt and a magazine with footballer stickers she knew he'd like.

Outside the shop she sat on a bench, and by the time she had packed everything in it, the case was full. Sonja stood up and wheeled it behind her to the perfume shop, as it went without saying that a woman passing through an airport should treat herself to something.

Sonja's favourite moment on these trips was the aircraft roaring towards take-off. Maybe it was the awesome power of the engines as they forced her helplessly back into her seat, or the knowledge that she had made it safely through one more airport. Or maybe it was because ahead of her was a relaxed trip through the sky, outside anyone's jurisdiction. She popped a piece of gum in her mouth and put the paperback into the pocket on the back of the seat in front before going through the options on the screen to see if the European flights were showing any new movies. The choice only changed once a month, and as she flew every couple of weeks, she'd often seen them all already. She had, so this time she'd read. The aircraft was quiet now; the flight attendants hadn't begun serving meals yet. Sonja leaned into the gangway to see how many hands were tightly gripping armrests. It was strange to think that she had once been scared of flying herself. But that had been before all this had started.

4

Bragi pulled the knot of his tie tight and ran a comb through his stone-grey hair. He always relaxed when he arrived at work, as if a burden had been lifted from his shoulders. He couldn't understand people who were reluctant to turn up for work, and he was always irritated by the younger customs officers' eagerness for time off. He enjoyed every minute of his job. There was always plenty to be done, and even a late shift on a quiet night could spring a surprise. It was unbelievable, the things people tried to smuggle in. Just last week he had stopped a shifty character who turned out to have several hundred live frogs in plastic containers in his luggage; and last month there had been the woman with that huge cheese hidden under her clothes. The cheese was made from unpasteurised milk, so Bragi had no choice but to confiscate it, writing out a fine ticket for the woman, who made sure she gave him a piece of her mind as he did so. But those were just the weirdos, and they weren't such a problem compared with the more serious, professional smugglers. Much had changed in his thirty years with the Directorate of Customs, though. Back when he started it had been mainly beer and a little hash that people tried to sneak past customs; that and ham sausage. It was as if Icelanders back then developed a collective madness for ham sausage as soon as they left the country.

These days you could buy Danish ham sausage in any supermarket, it was legal to bring beer into the country and hash smuggling had given way to harder drugs. So now, much of their work involved working closely with the police and their analysts, who monitored the movements of suspects as they left and entered the country. Yet, despite all the infra-red gear, CCTV and sniffer dogs, the smugglers always seemed a step ahead. He couldn't understand why people complained about the police using pre-emptive warrants to investigate potential criminal activity; he felt it was perfectly acceptable in the circumstances. He and all the customs officers were aware there were travellers who were constantly up to something dubious, but neither they nor the police could nail them down. It seemed that the dope business was able to adjust to changing times. He had a strong feeling that these days the small-time mules were no longer trusted; instead they were used as decoys – sent through customs with a few grams, to draw attention away from the real carriers with the large amounts. And the people who were bringing in these serious shipments weren't the junkie kids who were being served up as sacrifices; they had to be ordinary people. Bragi punched his card into the time clock and the click gave him a comfortable feeling of well-being. The time clock had come with them from the old airport building. It was a constant, while everything else around it had changed.

The airport was quiet, with only scheduled flights due to arrive that evening and into the night; Amsterdam, London, Copenhagen. However, an unusually virulent flu epidemic had left them short-handed, so Bragi decided not to make any spot checks that night. There had been nothing flagged up as suspicious by the analysts, so it looked to be an ordinary Tuesday-night shift. There were two officers in the baggage hall, and he sent the young temporary girl, whose name he failed to remember, off to make coffee while he took his place by the window to watch the recent arrivals coming down the staircase.

The crowd walked past it in its usual way, and he reflected, not for the first time, how similar people were to sheep when they moved in a herd. He observed the flow without concentrating on anyone in par-ticular, instead waiting for any warning signs – someone who stood out, who moved out of sync with the rest of the group; anyone looking anxious. As usual, the flow of people divided at the bottom of the steps, with around two-thirds heading for the duty-free shop and the rest going straight to the carousels. As people began to pick up their bags he tried to gauge how many there were for each person; but there didn't seem to be anyone with too much luggage, apart from families with children, of course. With the state the economy had been in since the crash he couldn't blame people for stocking up on cheap children's clothes when they went abroad. One family had eight bags – heavy ones, clearly – but he let them pass through with their sleepy children.

If he were honest with himself, though, he just couldn't be bothered to stop them.

Tonight nobody stood out from the crowd. The arrivals hall filled up – with tourists, mostly, and a few regular customers, too, people who travelled frequently. These were faces he recognised: the President's wife; a violinist who flew to London every week; the good-looking woman with the overcoat, who must be working overseas as she travelled several times a month. She always caught his eye – a petite woman with a glamorous quality about her, like a film star. Every time he saw her he wondered if that was why she was so smartly dressed or if there were some other reason.

It was all much as usual, there was nothing out of the ordinary. Bragi grunted to himself in satisfaction. He was exactly where he belonged and he had every intention of staying here as long as he possibly could. They could make all the fuss they wanted about retirement. He was going nowhere.

5

As soon as Sonja stepped off the aircraft at Keflavík, her heart began to pound. Having felt perfectly relaxed on the flight, she now had the feeling that her chest was ready to burst. She often wondered where the police would wait to pick her up if they were ever to find out about her. She always half expected that it would be right here, on the gangway, although customs would be a more likely place. In reality it wasn't until you passed through customs that you entered the country. She had no idea why these thoughts flew through her mind every time she landed, as there was nobody who knew of her movements; she had told nobody when she would be arriving with the goods and she always worked alone; completely alone. Those were the terms she had insisted on when she had first become tangled up in all this, if they could be called terms. It wasn't as if she had been in any position to set any terms. But she had told them that she had to do things her own way, and, for more than a year now, they had been satisfied with the results. The goods were delivered in the required week, and nothing had ever gone wrong. And they knew they could trust her completely, because of Tómas. Because they knew where Tómas lived.

The walkway was important. This was where there was CCTV, so it was important to do nothing suspicious; no going to the toilets right after leaving the aircraft and no sitting down to rearrange any hand luggage. And there should definitely be no looking around or indicating that you knew where the cameras might be. There was nothing wrong with being a little stressed before departure, but not after landing. And all this had to be achieved without looking too stiff or rushed. The best thing was to walk briskly along the walkway, yawn a few times to look suitably tired after the flight, stop maybe once to tie a shoelace, and be sure to greet happily any old friend you might meet along the way.

Sonja took on her persona on the walkway, and it was for this reason that it never seemed to her to be quite long enough. She glanced at the first advertising poster she came to, not to look at the advert itself, but to check her reflection in the glass. She ticked off the dark, narrow skirt, the white blouse and the woollen overcoat. She was an executive, a businesswoman, travelling for work. She bent over to adjust the right heel of her tights; it had twisted slightly when she had put her shoes back on, having kicked them off during the flight. These shoes were Italian leather, glamorous without being overly sexy, the kind that any woman in the business world would wear.

She straightened up and continued walking, rehearsing her cover story as she went: she ran her own company, SG Software. It was small but was doing well – active both in Iceland and abroad. She mainly offered consultancy work, but also system maintenance – all this information could be seen on her company website. When she was doing well, she could almost believe in the alter ego she had created for herself, but other times she wanted to stop at the end of the walkway and look into the eyes of her own unremarkable self, the woman who had never done any kind of business, the woman who had commissioned someone to create a fake website, the woman who couldn't, in fact, do anything.

Tonight, though, Sonja could feel the self-confident aura around her. Near the end of the long walkway she increased her pace in order to keep the blonde woman in sight, and was relieved to see her heading for the duty-free shop. Sonja took her place close to the start of the baggage carousel, knowing that soon enough there would be a crowd of people with trolleys and bags who would shield her from the customs window she knew overlooked the baggage hall.

The blonde woman's Samsonite case didn't show up until a crowd of people were already gathered, jostling to get to their baggage. Sonja pulled the case off the carousel and put it next to her own, identical case, as if trying to decide which was hers. Finally she put her own case back on the conveyor. Then she went to the duty-free shop and bought a few items – just for show, finding herself in the line, a few places behind the blonde woman, who seemed to be stocking up with a year's worth of sweets.

While Sonja paid for her purchases, she saw that the blonde woman had had time to collect her bag. Sonja watched her stride purposefully towards the customs gate, untroubled by what she might be carrying. Sonja followed behind her, relaxed and secure knowing what wasn't in her own luggage. The arrivals hall was crowded with people, as always at this time of night. Passengers crossing the Atlantic were increasingly choosing to break their journey with a couple of days' stopover in Iceland. Many Icelanders were amazed that travellers might want to spend a few days there in the depths of winter, but Sonja thought that clear, cold nights alive with dancing northern lights were the perfect reason.

Sonja couldn't see the woman with the mousy-blonde hair anywhere in the crowd. She hurried as fast as she could through the building and out into the car park. The woman didn't seem to have come through the left exit, so Sonja ran as fast as her shoes would let her around the building to the right exit. There she caught sight of her with a man who seemed to have come to collect her.

'Excuse me!' Sonja called. 'I'm sorry, but I think we have the wrong bags.'

The woman stared at her in surprise and then at the suitcase the man was pulling behind him for her. 'What?' she asked in confusion, not seeming to have understood.

'I think you took my bag off the carousel, and I took yours,' Sonja explained with a cheerful smile.

'Oh my God!' the woman yelped. 'I'm so sorry!'

She took the handle of the case from the man and began a flustered account of not having been thinking straight when she collected it from the carousel. Her boyfriend leaned forwards and looked at the label on the woman's case before handing Sonja hers.

He's the same as I am, Sonja thought. *He wants to be sure.*

She waved amicably to the couple as she walked towards the long-term car park where her car was waiting for her, covered with a thin layer of the volcanic ash that still hung heavy in the air of southern Iceland following the Eyjafjallajökull eruption a few months before.

6

Tómas wept silently under his duvet. It was strange how intensely he missed his mother the closer he drew to meeting her again. The waiting was just so hard. It was only two days until Friday but it felt a whole lifetime away. Everything was ready. His packed bag was under the bed. He had even fetched his passport from the living room and hidden it under the false bottom of his case, just as she had shown him. It was their secret. He didn't really know why his mother always wanted him to bring his passport; she just said she felt more secure if he had it with him. It was safer if his passport stayed with him, she said.

'Good night, Tómas!' his father called around the bedroom door, and Tómas mumbled a reply from beneath the bedclothes, hoping his father wouldn't hear the catch in his voice.

Dad sat on the end of the bed and pulled the duvet from over his face.

'You're crying, son?' he asked. 'What's the matter?'

'Nothing,' Tómas, answered, wiping his nose.

'Is it a problem at school?'

'No.'

'Something wrong at football? Somebody been teasing you?'

'No.'

Tómas shook his head and looked at the wall behind his father's head in the hope that the questions would stop. Dad shouldn't ask them; he certainly wouldn't want to hear the truthful answer. He wouldn't thank Tómas for saying that he missed his mother and wanted to be with her all the time.

His father put a hand under the duvet and rubbed his leg, muttering that everything would be fine and he was just tired. He should get to sleep and everything would be better in the morning. Dad tried to do his best. He did pretty much everything that dads are supposed to do. But although he would sometimes rub his legs, it was as if he could never make real contact with him.

7

Sonja took a longer route home than was necessary, to be sure that nobody was following her on the drive into Reykjavík from the airport at Keflavík, past the featureless lava fields and the aluminium smelter on the edge of town. She went via the streets of Hafnarfjörður lined with old-fashioned, timber-framed houses, then headed back to the main road and took a right turn, which took her near IKEA. She had just passed Iceland's favourite retail outlet, decked with Christmas lights, when a shower of hail rattled on the car's roof. She wondered if this might be the precursor to a blizzard, but the downpour ended with the same suddenness as it had begun, and Sonja again turned off the main road, this time into the Heiðmörk Park. She drove slowly along the narrow lanes, wondering idly how much damage the birch branches that scraped against the car's sides were doing to the paintwork.

As Sonja pulled up outside the shabby block where she rented an apartment after her long round-about journey home, she saw Agla's car was already there. She really had a knack for turning up at the wrong time. Sonja parked as Agla was getting out of her car and they met on the steps of the block.

'I've missed you,' Agla said, kissing her.

Sonja could smell the booze on her breath. It was no surprise. Agla never showed up unless she'd had a drink or two.

'You drove here drunk?' Sonja asked as they climbed the stairs to her apartment.

'I had a drink after work, and then I started to miss you.'

'Drinks, you mean, judging by the smell,' Sonja said, putting her key in the lock.

Agla followed her in, shrugged off her coat and dropped it on the hall floor.

'Come here.' She pulled Sonja to her and her hands slipped inside Sonja's clothes.

'I need to sort stuff out after the trip...' Sonja protested, but Agla interrupted.

'Don't talk shit,' she ordered. 'Kiss me.'

Sonja gave in and for a moment she wondered whether or not to break her routine and keep the case with her in the apartment overnight. She could jump into bed with Agla right now and deal with it in the morning. Surely her rigid safety measures were overkill? They probably bolstered her feeling of security more than they reduced the chance of her being arrested. Just as she switched cars regularly and changed the way she carried the goods, so she had a rule of keeping nothing at home and showering and changing clothes straight after handling the gear. But she had promised herself to do everything to make sure this worked out. A careless slip because she couldn't keep her hands off Agla wasn't an option. She had burned her fingers once before, badly.

'Get into bed and wait for me,' she said, pushing Agla away. 'I need a quick shower.'

Once Agla had disappeared into the bedroom, Sonja picked up her keys and the Samsonite case and quietly opened the flat door. On tiptoes, she descended the carpeted stairs to the basement, where the flats' storage areas were. However, once there, she walked past her own storage area, and moved on to the one owned by the couple from the third floor who were spending the year in Spain. The smallest key on her ring opened the lock. She pushed the case into the full-to-bursting space and clicked the lock shut again. This was another of her precautions to minimise risk. If the police were to call that night, then there would be no case to be found in her flat or in her basement storage. It had been convenient when the people up on the third floor had rented out their flat but not the storage space. Sonja had sawn off their padlock and replaced it with a new one, giving her a safe hiding place not directly linked to her.

She jogged softly back up the stairs and into her flat, shutting the door quietly behind her. She undressed quickly in the bathroom and stood under the shower. By the time she crawled into bed, Agla was lying on her side, already snoring. Sonja made herself comfortable against the warmth of her body and closed her eyes. This was as good as it could get, lying close to her, deeply breathing in the aroma of her hair.

8

Sonja woke suddenly the next morning to find Agla trying to slide out of bed without waking her.

'Where do you think you're going?' she asked, catching her arm and pulling Agla towards her. She wasn't going to let her get away with this. She had done it too many times – turning up in the evening drunk and full of passion, and sneaking off in the morning without a word.

Sonja put out a hand and smoothed down Agla's hair, which stuck out in all directions. It was coarse, unlike her own hair, and Sonja wondered if that was because Agla dyed it blonde or if it had always been that way. Agla always denied that her hair was dyed, although there was no mistaking those roots. But Sonja had no intention of having an argument about it, forcing Agla to admit that her genuine hair colour was anything other than what it first seemed. There was so much else that she would have liked Agla to be more open about than the trivial matter of her genuine hair colour: being more willing to display some feelings, for example – lower her defences and show the depth of emotion that had to be somewhere inside her. She had to have some feelings, although she kept them quiet, otherwise she wouldn't keep climbing into Sonja's bed, bringing her gifts and calling at night to find out where she was.

On the other hand, there were the clues that hinted Agla was less than serious about their relationship: the shamefaced looks in the mornings; the days when Sonja heard nothing from her; the snort of derision she'd give every time Sonja suggested that Agla might be a lesbian as well.

Sonja hated the pattern that had developed, but since she had been caught in the snare she had no option but to live her life differently. So it was convenient, in fact, that Agla had no interest in anything permanent – remained unwilling to commit to a proper relationship. For Sonja it was a relief not to have to be mindful of anyone's welfare but her son's. The snare was wound round her tightly enough, without Agla adding further complications to her life.

Sonja rolled onto her back and pulled Agla down on top of her. She liked it that Agla was bigger and heavier than she was, pressing her down into the mattress.

'Wait,' Agla said, reaching to twitch the curtain closed, shutting out the little light that made its way in. She never liked to have light in the bedroom, preferring darkness for their lovemaking. Sonja had once lit a candle on the nightstand, but noticed that Agla avoided looking into her eyes. After that she accepted the need for darkness. It was a refuge of sorts, from the shame that she knew plagued Agla, as well as from her own fear.

9

Bragi was enjoying his walk in the cool morning. A rare tranquillity seemed to have settled over the western district of the city, and he wished that Valdís could be there to enjoy it with him. The dark-grey render on the walls of the houses in this part of town glittered as the lights of passing cars flashed across them, their studded winter tyres rattling on the street as they swept past. Most people were at work by now, even though it was still dark. At this time of year mornings were depressingly gloomy and there was little hope of much daylight before midday.

He and Valdís had walked a great deal together in the last few years, even after she had started to lose her way. Then he had guided her through the streets, pointing out details that caught his eye – an intriguing moss pattern on a wall, a cat hiding under a car, rust-red leaves that filled the streets on gusty autumn days.

Today he would be able to see her twice. By visiting early it shouldn't be too obvious that he was returning again later in the day, as by then the shifts would have changed. Nobody would look at him with those pitying glances that said there was no need to come more than once a day, that there was no need to be there so often. He knew well enough that he didn't need to; he simply wanted to come. He wanted to be either at work or with her. He hated being alone at home.

When he arrived she was sitting at the breakfast table. He sat next to her, helping himself to a cup of coffee.

'Hæ, my love,' he said.

'Hello,' she mumbled back, looking up sharply.

It was an ordinary conversation between a normal couple – almost. Maybe a little dry, between a couple with a long history; it was not the way it had been between them before her illness had taken hold. She had never greeted him without a smile, without an endearment, without *'my sweet', 'my darling', 'my heart'* added to her words. She had called him every one of those names in the fifty years they had shared.

Bragi picked up the bowl of porridge that was already on the table in front of her and fed her, a spoonful at a time. She looked at him with a flicker of gratitude in her eyes and he hoped that she still had a little tenderness for him inside her. He hoped that she was still able to register his affection, even though she didn't recognise him any longer. She finished the porridge, but Bragi knew better than to ask if she wanted more, now that she had lost the ability to know if she was still hungry or not; she simply ate what was put in front of her regardless of how much food there might be. He gently wiped her mouth and took off the bib, the sight of which infuriated him. It was a child's bib, decorated with smiling baby elephants, and although he knew it protected her clothes, he felt that there were better ways to do this than to put a child's bib on a grown woman. There was a great deal about this institution that infuriated him, in fact, especially since he had discovered the bruise. But he was in no position to let his anger show. His only option was to be grateful; grateful that she was safe, in a secure place where her needs were catered to. The healthcare system had no interest in the fact that he missed her.

'Now we'll go for a walk,' he said, and helped her to her feet. She allowed herself to be led without any change to her expression, completely docile, with no sign of expectation or dismay. She was easily handled now. In some ways it had been a relief when she had turned entirely inwards and stopped crying when he left her, stopped feeling frustration at her own weakness, when the occasional outbursts of anger had stopped, even though it meant that she no longer knew him.

They took the lift down to the ground floor and went out into the garden. He draped his jacket over her shoulders and they walked a few circuits. He no longer dared take her further than the garden, he never knew when she would be overcome by fatigue, so they walked round and round the garden, three little steps of hers to one of his. For a while, for the time they were there together, the loneliness left him, even if neither of them spoke. They didn't need to say anything, there was nothing that hadn't already been said between them. The only thing that had any meaning now was her touch, the warmth of her hand on his arm. That was all that remained, the only thing there could never be enough of.

10

Agla searched hurriedly through her handbag for something that would disguise the flush on her face. She couldn't control it. Just the thought of what had taken place in the bed a moment before was enough to set her cheeks glowing. The pounding of her heart was accompanied by the same guilt that had plagued her as a child. She had thought she'd grown out of it, but since she had got to know Sonja it had returned to her life, taking up residence like a guest outstaying their welcome. To start with there had been no hint of shame, only an overwhelming excitement that took root deep in her belly every time she thought about Sonja and then found its way to every part of her when they met. It was a burning excitement that set them both alight, producing kisses that had no end, touches that seemed to live on long after they had parted. But when Sonja's husband, Adam, had walked in on them in the heat of passion, leading little Tómas by the hand, Agla felt as if the reality of what they had done had been poured over her like shit from a bucket. She had hardly felt clean since. Their whole relationship had been poisoned by that moment: the questions in the child's expression, the devastation on the husband's face, the confusion in Sonja's eyes, which had shown she knew that her life would never be the same again.

'Toast?' Sonja called from the kitchen.

Agla cleared her throat and shook her head. 'No thanks.'

'Coffee? Surely you want some coffee?'

'No, I'll keep that for later.'

'Come here and have some coffee. You're not in a hurry. I know for a fact that you're not in any rush.'

Agla shuffled awkwardly into the kitchen, and as her eyes met Sonja's for a moment, her heart jumped that extra beat, as it always did when they looked at each other. But this heartbeat came with a wrench in her belly, her conscience gnawing at her – the shame that coloured everything. It was incredible how matter-of-fact Sonja could be. A few minutes ago they had been in each other's arms, and now Sonja was munching toast and reading the paper as if it were the most enthralling thing in the world.

'He's an absolute bastard,' Sonja said, tapping her finger on a full-page advert placed by supporters of Húni Þór Gunnarsson, the young MP who had sailed into Parliament on the strength of his father's reputation, a man who had been an MP himself for decades.

'Yeah?' Agla said absently, her face still burning.

'He and Adam, my ex, are friends. So I know what kind of a guy he is.'

If there was anything bound to unsettle Agla even further, it was a mention of Adam. The 'my ex' qualifier, as if she didn't know who they were talking about, made it even more aggravating. She had known Adam well, long before he had walked in on them in bed together. She had worked with Adam at the bank for several years, and now, after the financial crash, their shared fate was that they were both being investigated by the Special Prosecutor. Adam had been the one who had introduced her to Sonja.

11

He always chose the place, she the time. Sonja had only just switched on the pay-as-you-go mobile when he called and suggested a particular clearing in Heiðmörk, the thickly wooded stretch of National Park surrounding the Elliðavatn lake on the edge of the city. They had used the place before, so Sonja knew she would not need much time to check things out. On a weekday at this time of year she could be almost certain that the area would be deserted; the Heiðmörk woods seemed to fall into a trance during working hours, only coming alive again at weekends when people walked their dogs there.

'Two o'clock,' she said. That would give her four hours to dilute the powder and then find a good hiding place for the case in the under-growth around the clearing.

'See you then, sweetheart,' he said smoothly, the sound of his voice making Sonja's skin crawl.

She would have liked to have had a day off, but she knew she would be unable to relax until the handover took place. Until the shipment was in the right hands, she would remain a bag of nerves.

She pulled on jeans and a T-shirt, and twisted her hair into a knot. It was too much trouble to comb it out; she had fallen asleep with wet hair the night before, and this morning's passion with Agla hadn't helped matters. The memory brought a smile to her face and she promised herself that she'd have to manoeuvre Agla into bed sober more often. There was a seriousness to it that way, reminding her of when they had been just starting out together, before everything had changed. She grabbed her coat and stepped into the stairwell outside her flat, and found herself facing the woman from next door, who was standing there in her dressing gown. She had a towel wrapped around her head as if she had just stepped out of the shower, and her face was red and puffy. She was a pleasant neighbour, although Sonja found that she could often be trying.

'I'm sorry to trouble you again,' she said in the wheedling tone that always meant yet another laptop problem she needed solving.

'The computer again?' Sonja asked with a polite smile, hoping that today's tale of electronic woe wouldn't be too involved.

'It's just confuzzled itself.'

'Confuzzled?' She wondered how this odd expression could be applied to a sick computer.

'Yeah. It doesn't matter which buttons I press, nothing happens. And I can't even switch it off.'

'Let me have a look.'

Sonja knew from bitter experience that there was no point explaining yet again to the woman that she didn't repair computers. It was quicker to just take the laptop, fiddle with it for a little while and then hand it back. Normally it was enough simply to restart it, and her neighbour would imagine that she had spent an hour or two working some magic on the sick machine. She had no idea how the woman had stumbled across the website for her fake software development company, as Sonja had taken care to keep it off any search engines.

Nevertheless, the woman was firmly of the opinion that anything Sonja didn't know about computers wasn't worth knowing.

'You're an angel!' the woman cried, reappearing in the corridor with the computer. 'If only all computer people were as helpful as you are.'

Sonja took the laptop and swiftly disappeared into her apartment, clicking the door shut behind her, realising that her neighbour had begun to hurry after her, clearly looking for an opportunity to follow her inside. Under normal circumstances it would have been a pleasure to have a garrulous neighbour to share coffee with, and Sonja hoped that one day she would be a warm-hearted woman, happy to invite visitors in. But not now. There were a few things that needed to be sorted first and merchandise to be handed over to its owner.

12

The lifts doors opened and Agla swept straight past reception and into her office, shutting the door behind her. She had a killer hangover. Sonja was right, she had been hitting the bottle harder than she should. But without a drink, she was struggling to sleep. Ever since the financial crash she had felt she was hanging in thin air, waiting for some sort of a resolution to take place, without a clue as to what that might be.

She had kept her job, shifting over to the new bank that was built on the ruins of the old one, but she had practically nothing to do. Nobody trusted her. She signed things off, authorising loans for small businesses almost as if she was working on a conveyor belt, but apart from that she was given nothing to do, nothing challenging, nothing at her skill levels. And there was nothing that sparked her enthusiasm. Everyone was waiting for the Special Prosecutor, appointed in the wake of the financial crash, to publish his findings. Until he reached his conclusions, the resolution committee that had taken over the bank to manage its bankruptcy would keep her as far as possible from any real business. Not a word was said to her about all this, but she could see the blend of disappointment and loathing in her colleagues' eyes, as if she, along with the other senior staff at the bank, had been personally responsible for the misery that many Icelandic families were now having to endure. The only thing that made her turn up at the bank every day and submit to the judgemental gaze of her fellow workers, rather than handing in her notice, was that stubborn streak deep inside her.

Agla hung up her coat, and, seeing how creased it was, wondered if the reception staff had noticed that she was still wearing yesterday's clothes. She sat at her desk, started up her computer and went through her emails. By the time she had deleted the usual announcements, junk and adverts, there were just three messages left. It was so little, she couldn't be bothered to deal with it. Before the crash she had been in a constant race to keep up with her emails and in those last few years she had even had a secretary who would keep on top of everything. Agla pulled open her desk drawer and stretched for the bottle of Jägermeister – the morning hair of the dog she was always careful to have ready for when it was needed. She unscrewed the cap and took a swig. The bitterness of it burned its way down to her stomach with an agreeable warmth. Once she had enjoyed the feeling for a short while, she was ready to go out and meet her colleagues' gaze.

She went into the bathroom to touch up her lipstick, not that it made much of an improvement, and she had to admit to herself that she wasn't looking her best. The last few years had taken their toll on her. The drinking was having an effect, although she needed it to calm her nerves. The anxiety over where the Special Prosecutor's investigation would lead was making the atmosphere at the bank unbearable; and then there was Sonja. Sonja was driving her crazy.

The two resolution committee guys, Gummi and Palli, were standing by the coffee machine when she reappeared from the bathroom. These two were so alike that it had taken Agla the best part of a year to tell them apart; she could still hardly believe they weren't related. What's more, they dressed exactly the same. Today they were wearing identical pastel-shade pullovers over open-necked shirts. This was one of the meaningless changes the crash had brought about. Before, men had worn ties; now it was all open-necked shirts. Gummi put a paper cup in the machine and punched the latte button. The machine's latte was undrinkable – instant coffee with powdered milk dissolved in piss-warm water, another glaring symbol of the bank's fall from grace. Before the crash the top floor had its own barista, who drew hearts and clover leaves in the froth.

'You heard about Jóhann?' Palli asked, putting a copy of the *Fréttablaðið* tabloid newspaper under her nose.

The face of the former chief executive of the old bank jumped off the page at her. 'Jóhann Jóhannsson's status is now officially that of a suspect in the Special Prosecutor's investigation', the caption announced.

The circle was closing in. Tightening ominously around her.

13

Sonja placed the package on the kitchen table and opened it cautiously. There were three plastic wrappings; two vacuum-packed layers and one outer layer, securely taped. She cut through each covering in turn with the kitchen knife and then spooned the contents into a Tupperware box. She took care to scrape all the powder from inside the wrappers and then used a dry paintbrush to make sure she had extracted every grain. She put the box on the kitchen scales and noted the reading: one kilo, one hundred and twenty grams. The box weighed a hundred and eighty grams, so that left a little short of a kilo. That meant she could take fifty grams for herself. She spooned it into a small plastic bag. That went into the freezer where it would stay until she could put it safely in her bank deposit box. She used baking powder to make up the weight to a kilo and then carefully stirred the contents. The last thing she wanted was an accidental sniff of coke, followed by a sneezing fit and a buzz. It was strange, but smuggling cocaine had killed any interest she had in getting high. Occasionally she'd have a glass of white wine with Agla, but that was rare, and it was more than a year since she had snorted anything. Being caught in the snare had given her a definite need to be in control of herself, to keep her judgement unimpaired. It wouldn't be smart to get hooked on the stuff; the feeling of invincibility that came with a coke buzz wasn't conducive to successful smuggling trips. A good few people had been burned that way.

Sonja closed the Tupperware box, secured the lid with lengths of broad tape and put it back in the Samsonite case, which she then filled up with all the newspapers that had collected in her post box while she had been away.

She was in Heiðmörk just after twelve. It was later than she would have liked so she scanned the woodland around her, to make sure that there was nobody about. This was a convenient spot. While the deciduous trees stood bare, having shed their leaves, there were a few evergreens among them, and the dense tangles of birch wood were thick enough to screen what she was about to do from any curious eyes that might be passing. It wasn't as if there was a shortage of lonely spots to be found in Iceland, but going far beyond the city limits to find places that hardly anyone ever visited would require a four-wheel drive.

She parked the car a kilometre from the meeting place, took out the suitcase then walked briskly towards the clearing with it. When she was close, she stepped onto a narrow dirt track that led into the bushes and followed it in the shadow of the trees parallel to the road until she was alongside the clearing. She found a space for the case in the bushes, took a length of red ribbon from her pocket and tied it in a bow to a branch over the hiding place. Then she took long strides towards the clearing, counting one, two, three ... She counted thirty-two long paces to the clearing. Then she walked back along the road, got into the car, drove to the clearing and waited.

Waiting was the worst part. All the same, she never dared to be just in time. There was a certain security in being there early, being there first, the merchandise hidden away. Her meticulous preparation made her feel she had at least a semblance of control over the situation. But it was still difficult to wait. She had done this more times than she could count over the last year, yet it was still something she couldn't get used to. She found it hardest of all to deal with Ríkharður – the man she always met. Several times she had suggested to Thorgeir – the lawyer who took care of the cash side of the business – that she could make the handover to someone else, or stow the goods away somewhere to be collected, but he wouldn't hear of it. For some reason, she always had to make the handover to Ríkharður. She wondered if this was their way of reminding her of her position. Reminding her that such decisions weren't hers to take. Every time they met, Ríkharður did his best to scare and shock her. The first time, she had been so frightened that she had vomited after meeting him. Now she was able to contain herself, keeping her fears hidden. She was determined not to let him see that she was scared of him; she had no intention of giving him that power over her.

It was four minutes to two when a car drove into the clearing. He was punctual, you could say that for the bastard. Sonja took a deep breath, got out of the car and took a few steps towards Ríkharður and his apprentice. He had a different accomplice every time, but somehow they were always the same: young, muscle-bound, nervous and too well dressed for such youngsters.

'Hi, honey,' Ríkharður said and his eyes scanned her leisurely, from top to toe, as if he were a feline predator and she were the unwitting prey he had decided to tear apart.

'Good afternoon,' Sonja answered, stiff and formal. It was a question of sticking it out, keeping her eyes on his face the whole time, not leaving him an opening and showing no weakness. She didn't even look at the toy soldier beside him, acting as if he wasn't there.

'Got some sweeties for us?' Ríkharður asked, licking his thick lips so that they shone. It was such an overplayed performance, exaggerated to the point of ridiculousness, she would have laughed if she hadn't been so frightened. She'd have loved to have a fit of giggles, right there in front of him, dropping to her haunches and wetting herself laughing. He was the complete gangster stereotype, so much so that at the beginning she had sometimes wondered if he was simply playing a part, had been brought in to make sure she stayed scared. His head was closely shaved, and he had a thick neck, tattooed knuckles and eyes set so deep in his head that the whites of them could only just be glimpsed. His face was pitted with scars, and his body was so swollen with muscle and his thighs were so thick, he had no option but to stand with his legs spread wide.

Sonja's expression remained impassive. She sighed to indicate her irritation at the usual reception. 'Thirty paces, that way. There's a red ribbon on the tree.'

'The same old parlour games,' Ríkharður sneered. 'You couldn't just say "here you go" and hand me the fucking packet?'

'No,' Sonja replied. 'It didn't even cross my mind.'

'And don't you think it'd be an idea to suck my dick as a little bonus? There are plenty of girls who do.'

'There's even less chance of that,' Sonja told him, but her eyes dropped of their own accord to where his hands were provocatively cupping his balls. He grinned and she felt cold sweat trickle down her back. It had taken the snare to convince her that cold sweat was more than just a myth.

'Get the gear, boy,' Ríkharður said, and his accomplice set off into the scrub, returning a moment later with the Samsonite case.

'Call Thorgeir,' she said, staring, unblinking, at Ríkharður's face.

'I should check the merchandise first,' he replied, running his tongue over his lips again.

'That's just great. You go sticking your nose into the stuff the moment you get your hands on it,' Sonja said, squeezing out a humourless smile. 'Call Thorgeir.'

Ríkharður took his phone from his pocket, slowly selected a number, and put it to his ear.

'Hi,' he said. 'She's delivered. All good.'

Sonja turned on her heel, forcing herself to take measured steps back to her car. She got in and drove away. But it wasn't until twenty minutes later, when she was already in the Skeifan shopping district that her heart rate started to slow down.

14

Bragi was pushing one of the big trolleys around the Mela-market, in spite of the difficulty of manoeuvring it down the shop's narrow aisles. Once a week he went there and bought precisely what was on his shopping list – the same items every week. He had discovered when Valdís's illness became increasingly debilitating that if he wasn't going to starve, he'd have to learn to cook for himself, so he had learned to prepare six recipes. Monday was boiled haddock and potatoes, Tuesday was lamb chops in breadcrumbs. On Wednesday he treated himself to a seared sheep's head that he could buy ready to eat. On Thursday he fried some salmon, on Fridays he'd make some French toast and tea. Saturday was roast lamb, and the leftovers would then last through Sunday. When he was on night shifts he cooked in the evenings before work, and when he had day shifts he'd take leftovers with him or buy himself something for lunch. The menu at the airport wasn't tempting. Normally he tried to buy everything on his weekly shopping trip, apart from fish or milk, which he'd fetch as he needed them.

The sheep heads were piping hot, straight from the pot, and Bragi felt his mouth watering at the prospect. He took a carton of ready-mashed swede to go with his meal and filled the trolley with the items on his list. There was something comforting about shopping at the small Mela-market. He knew the staff, and this place was one of the few shops left in the city that were reminiscent of the typical grocer's shops he remembered from the old days. Here there were people serving at the meat and fish counters who were happy to give him exactly the weight he asked for, meaning he didn't have to pluck pre-packaged portions in polystyrene cartons from the chiller cabinets like in the modern supermarkets. The Mela-market always had food that matched the time of year, too. There was hot liver and blood sausage, and soon the aroma of smoked lamb would fill the place. In the spring he could look forward to cod roe and cod liver with his haddock fillets, and there would be guillemot eggs in May. Bragi stuck firmly to the food he had grown up with – the kind of fare he and Valdís had always preferred to eat. He had never acquired a taste for the pasta and pizza that the younger generation were so fond of. In fact, he wasn't even sure it was healthy for Icelanders to live on a diet heavy in wheat.

There were two people ahead of him at the till, so he reached for a magazine and thumbed through the pages. It never ceased to amaze him that such a tiny country should have so insatiable a market for glossy magazines, which to him seemed to all be more or less the same. He flipped through the pages without paying much attention until it was his turn at the till, where he carefully stowed his purchases in one carrier, putting the hot food in a smaller bag.

He had only taken a few steps from the shop door when a strange idea occurred to him. It wasn't a conscious thought, more an unconscious impulse, the result of who knew how many unrelated images that all of a sudden coalesced into something whole. He turned round, went back to the shop and bought the magazine. On a bench outside the store he sat down, his bags beside him, and scanned the pages a second time.

There it was: 'How to dress for business and pleasure this winter'.

It wasn't so much the article that attracted his attention as the photographs – pictures of elegant beauties, as always in these magazines. According to the article, they were all dressed in fashions designed to allow them to head directly from work and out for a night on the town; presumably it was some kind of office work they all did, as these weren't the kind of clothes that would be much use for anything else. Bragi examined the pictures closely, and gradually the thought crystallised in his mind. The beautiful lady in the overcoat – the one he felt had a star quality about her as she so often passed through the airport terminal – dressed in the same way as these girls on the pages in front of him; precisely the same, as if she had followed the magazine's instructions to the letter. She wore the same trousers, the same style of shoes, alternating a blue or a grey overcoat. Occasionally there would be a chequered cashmere scarf folded over one arm. Of course, this was the style that a certain type of woman affected, but the odd thing was that the woman he had noticed at the terminal never deviated from the script. There was nothing about her that he generally saw other passengers carrying with them: shabby scarves, maybe, or an old but comfortable jumper; shoes that were perfect for walking those long airport corridors on sore feet. She was always perfectly turned out, as if she had prepared for a fashion shoot, or, as the article pointed out, was ready to head for the bright lights. The truth of it was that nobody was ever that perfect. It had to be a disguise. This had to be a particular persona she wanted to display. And if that was the case, then she had been very successful.

15

Jóhann was a changed man; it was a shock to see him. He had always been so solid, but now he looked as if his torso had gone soft, the flesh flabby under his tight shirt. He had also lost most of his hair; just a few straggling strands remained on top, and the strips above his ears weren't looking good either. He was someone who still wore a tie with his shirt, though, and when Agla hugged him she recognised the familiar aroma of the aftershave he always used.

'It's a real bastard,' Agla said, taking a seat opposite him.

Lunch at a quiet downtown restaurant had been his suggestion, and he had found a table in a corner, half hidden behind a large potted plant. The man who had once taken every opportunity to hog the limelight was now avoiding attention, the result of being one of the most recognisable faces behind the financial crash. Agla thanked her lucky stars she wasn't in the same position. The sideways looks she got at the bank and the way her colleagues treated her like a pariah seemed a walk in the park compared to being spat at in the street like Jóhann was.

'Yeah. It's a pain in the arse,' Jóhann said. 'Lousy for the kids, seeing all this stuff about me on the front pages. It doesn't make anything worse for me though. Now at least I can refuse to answer questions.'

'I was told when I was being interviewed that I couldn't refuse to answer unless I had been formally charged.'

'Every job has its perks.' Jóhann raised his glass, and Agla saw he was drinking water.

'You're not going to join me for a proper drink?' she asked, waving to the waiter.

'No.' Jóhann smiled apologetically. 'My health's already too screwed up for any more drinking.'

'Unlike me,' Agla said, ordering a large beer and a chaser to go with it. They both ordered the fish of the day – pan-fried cod with shrimp and potatoes.

While they ate Agla enquired after Jóhann's children, and he asked what had been happening at the bank. When the waiter came to take their empty plates, Jóhann fell silent, waiting for him to leave them alone.

'We have to make sure our stories tally,' he said at last in a low voice.

Agla nodded her agreement. 'Just enough,' she said. 'They mustn't tie up too closely. Too perfect looks suspicious.'

'It's no good if we're at cross purposes, though, and contradict each other's versions.'

'My version of events is all worked out,' Agla said, hoping to sound suitably sharp. It felt as if Jóhann were checking up on her. 'Nothing's changed at my end,' she added, making her voice gentler and adding a smile.

'Of course. Of course,' Jóhann mumbled apologetically. 'We can't be too cautious.'

'Never too cautious,' Agla agreed and stifled her longing for another beer. It wouldn't do to be hammered right after lunch.

'It would be useful if you could outline for me the route ... y'know ... that the money took. I never looked too closely at that offshore fund. And now ... I'm at a disadvantage not knowing.'

'Believe me, my friend. Not knowing is bad, but knowing is worse. The best defence is to know nothing. While we each have just a piece of the puzzle, there's no way to see the overall picture. And the reality is there's no picture to see.'

'But to avoid casting suspicion, it would be useful to know which fund not to mention.'

'There's nothing you need to avoid mentioning,' Agla said. 'I'm ... I *was* good at what I did. There's no way it can be traced. And as long as it was an ordinary deposit, as far as I'm aware, you don't know through what fund the cash left the country. And as long as neither of us knows how the money made its way back, there's nothing to be worried about.'

'You're right,' Jóhann sighed. 'Quite right. I reckon my nerves are starting to fray at the edges. My blood pressure's off the scale these days.'

'I reckon you need a stiffener,' Agla said, catching the waiter's eye.

16

There was a bitter smile on Sonja's face as she ascended the twelve steps to Thorgeir's legal practice in Lágmúli. The practice was located on the eastern side of Reykjavík, in one of the many architecturally dubious 1970s buildings in the area that had not aged well. The steps were worn, the linoleum was cracked, as if it had been polished too many times over the years, and the air of the building had a slight whiff of mould about it, which Sonja felt was entirely fitting. She had been such an innocent the first time she came here, so full of hope. She had quite simply believed that Thorgeir wanted to help her. Now though, if there was anything she was determined to teach Tómas, it was that, when you're in trouble and someone comes to you offering to help, it's best to send them packing. She would teach Tómas to rely on himself, to learn to deal with his own problems and, above all, not to get into any kind of a fix that he'd need help to extricate himself from.

She had first come here a few weeks after she and Adam had parted company. Thorgeir had called her out of the blue, and to begin with she hadn't realised who he was. They had been only vague acquaintances – Thorgeir and Adam had studied law together, and she had met him once or twice at their reunions. The call should have aroused her suspicions, she realised now. Lawyers don't usually call to offer their help.

'I hear Adam's playing dirty over your divorce,' he had said, offering his sympathy. 'Let me help you out.'

He had a warm voice with a comforting tone to it, so, without thinking twice, she had put her fate in his hands. On reflection, this was typical of the way she had lived her life – going with the flow, letting the tide carry her along with it.

Sonja wasn't able to judge just how well or badly Thorgeir had acquitted himself as a divorce lawyer. Adam's and her debts combined had been roughly equal to their assets, so Adam took on both. She therefore found it fair that he got to keep the house in Akranes and the car, while she moved out, which was what he wanted. She was the guilty party, after all. She was the one who had screwed up. She was satisfied coming away with zero, owning nothing and owing nothing, but it had hurt to leave Tómas behind with Adam. She had been unable to demonstrate that she could provide Tómas with a decent home, so Thorgeir had advised her to agree to Adam having custody for the first two years – giving her time to get back on her feet and his anger to run its course. Then there might be a way to negotiate joint custody, Thorgeir had said. Until that point she would have access of the kind that divorced fathers usually have: every second weekend and part of the Christmas and summer holidays.

She wasn't angered by Thorgeir's advice, thinking back then that he was probably right. She had nothing and nobody. Agla had made herself scarce the moment things started to get nasty with Adam, and Sonja herself was half paralysed with fear. The opportunities for earning her own living were looking increasingly rare, and it didn't help that Adam was threatening to shout from the rooftops exactly how he – and their son – had found out about her affair. She didn't think she had actually broken any laws, but, it was still a potent threat; one that she didn't dare ignore.

She rented the cheapest flat she could find and found a secretarial job with a wholesaler. The wages weren't enough to cover both the rent and the child support, but that stopped being a problem when she was let go once her probation period was over. That was when she found herself sitting in Thorgeir's office in tears, unable to pay his legal bills. That was when he mentioned that he had an idea. She recalled having a moment's doubt, but it was instantly swept aside by her gratitude. In hindsight, she'd been far too grateful.

Thorgeir's idea was that she could travel to Denmark on behalf of an acquaintance of his who needed a favour. This man was stuck with a pile of foreign currency that he couldn't get out of the country due to the money exchange restrictions that had been imposed after the financial crash. For her efforts she would be paid enough to keep her afloat while she was looking for work. Sonja went home, ostensibly to think about the offer for a couple of hours before calling Thorgeir back. She had actually made her mind up to say yes before she had even left his office but hadn't wanted to appear too keen. If only she hadn't been so gullible. If only she had known that this was how people were trapped in this business.

17

Sonja filled in an SG Software payment form for half of her fee for the shipment and handed it to Thorgeir. He took it and nodded, before swinging his office chair around in a half-circle to open the safe behind him. His quick movements and slim build were at odds with his lined face and thinning hair. He was one of those men who become old in their mid-twenties and stay that way.

'And the rest in cold, hard cash?'

'You don't need to ask, Thorgeir. Always the same. Unless you want to make it more.'

Thorgeir turned back with a smile and handed her a thin wad of five thousand-krónur notes. She didn't need to count it. The amount would be correct; as far as money was concerned, Thorgeir was always straight with her.

She was about to stand up when he gestured to her to stay in her chair. 'Wait a minute, my friend,' he said.

Sonja snorted. She was no friend of his, and he was certainly not hers. He had put himself out of the running for that relationship when he sent her to Denmark with a suitcase full of cash to be met by men in suits who, it subsequently turned out, were not the right men in suits – or so Thorgeir had said afterwards. Of course, she knew now that the whole thing had been carefully stage-managed. It had been a play performed to ensnare her. Thorgeir's fury that she had delivered the case to the wrong people and Ríkharður's lurid threats, which then turned into a suggestion that she could work off some of the debt by taking a few trips to fetch coke, had all been scripted beforehand.

'I'm not your friend,' Sonja said drily. 'What do you want?'

Thorgeir looked at her with a broad smile, and once again she saw that sincerity in his eyes, an expression he seemed to be able to summon at will.

'I reckon it's time for you to take a big shipment,' he said.

'How big?' Sonja asked, her heart lurching inside her chest.

'Two or three Ks.'

'That's on a completely different scale,' Sonja said, alarmed. 'How am I going to bring three kilos into the country?'

'You've been resourceful up to now,' Thorgeir said, the smile reappearing, as if they were simply chatting about the weather. 'Imagination is your strong point. You'll think of something.'

Sonja said nothing. She had been half expecting that a proposal like this would come her way. She'd long had the feeling that she was being put through a series of trial runs, that they wanted to find out if she would mess up with a one-kilo shipment before giving her something bigger.

'I don't have to tell you that the remuneration for your efforts is in proportion to the volume. But it has to happen next week.'

'Send me the contact numbers,' Sonja said, standing up.

More money would do her no harm, as well as more white powder to skim off. That would bring her target closer, along with the day she could be free.

18

Sonja held the handles of the shopping trolley tight and made an effort to control herself. Her heart was hammering as if she had sprinted from Thorgeir's office, when in reality all she had done was get in her car and get out again at the shop. Shifting three kilos seemed to require a change of strategy. Perhaps there wasn't a great deal of difference, though; maybe she could simply adjust her methods to suit the larger amount. As she went through the shop dropping items into her trolley, her mind was working overtime to find a solution. She knew that the largest amounts came in by sea, but this delivery had to happen next week, and she had no time to organise anything that would involve a ferry crossing. And anyway, she knew little about the ferries, except that they didn't run in the dead of winter. Apart from that, she had no shipping contacts that could be of any use. She'd have to work things out for herself, as usual.

She picked up buttermilk and bananas for Tómas's breakfast and dropped them in the basket, along with a frozen pizza that they could share tomorrow night and coffee to replenish her stocks. She had no idea what to have for dinner on Saturday; maybe she and Tómas could go out somewhere to eat. He liked fish, so they could go to the Sægreifinn fish bar down by the harbour for grilled fish on skewers and paper cups of creamy langoustine bisque. She knew he would enjoy that. He loved Reykjavík harbour; it was so much livelier than the harbour in Akranes, where he lived – out of town, on the other side of the bay. It was a long time since they last went downtown together and he always seemed to enjoy everything she suggested. He had always been an exceptionally agreeable child, in fact, and since the divorce he had been even easier to be around, never asking for anything or making demands. Sonja knew that he wanted for nothing, living with his father, and she wondered if, by never asking for anything from her, he thought he was protecting her. Thinking about Tómas gave her a stab of anguish, making her force her mind elsewhere. Somehow it was easier to concentrate on how she was going to bring a suitcase full of cocaine into the country than to consider what impact the divorce had had on her son.

The pain in her belly had gone by the time she reached the check-out, her heartbeat had returned to a reasonable rhythm, and she was calm again. While there was no doubt that more kilos were going to be less easy to carry, and the risks would be greater, she felt a certain security in carrying the larger quantity. It meant that she could be sure she wasn't being used as a decoy. Decoys always carried the small amounts. A big shipment meant there was more at stake for everyone concerned.

19

Tómas was almost sick with anticipation. It was Thursday. Tomorrow, after lunch, his mother would collect him and he would spend the whole weekend with her. He never expected her to give him anything special or take him out. Normally they just spent time at her place, maybe going for a walk around the district, and sometimes all the way up to the slopes at Öskjuhlíð, which Tómas called 'the forest' because of the birch scrub covering the slopes leading up to the glass dome of the Pearl building. Sometimes they went for a drive, and saw how many yellow cars they could count. Today's excitement was even greater because weekends with her were perfect. Mum simply did everything just right. On Friday evening they'd put some lively music on and dance around the living room. The movement and the loudness of it all was just what he needed to release the tension, having spent so long anticipating his time with her. After that she always made popcorn and then they'd watch a movie. At Dad's place he was allowed to watch any cable movie he wanted, but Mum always chose films she thought would be good for him – educational ones. Even though these films weren't always particularly fun, it was still something to be able to sit on the sofa, munch popcorn and watch a movie with her. It was the same with breakfast. Dad always bought Honey Nut Cheerios or

Lucky Charms, and he did try to get the right mix of buttermilk, but it was never quite the way it should be, however much Tómas tried to tell him how to do it right. Mum could do it perfectly, though. She'd pour the buttermilk first, sprinkle it with just the right amount of brown sugar and then slice a banana on top. Somehow she got the banana slices the ideal thickness; not so heavy that the banana flavour overwhelmed the buttermilk, and not so thin that the slices turned slimy. Mum's version was always just so.

Now there was one more sleep and one day at school before Mum would collect him, and he would sit shyly in the car on the way through the tunnel that connected Akranes village to the capital, while she asked him about school and football. Later, when they had closed the front door of her flat behind them, the tears of joy would be free to roll and that's when they'd crank up the volume and turn the living room into their own dance floor.

20

Sonja tapped on her neighbour's door, half hoping that there would be nobody home, in which case she could just hang the laptop in a bag on the door handle. She had restarted it, and the machine seemed to be more lively now. If it didn't improve its mysterious reluctance to perform, though, she would have to pay for it to be mended herself; she couldn't let the secret out that she wasn't able to fix it herself, and that she in fact knew nothing at all about computers.

'Thank you, darling!' her neighbour whooped as the door opened.

'It should be better now,' Sonja told her. 'But maybe you ought to think about replacing it with something newer.'

'I thought about it after what you said the other day, but I can't get over how quickly this stuff wears out.'

'This one's three years old,' Sonja said. 'They don't last much longer than that.'

This was no special wisdom she was imparting, but her neighbour looked at her as if she was a rocket scientist. 'And I though this one would last me out!'

'Computers are tools,' Sonja said, trying to sound professional. 'They wear out just like any other tool.'

'I've never thought of it like that, but you're right, of course. I suppose it gets more wear and tear than other electrical gadgets do – like a radio or something.'

'Yes,' Sonja said, starting to edge backwards across the passage towards her own flat. 'The radio just has to produce sound, but the computer has to...' she searched for the right words, '...think. The computer has to think.'

'You explain it all so well, you know, in layman's terms,' her neighbour said with satisfaction. 'If only there were more people like you in the computer business.'

Sonja smiled and nodded a goodbye. Then, just as she was shutting her own door, her neighbour called out – something about bugs.

'What did you say?' Sonja asked, pulling the door open.

'I was just telling the chairman of the residents' association that we need to put down insecticide in case we get silverfish again. It's been a year since we had them in the cellar; we don't want another infestation.'

'Insecticide?' Sonja stared questioningly at her neighbour, who stared back, clearly expecting an answer.

'That's right. We need to put insecticide down for the silverfish. Don't you agree? I know you young people aren't as bothered by bugs as we old people are. You've travelled so much, and with the global warming and all those new insects coming here you probably don't mind silverfish. But I can't stand creepy crawlies. Especially the ones that hide in the dark. Shall I tell the chairman that's all right with you?'

'Absolutely. Yes,' Sonja said with an apologetic smile and closed the door, her mind elsewhere. Now she knew how she would bring the shipment into the country.

21

It was as if apartments that were empty for too long acquired a deep sadness. The air became stale, the curtains were half drawn, and there was a fine layer of dust over everything. This sadness was what Agla often encountered when she went home, so she avoided the living room with its minimalist, Scandinavian-style furniture, which she had chosen with little thought from a Danish catalogue, instead going straight to the bedroom, which she had painted herself in dark grey to counter the unbearable summer light that started seeping in through the curtains every April. She usually ate her takeaway meal in bed – noodles maybe, or a meat soup, in front of the television. For ten years she had been fine being alone. She liked coming back to find things exactly as she had left them, and, apart from Fridays, when the girl came in and cleaned, nobody ever came to her flat. Even Sonja had only come home with her on a handful of occasions. Even though it was ten years since her divorce, she still felt a particular pleasure in dropping her underwear on the floor, scattering cosmetics around the bathroom and leaving the bed unmade knowing no one was there to point out her domestic shortcomings.

Agla ate while the bathtub was filling up, looking forward to lowering herself into water so hot it made her gasp and feeling it envelop her like a scalding embrace. While she enjoyed her solitude, she thought, as she turned off the taps and stepped into the water, loneliness was something quite different. That was more like a kind of melancholy longing – a desire for something she was on the point of discovering, but never actually managed to find.

She let her thoughts wander, floating between sleep and wakefulness in the hot water. Left to itself, her mind inevitably turned to Sonja, the woman who exerted a pull on her that she could not explain. The feelings she had about her were like nothing she had experienced before. It was some kind of sorcery, an enchantment that would not leave her in peace. She would have sacrificed anything to be free of it. She had little in her life that she could sacrifice, though – except Sonja herself. She was the only thing that sparked in her any desire, any kind of fire. Yet at the same time, she felt such an endless shame for what she wanted from this woman. It couldn't be healthy. It had to be her hormones going haywire, the menopause kicking in. Time and again she had tried to cut off all connection with Sonja, but she'd never been able to do it. She was hooked. Hooked on her smile, hooked on the fast breath in her ear, hooked on licking the sweat from her breasts, hooked on the way she gasped as she came.

The flow of her thoughts was interrupted by a sharp ring on the doorbell. Agla started and quickly sat up in the bath. Then she decided to wait. It would be someone hawking dried fish or lottery tickets; nothing worth getting out of the bath for. But when the bell chimed a second time, she hauled herself out, wrapped herself in a dressing gown and went to the door.

It was Jóhann. He was standing outside, three other men with him. Two of them she knew as his lawyers – one of them had also worked for her – but the third man was a stranger.

'You could have picked a better moment,' she said, wrapping the dressing gown more tightly around her.

'We won't stay long,' Jóhann said, stepping inside, the other three following behind.

Agla went ahead of them and sat in one of the living-room chairs.

'Sit down,' she invited, gesturing at the sofa, but Jóhann shook his head.

'Just to underline what we discussed today—' he began.

But Agla interrupted him. 'Does what we talked about need to be underlined?' she asked. 'And who's listening?' Her eyes rested on the third man who hadn't introduced himself.

'Sorry. Guðmundur's the lawyer representing Adam.'

Agla's hand rose instinctively to her chest and tried to stretch the gown to cover her better. With wet hair and wrapped in a dressing gown while Adam's lawyer stood over her, she felt suddenly defenceless.

'I confirm what I said today; nothing has changed from my perspective,' she said.

Jóhann smiled awkwardly and looked from one lawyer to the other.

The older of the two then spoke. 'As there are, shall we say, three links to this chain,' he said, 'we can't emphasise enough how important it is that each link remains ... strong.'

Agla got to her feet, glaring at Jóhann. 'You and Adam have clearly put your heads together, and, seeing as his lawyer is here, I assume that he's being kept informed. But what the fuck makes you imagine that *I'm* the weakest link?'

The lawyers remained as impassive as if they had been moulded from porcelain; Jóhann gnawed his lip and beads of sweat could be seen emerging on his forehead.

Then it dawned on her. It was clear that, should things come to a head, *she* was the one who would be expected to fall on her sword.

22

Absorbed in looking up different kinds of poison on the internet, when her phone rang, Sonja neglected to check the caller's number before answering it. Greeted by Libbý's cheerful voice she immediately regretted being so absent-minded. Libbý was one of a group of her old friends from her home town of Akureyri in the north of Iceland; the group who referred to themselves as the Sewing Circle. In reality their gatherings were far more about having fun over a meal than any kind of needlework.

'Hi-ee!' Libbý trilled. She was the only person on the planet who could stretch that tiny word to two syllables. 'I've finally caught up with you at last. Have you been busy?'

'Yes,' Sonja replied, 'you could say that.'

'I ran into your mother at Glerártorg the other day and she said you were working for some computer company.'

Sonja gritted her teeth at the thought of her mother and Libbý discussing her affairs in the middle of Akureyri's shopping centre.

'Well, yes. But it's pretty much my own company. It's quite small, so I'm sort of working for myself.'

'Yeah-eah,' Libbý said, stretching another short word beyond the usual single syllable. 'Your mother said that you're abroad a lot.'

'That's right. A bit,' Sonja agreed, desperately trying to think of a way to turn the conversation in another direction.

'Who would have thought that you'd turn out to be some kind of computer guru?' Libbý said with a laugh.

'And you?' Sonja asked. 'What's new?'

'Fine,' Libbý replied. 'The same old story, you know. The old man, the kids, the gym. And I'm still at the bank. One of the few cashiers who hasn't been made redundant.'

Sonja was about to congratulate Libbý on her good fortune in holding on to a bank job with things as they were, but her friend hardly paused for breath.

'It was so good to see your mother; hasn't changed a bit, still so young looking, I hadn't seen her for a while, which is strange in a little town like this, but she has her account at another bank so I wouldn't see her at work, and she said she usually does her shopping out in the village, and she was so sweet and invited me round for coffee, said she'd even do some of those pancakes of hers that I always loved so much.'

'How lovely,' Sonja said sharply, visualising her mother making pancakes for Libbý when she had no inclination to speak to her own daughter. Her sarcasm went straight over Libbý's head.

'She's such a darling, your mother. Wonderful to see how she looks after herself. How old is she now? Sixty, seventy?'

'She's sixty-three,' Sonja replied, surprised that she knew the answer without having to think about it. Her mother still had a place in her heart even though it was almost two years since they had last met.

'Oh, and your mother said that Adam has custody?' Libbý's tone was questioning, and Sonja immediately understood what she was fishing for. The Sewing Circle was about to meet and Libbý was in need of some juicy gossip for the other girls.

'Yes, that's right,' Sonja snapped, and then immediately realised how rude she must sound. But it was too late. Libbý would relish telling the girls how grumpy Sonja had become.

'Er, but … is there some special reason? I mean, you and Tómas were always so close…'

Hearing the hesitation in Libbý's voice, her curiosity blended with trepidation, Sonja felt herself softening towards her old friend. 'It's just temporary,' she said. 'Adam and I agreed on two years, which is almost up, so we'll probably be rethinking the arrangements soon.'

'OK … And you were happy with that?'

'No,' Sonja replied quickly. 'But it was … just that … I couldn't. It was about money, mainly. I was pretty skint right after the divorce.'

That was putting it mildly, she thought. The day before she signed away custody to Adam, on Thorgeir's advice, she had stood in the food bank in the hope of coming away with a bag of provisions so that Tómas would not go hungry. There was no way to describe the depth of humiliation that had engulfed her during the hour she had spent waiting there. Finally she couldn't stand it any longer and had broken free of the queue and gone to the Nóatún supermarket, where she had shoplifted frozen chicken, biscuits and milk. There was also no way to describe the emotion that had swept over her when she returned home and looked into her own tear-laden eyes in the mirror, wondering who this woman in front of her was: someone who would rather steal than ask for help.

No, there were no words to describe to Libbý those first few months after the divorce, so instead she simply repeated herself: 'I was pretty skint.'

'Darling! Did he treat you that badly?' Libbý said, sounding shocked and speaking as she breathed in.

Sonja felt a touch of pleasure in complaining about Adam like this – complaining and receiving a little sympathy in return. All the same, she knew that, if Libbý ever discovered the whole story, her compassion would be short-lived.

'Yes, he treated me very badly,' she said.

Libbý drank it all in. 'I can tell you now that I never liked Adam. I never thought he was right for you, always so reserved and arrogant and sulky. We girls were always wondering what you saw in him, because even though he's good-looking, we could see that you were never yourself around him. Isn't that right?'

'Probably not,' Sonja replied. 'I thought that I loved him, and maybe I did, but now I feel it was all one big misunderstanding.'

23

'We're running a book,' Bragi's colleague Atli Thór told him when he appeared in the customs officers' canteen at the airport.

Bragi said nothing and went to the coffee machine, half filled a cup, added a few drops of milk and waited for Atli Thór to explain.

'This week's day shift has a bet with the night shift over whether or not you'll turn up at the Christmas staff party,' Atli Thór said with the audacious glint in his eye that gave him a juvenile look, but which made him pleasant to work with.

'Really?' Bragi said, taking a seat next to this young man, who had only recently completed his customs training and seemed to look up to him, watching his every movement like an excited puppy. 'And which way did you bet?'

'We reckon you'll come, but the night shift's bet is that you won't.'

'Ah,' Bragi said. 'And what's at stake?'

'There's plenty at stake, I can tell you!' Atli Thór's hands pattered across the table in front of him as if he were playing a drum roll as the prelude to a death-defying circus act.

Bragi was almost sure that the story of the bet was a simple lie to get him to come to the staff party, although he couldn't be completely certain. He had become used to Atli Thór's games; he always seemed to have some running joke on the go.

'The losing shift buys a bottle of Rémy VSOP for the winning shift, no less.'

'That's a bet worth winning.'

'That's right, my friend. The finest cognac. Top quality and well matured, just like you.'

Bragi smiled. He could see the look of expectation on Atli Thór's face and sighed to himself. He would probably have to make an appearance at the staff party so that Atli Thór would win his bet. It wasn't as if he had anything else to do, other than sit with Valdís and dream of a future far from the clinic's sterile walls. That future would be one in which he could ensure that every one of the precious minutes she had left would be perfect and peaceful, and, not least, secure. But he knew perfectly well that sitting with her for an evening, those dreams coming to him in the stillness, would only bring on a depth of sadness. He always found it harder to leave her in the evenings, and even more difficult when the staff decided that it was time patients should be on their way to bed for the night and encouraged him to go. So he might as well take part in the party, he thought, even though he had no desire to do so.

'I have no comment on the matter,' he said to the group at the table. 'Might as well keep things tense, right up to the final moment.'

24

Jón, the Special Prosecutor's investigator, placed the camera on a small tripod on the table, but he looked defeated when he tried to switch it on and it didn't work. He had to fetch someone to help him out.

'The recording equipment in the interview room isn't working,' he said, pointing at the camera in the corner of the room.

The young woman with a blonde fringe who had come to his aid set the camera up and trained it on Agla. 'Can I bring you a coffee or anything?' she asked sweetly.

'No, thank you,' Agla replied, hoping that her words sounded just as amiable. She had nothing against the Special Prosecutor's staff. These were only people doing their jobs and Agla would get what she deserved; and maybe something a little more too. Jóhann and his legal posse would see to that.

Outside the window the surface of the bay was placid and the higher slopes of mount Esja were dusted white with snow. The cold blue light of the low winter sun cast long shadows as it streamed through the window, turning the scratches in the pine tabletop black and highlighting the dust on the blinds. This light was merciless; it left nothing hidden. It would be clear on the recording that Agla had a hangover.

She knew it was not a good move on her part to be here without legal representation, but the Prosecutor's investigator had said that they only needed clarification on a minor matter – an extension of her statement. Besides, following the visit from Jóhann and his associates, Agla was determined to get a new lawyer. Her current one had been appointed as part of Jóhann's legal representation package, but now she had the feeling that she would be better off striking out on her own.

'So, Agla,' Jón said as he took a seat, 'thanks for coming in again.'

Agla nodded and squeezed out a smile for the camera as Jón rattled off the case number. Agla knew the number off by heart; remembering numbers had always been something she found easy.

'Continuation of Agla Margeirsdóttir's statement. Jón Jónsson present. For the record, I would like to state that Agla has not requested the presence of a lawyer.'

Agla shook her head. 'I'm between lawyers right now.'

'Let's make a start. There are certain circumstances regarding three investment funds and I would like to hear how you interpret them.'

'I can try,' Agla said, unfolding her reading glasses.

Jón pushed a stack of paperwork across the table to her. 'I'd like to know what you make of the items highlighted in yellow.'

Agla liked Jón Jónsson and always thought of him as 'Inspector Jón', never quite sure whether he was a police inspector or an investigator for the Prosecutor's office with a police rank. He was always suitably reserved. She liked that better than when investigators started off friendly, but, at the slightest provocation, turned into baying hounds. Normally there were two investigators, and under usual circumstances she would have brought a lawyer with her. But as she had come here unaccompanied, she appreciated the consideration he was displaying in speaking to her alone.

Agla took the pile of papers and flipped through a few pages. It was a list of transactions covering the bank's overseas investments, alongside a register of share purchases in the bank itself. The first entry was from March 2007 and the last from February 2008. This was how most of her statements had been taken: she sat and read through documents that were a few years old and gave her best guesses of what was what.

Jón placed a finger under a yellow line in the transaction list of overseas investments. 'I'd appreciate it if you could explain this transaction.'

'October three years ago,' Agla said drily. 'I can't say I have it at my fingertips. There were quite a few risky investments going on at that time.'

'It's eight hundred thousand dollars,' he said in a tone that clearly indicated that the amount should be enough to jog her memory.

'It doesn't ring any bells,' Agla replied. 'Amounts like that were not unusual back then.'

'Maybe it'll help if I tell you that a similarly sized transfer was made every week over the next few months.'

'No. That doesn't help. I don't remember anything regular of that amount.'

'Not exactly that amount, but always between seven and nine hundred thousand dollars.'

'At that time I was responsible for around three million dollars a week of investments, so figures like that are nothing special.'

'Would you take a look at the fund this payment went into, and the transfer the following week, and again the week after that?' Inspector Jón placed a precise finger on the lines highlighted in yellow as Agla flipped through the pages.

'Iceland Trading Ltd, ML Holding, Avance Investment,' she read out. 'These are all funds I used regularly. The first one was an agency fund, the other two were investment funds.'

'If we examine a period of several months, then we see there's a pattern – with similar amounts going into this same fund every week.'

'My work patterns were also similar from one week to the next. In my experience these were good funds, which is why I used them frequently.'

'Let's leave things there,' Jón said.

Agla felt a shiver run through her whole body. That phrase meant that he was about to start making connections.

'What's so striking,' he said, 'is what's revealed when this list is compared to the other one.' He tapped a fingertip on the stack of share registrations.

'I know you dream of neatly linking these two together, but you know I can't help you much with share trading at the bank; I never had any part in that. That was Adam's department entirely.'

'When the money that goes into foreign investments over this period is compared to foreign purchases of the bank's shares, then we see similar amounts at similar intervals.'

'So shouldn't we conclude that everything seeks equilibrium?' Agla sat back in her seat and folded her arms. Now it was time to cross swords with Inspector Jón, it seemed.

'That's what you all keep telling us,' he said.

'Meaning who?'

'You, Jóhann, Adam and your people.'

'Maybe because that's the way it is.'

'Maybe, and maybe not.'

'What basis do you have to disprove it, other than figures on a list?'

'Suspicion and experience,' Inspector Jón said, following her lead by leaning back in his chair so that they faced each other like well-fed guests after a monumental banquet. 'We suspect that the money flowed through the equity fund and then from one fund to another in order to cover the trail, and that in reality this cash came right back in the form of shares in the bank, to keep the share price up.'

'I can't confirm or deny your suspicion,' Agla said. 'I can say truthfully that I was only in charge of investing on behalf of the bank and its more prominent clients in overseas funds. I have no idea if or when this money might have come back into the bank. That's the honest truth.'

The best defence was ignorance. There was a soft click as Inspector Jón switched off the camera.

On her way out to her car, Agla couldn't help being aware of the connection between this session and the visit from Jóhann and his troop of lawyers. Was it coincidence that had taken Inspector Jón straight to that particular fund? Or could one or other of the boys have leaked something? At any rate, they were finding themselves in increasingly hot water.

Agla sat in the car and wondered whether to stop off at the state-run off-licence on her way to the bank. She couldn't remember what she had left in her desk drawer, but right now she certainly felt in need of a stiff drink. If only Iceland was like other countries, where you could buy booze in supermarkets. She still hadn't made up her mind when her phone rang.

'Hello?'

'What the fuck were you doing at the Prosecutor's office without a lawyer?'

Jóhann's voice was so angry that it was almost a squeak. It was astonishing how quickly bad news could travel.

25

Sonja was perched on the edge of Tómas's bed, watching him sleep. She could have left him a while ago; it was some time since he had fallen asleep in the middle of the thrilling story about trolls she had been reading for him, but she found herself unable to tear herself away from him. She savoured the pleasure of being so near him, feeling the heat from his body through the bedclothes, listening to his steady breathing. It was startling how absence triggered such thankfulness for his presence when it came. She couldn't remember having sat and watched him sleep when she had the opportunity to do so every single evening.

Everything she was doing now was for him; she remained in the snare in the hope that they would have an endless row of such evenings – him at her side, falling asleep with his little hand in hers. All these trips that carried with them the risk that she could lose him entirely were what gave her hope for a future in which she would be able to do everything to make sure he stayed with her more often, so that she could seek custody of him.

The flow of cash into her fake company's account was gradually providing a basis on which she could support him financially. And then there was the deposit box. That was where she had a bundle of notes in different currencies that was getting steadily fatter, a little box of gold coins that Agla had told her was a secure investment after the financial crash, as well as the bag of powder that she had collected by harvesting a few grams from each shipment. The bag was pretty big now; it had to be getting on for a kilo. This was the kilo that would get her out of the snare.

The doorbell chimed and Sonja leaned over Tómas to kiss the top of his head. There was a delightful aroma to his hair and, even though he was growing fast and she could see new aspects of him in his face every time they met, that aroma always remained the same.

It was Agla at the door. Sonja could see from the way she leaned against the doorframe that she had been drinking.

'You know Tómas is here with me this weekend,' Sonja said.

Agla followed her into the living room and sat next to her on the sofa. 'He's asleep, isn't he?' she whispered, reaching for Sonja's top button and trying to open her shirt.

'Yes, but he sometimes wakes up in the night,' Sonja said. 'And you'll have to say hello to him and look him in the eye in the morning.'

Agla sighed and dropped back into the sofa's embrace. 'OK, I'll go. But tell me something interesting first,' she said. 'Talk to me.'

'About what?' Sonja asked.

'Anything but investment funds. Tell me a Sapphic secret.'

'What do you mean?'

'Something that all lesbians know.'

Sonja thought for a moment and decided to tell her about the gaydar, figuring it would be good for her to understand her own instincts.

'Lesbians have an extra sense that makes it easier to find and recognise each other. Gay men have the same sense for other gay guys. It's called the gaydar, you know – the gay radar.'

'And how does it work?' Agla sat up and looked at Sonja, her interest sparked.

'It's as if you have a feeling that you connect with another lesbian, something that's different to what you get with other people. It's somehow stronger, as if you have a greater affinity with that person. I wouldn't say that there are alarm bells going off in your head, but that's not far from the truth.'

'Isn't that just being horny?' Agla sniffed, sinking back into the sofa.

'No, it's nothing to do with wanting to fuck them. It's more an instinct when you know you have something in common. Maybe it's derived from some kind of mating call, I don't know. It's something that helps you find love and security.'

'Weird.' Agla was clearly thoughtful.

'That's right,' Sonja said. 'Sometimes I feel it's almost supernatural. But it's not safe to trust it completely. Sometimes your gaydar goes off and the other woman isn't ready, or isn't aware what kind of signals she's giving off. Some women give out mixed signals. The body language and the electricity say one thing, but the words say something else. Just like you did to start with.'

'You couldn't have got strong signals from me.'

'Yes, I did. I had an overwhelmingly strong feeling about you.'

'Then there's something wrong with this radar of yours,' Agla said with exasperation, sitting up straight. 'I'm not a lesbian.'

26

'You asked for a Sapphic secret, so don't get in a state when I tell you one.'

'I'm not in a state,' Agla hissed, struggling to keep her balance as she put her shoes on.

'Don't be like that, there's no need to leave in a huff. I was just telling you an amusing story. I'm no expert on lesbians.'

'You seem to know quite a bit.'

'Come back and talk to me. Let's be friends.'

'How many have there been before me?' Agla asked, her accusatory tone warning Sonja that a rough ride was coming.

'Don't start on that.'

'I'm not starting anything. I'm just asking.'

'I can't be bothered to argue over something that isn't important.'

Sonja turned away, but Agla pulled her back.

'Tell me,' she said. 'I want to know.'

Sonja sighed. The feeling that they were in deadlock sometimes gripped her; it was as if the two of them stood on the brink of a precipice, unable to move either forward or back.

'There were two women before Adam, while I was at college. After things turned bad and you ran for it, then there were a couple more.'

'A couple? What do you mean by a couple? And I didn't run for it. I'm here, aren't I?'

'Oh, Agla,' Sonja said with a heartfelt sigh. 'Don't, please.'

'How many?'

'I don't remember!' Sonja pulled herself away. 'After Adam walked in on you and me, when everything turned to shit,' she hissed, 'I was lonely and broken-hearted. All of a sudden you didn't want to know me. Life had become a disaster, so I had wild nights a few weekends in a row and took someone home. OK?'

'Broken-hearted? Why was that?' Agla asked with a triumphant smile on her face.

Sonja's anger flared at this. She marched to the kitchen, turned on the tap and, trembling, filled a glass with water.

Agla followed and wrapped her arms around her from behind. 'Tell me about your broken heart,' she whispered; Sonja could feel the heat of Agla's breath on her neck.

'I was devastated without Tómas. As well as that I was desperate and lonely because you didn't want anything to do with me. And you can stop trying to stir it all up to get me to say that I love you. Try saying something sweet to begin with and maybe you'll get the response you're looking for.'

Sonja turned around and stared into Agla's eyes, but she looked away.

'Were many of them better than me?'

Sonja pushed Agla away from her. 'Better than you? What the hell are you talking about? There's something wrong with you if you have to ask something like that.'

'Were they better in bed?'

'I give up. You'd better go.'

Sonja went to the hall, took Agla's coat and handed it to her.

'I'm just asking so I know where I stand ... in comparison. Because I'm not used to this, am I?' Agla looked shamefaced, as if she was aware that she had gone too far but had been unable to hold herself back.

Sonja's anger evaporated; and she felt an urge to laugh but did not dare let herself. This couldn't go on, she told herself. She would have to set Agla limits; these games needed to stop.

'To be truthful,' she said seriously, 'you're about average.'

Sonja opened the door and Agla stepped out into the corridor.

'Do you mean that?' she asked.

'No,' Sonja replied.

'You're kidding, then?'

'Of course.'

'Can I come back in?'

'No. It's time to go.'

'Can I kiss you goodbye?'

Sonja gave in, and Agla kissed her, one hand straying to fondle a breast.

'Enough!' Sonja said, removing Agla's hand, even though her touch was tempting.

She could easily have led Agla back to the sofa, let her hands roam wherever they wanted. Agla's insecurity was infuriating, but the knowledge that she was the only woman Agla had slept with was something that always turned her on. She knew that in Agla's eyes she would always be perfect; and perfection was like a coke buzz – liberating, satisfying and dangerously addictive.

27

'Her, ba, mi ... mis,' Tómas spelled out, concentrating on the bottle.

'It's Herbamix,' his mother gently explained. 'Remember, the X is like a K and an S together.'

'Herbamix,' Tómas repeated. He was sitting inside the shopping trolley. He was too big to sit in the child's seat, but his mother had said there was nothing wrong with him climbing into the trolley and sitting there as she pushed it around the Garðheimar garden centre. He was so big now, he practically filled the trolley, but it wasn't as if Mum was buying much; just a few candles, flower pots and that bottle.

'What is it, Mum?'

'It's weedkiller.'

'Weedkiller?'

'That's right. It kills off weeds. You put it on the garden and it kills everything except the grass.'

'What grass are you going to put it on?'

His mother thought for a moment. 'I'm buying it for my friend in another country who has a garden.'

'Is there grass there now?' Tómas asked. 'The grass in Akranes is all dead and frozen. We can only play football on the indoor pitch at the moment.'

'In England there's grass all year round. And you can't get this stuff there so she asked me to buy it for her.'

Tómas recognised the look on Mum's face; it was the one that said he'd asked a silly question, so he decided not to ask anything else, even though he would dearly have liked to know more about the garden in a foreign country. He wanted to go with her to that other country and see her friend scatter the weedkiller all over her garden so it would look perfect. He wanted to go with her to England and drink loads of fizzy pop, like you always do on holiday, and play football on the emerald-green grass.

Back in the car his mother was cheerful again and they sang made-up songs all the way to the next shop.

'Once there was a monkey, always in a hurry, banana! Bananana! Bananana!'

This next shop was not like a normal shop; more like a workshop with a garage door and a smaller door next to it.

'Do you want to wait in the car?' his mother asked.

Tómas shook his head. He never wanted to wait in the car. He wanted to be with her every minute that he could.

'Come on, then.'

She opened the door and he followed her into the workshop.

'I'm after some rat poison,' Mum said to the old man who was sitting at a desk surrounded by huge shelves full of all kinds of stuff that Tómas didn't recognise.

'Rat problem, sweetheart?' the old man asked and his mother shook her head.

'It's for a friend in the country.'

'You're sure it's not mice?'

'No, definitely rats,' she said firmly.

The man shrugged, stood up and rooted through the contents of a shelf deep inside the shop. He took down a box, opened it and placed it on the counter in front of her.

'They're bait blocks. You'll have to be careful to wear gloves to handle them, and make sure children don't get near them, or other animals. Instructions are in the box.'

Mum counted out the notes and paid him.

Then the old guy handed her a sheet of paper. 'You'll have to sign for it. Name and ID number.'

'It's for my friend. Should I put her name?'

'Sure. Do that,' the old man said. 'I'm supposed to ask for

identification. But since you're buying it for someone else, we won't worry about that.'

Mum wrote a name on the sheet of paper. She was so fast, Tómas wasn't able to read it.

They went outside again and before they got in the car she put the box of rat poison in the boot.

'Are there rats in your friend's garden in England?' Tómas asked.

His mother laughed. 'That's right. She's having a terrible time of it, what with weeds and rats.'

28

It was remarkable how alone one could feel in a crowd. Bragi stood at the bar, nursing a beer and watching the guests taking their places at tables for the annual Christmas party. Workplaces were now increasingly holding their Christmas parties long before Christmas itself, ahead of the frantic December madness that traditional Christmas preparations demanded. Some people would clean or paint their houses from top to bottom, buy gifts for dozens of people and embark on marathon baking sessions. Valdís had always kept on top of what was needed for Christmas. This year Bragi would be having a much simpler celebration.

He wondered if the awkwardness he felt standing by the bar stemmed from the fact that he was one of the few who had turned up unaccompanied. Or maybe it was the generational shift that had taken place within the Directorate of Customs – there were few people present he would call close friends. One or two couples were already on the dance floor and people were shedding their inhibitions, courtesy of pre-dinner drinks. The music, along with the chatter of countless voices in the hall, melded into a single babble of noise in his head. His patience for loud noise had been wearing increasingly thin as he grew older. At one time he would have relished all this. He would even pull Valdís onto the floor at dances, right up by the speakers, so there was no way they could exchange any words. They would communicate with movement and touch, developing a rhythm that would synchronise between them. Once the children had arrived, though, going to a dance became a rarer event. He regretted that now.

'The day shift wins the bet,' Hrafn, the Chief Customs Officer, said as he joined Bragi at the bar.

'I couldn't not show my face and let them lose,' Bragi said.

'No, we couldn't let that happen.' Hrafn coughed awkwardly. 'A shame Valdís couldn't be here tonight.'

'I know,' Bragi said. 'She doesn't go out these days.'

'Of course. I understand,' Hrafn said and sipped his drink.

'Indeed,' Bragi said. He never knew how to respond when people tried to show him sympathy for Valdís's illness.

'Don't think I'll be staying long tonight,' Hrafn said in a brighter tone. 'It's on the loud side for me, and we're not getting any younger.' The words sounded odd, coming from a man twenty years Bragi's junior. 'It's interesting to see how the younger generation matures and gradually takes over, though, isn't it?'

Bragi nodded his agreement but kept his thoughts to himself, aware of the subtext to Hrafn's words. The unspoken message was that it was time for him to stop being so stubborn, retire and let someone younger take over his job. He understood the sentiment. Every week there was something in the news about yet more rounds of redundancies, companies closing one after another, and the banks snatching whatever was left over as people were dismissed. With people who had families to support finding themselves out of work, his stubbornness did seem selfish. There was no doubt about it – he should step aside, leaving the way clear for a younger man with a fresh approach to the job. And, obviously, a younger man in his position would be cheaper for the Directorate. The customs service, like everyone else after the crash, was expected to make savings.

Bragi could see that Atli Thór and the others from his shift were taking their seats. He nodded to Hrafn and hurried over to join them. Since he was here, he was going to make the most of the meal. Even though it was not yet December it was never too early in the year for smoked lamb.

29

Tómas only began to cry when they were in the Hvalfjörður tunnel, on the way back to his father's place in Akranes, which lay a short distance from the capital. Sonja had expected tears earlier; they normally began before they were even in the car, so today he had done well. All the same, his silent weeping was like a knife in her heart.

'There, there, my darling,' she whispered, adjusting the mirror so she could see him behind her on the back seat.

There was no anguish in his expression, just a flow of tears down his cheeks and a trembling lip. Sonja longed to stop the car, sit in the back with him and hug the boy tight while she stroked his hair. She could think of no words that could comfort him, and she was on the verge of crying herself.

'Let's just look forward to next time,' she said.

'But that's such a long way away,' the boy sniffed.

'It seems like that,' Sonja said. 'But if you think of it the other way around then it's not so long. Think about our next time together, and then go backwards, and you'll find it's much closer than it seems. Before you know it, two weeks will have shot by, and then we can spend another weekend together.'

'Why can't I come and live with you?'

'It's not that simple, sweetheart. You know that.'

'I could live with you and just live with Dad when you're working abroad.'

'You know that wouldn't work out, what with school, football and everything else.'

'Why can't I have one week with you and one week with Dad? Then it would be fair, wouldn't it?'

Sonja had to agree that such an arrangement would have a

fundamental equality to it, but that was something that Adam would never agree to.

'I'll talk to your father about it,' Sonja said.

'You always say that, but you never do!'

Now Tómas was angry, and in many ways this was easier to bear than the sorrow. The anger was a defence mechanism, forming a hard shell around his little heart.

When they arrived at Adam's house, Tómas was about to jump from the car and run the moment she pulled up outside, but Sonja caught hold of his arm.

'I work and work so that I can make it possible for you to be with me. There's nothing in the world, Tómas, that I'd rather have than you with me all the time. But there are rules about that, grown-up rules.'

'Stupid poo-rules,' Tómas said. She could see he was holding back his anger to keep from bursting into tears again.

'Yes, that's right. Stupid poo-rules,' she said with a giggle that brought a smile to his face. 'I'm working as fast as I can to find something better for us, so that we can be together more.'

'Together all the time,' Tómas said.

'Yes. Together all the time,' Sonja agreed. 'That would be the best thing.'

'And just every second weekend with Dad.'

'That's right,' Sonja said and hugged the boy tight against her. 'But until then we'll both have to work hard. We'll have to be tough and do what has to be done.'

30

'This has to happen early next week.' There was a tension in Thorgeir's voice that Sonja hadn't heard before.

'I don't let myself be pushed around. You know that,' she replied.

She heard Thorgeir take a gulp of air. 'You're playing with the big boys now,' he said in a low voice, as if he was making an effort to keep his temper in check. 'That means new rules, you understand? A whole set of new rules.'

'Yes, I understand,' Sonja said, and put the phone down. She had avoided letting anyone interfere in her travels so far, but the size of this shipment provided a certain security. There was no chance that Thorgeir or Ríkharður – or whoever was behind them, pulling their strings – would risk jeopardising such a large amount.

It was dark when she emerged from the Hvalfjörður tunnel on her way back from Akranes, and the clouds were so low they seemed to have settled on the ground – she could hardly see the city lights on the other side of the bay.

She would have to dig deep now that this job needed to be done fast. She put her foot down and took advantage of a gap in the traffic to overtake the car that had been pottering along ahead of her. She set the wipers to full speed to clear the windscreen as something that seemed to be halfway between rain and sleet streaked down from the skies. She would be at the Nóatún supermarket in Grafarholt in ten minutes.

Standing at the store's meat counter, she felt overwhelmed by a sudden hunger, which was bizarre considering what she was about to do. She would have liked to have eaten these steaks herself. She would have loved to have grilled them and served them with gravy and a salad, eating them with Tómas and Agla at the table with a chequered cloth on it. Afterwards Tómas would watch television while she and Agla would wash up, and later they would all brush their teeth together, laughing with mouthfuls of toothpaste, dressed in soft pyjamas and with faces freshly scrubbed before bed.

'Anything else?' the man behind the counter asked, handing her the steaks packed in a plastic tray.

'I'll have two pieces of the grilled chicken,' Sonja said, shaking off the remnants of her daydream. There were no pink pyjama parties on the horizon. There was an uncomfortable evening ahead of her – gnawing the chicken off the bones, sitting in her car outside the homes where the sniffer dogs lived while she waited for the right opportunity.

31

It wasn't the first time she had watched this place. To start with she had sat here to monitor the comings and goings so she could get an idea of the schedule the dogs and their handlers worked to. While the ferry between Denmark and Iceland was running she tried to time her flights to coincide with the ferry's arrival days, so that she could be sure that at least one of the customs service's two dogs was busy over on the east coast. Now, though, in winter, the ferry wasn't running, so she couldn't afford to take a chance. One of the dogs might be used to sniff mail at the postal sorting office on a particular day, but she couldn't be certain of that, and, anyway things could always change. She had worked out that the customs services' schedule varied occasionally, so changes to the routine were difficult to anticipate.

A blue sheen lay over the windows of the house facing the street, but a bright-white light from the window at the back shone onto the grass. This must be the kitchen window. Occasionally Sonja could make out some movement inside; the occupants must be cooking a meal. It was dinnertime, but she didn't have any appetite, even when she bit into a chicken leg. She should have those steaks ready. The dog was always let out into the garden after the house's occupants had eaten, and again before they went to bed. It would be as well to get to him the first time.

She opened the boot and fetched the box of rat poison and the flask of Herbamix and got back behind the wheel where she pulled on the gloves. They were only ordinary wool gloves but they would have to do as she had forgotten to buy rubber ones. She cut holes in the steaks with a pocket knife and pushed the waxy blocks into them, as many as she could stuff into each steak. She placed the meat back on its plastic tray and poured a little of the weedkiller over it. It was an unappetising way to season a meal, but it would do the job.

Almost an hour passed before the kitchen light was switched off and the dog raced out of the back door. He always seemed so happy to be let out, the poor thing, Sonja thought. She left the car and padded across the street, making her way along the fence as if she were a perfectly normal neighbour taking an evening walk, while cautiously making certain that nobody was standing in the doorway keeping an eye on the dog. Surreptitiously, she threw one of the steaks over the fence. A moment later the dog was there, onto it.

Back in the car she peered into the darkness; as far as she could make out the dog ate every scrap.

At the second house she had to wait almost two hours. This one was more of a problem as the customs officer who handled this dog was more careful and had a habit of watching the garden while the dog was outside. At last the door opened and the dog came out to sniff its way around the bushes, seeking the right spot to pee in. As usual, the handler stood in the doorway and smoked.

Sonja started the car and moved it a short distance down the road, then hurried back towards the house with the plastic tray in her hand. As she jogged past the door she rang the doorbell. She heard the dog bark out in the garden. Looking around the corner, she saw, as she had hoped, that the man had gone back inside to answer the front door, shutting the dog out and leaving it barking in the garden. Sonja called to it, and it came running to the fence. She gave it the steak and a few kind words. It was a small dog with a mottled coat and long ears – and a good appetite: it swallowed the steak practically whole.

'I'm sorry,' Sonja whispered, stroking its head. Then she made herself scarce, back down the street, intending to make a circuit and come back to her car from the opposite direction. Her heart pounded as she walked, the guilt collecting inside her. There were plenty of things she could teach the customs service, including the invaluable advice that they should never take their eyes off their dogs in their own gardens, not even to answer the door. She was sure that procedures would be changed now that she had killed both of their sniffer dogs.

At the first set of red lights on the way home she punched a text message into her pay-as-you-go mobile, sending it to the number Thorgeir had given her: '*Hi. This is S. Text me an address please.*'

She thought through flight times all the way home, working out in her mind when it would be best to set up the decoy. Her train of thought only stopped when she saw the white envelope in her mail box. Post wasn't delivered on a Sunday, she thought, her hands trembling as she fumbled for the key to the mail box. Taking the envelope, she ran upstairs and shut the door behind her before opening it – as closed doors could provide protection from whatever threat it might contain. This was the worst thing about being caught in the snare, the worst thing of all.

The envelope contained a photograph of the Akranes Sports Club's junior football team. Tómas was kneeling in the front row, smiling as he looked into the camera. Behind the row of laughing nine-year-old boys stood a crowd of adults – parents, she guessed; Adam was among them, on the far right of the group.

At the far left stood Ríkharður, a grin on his face.

32

The atmosphere in the Special Prosecutor's office had changed beyond all recognition. There was a crackle of tension in the air, and the staff who usually sat quietly at their desks were excited, whispering and eyeing her as she sat and waited for the new lawyer. He had hardly had time to acquaint himself with the case – his appointment had only been confirmed on Friday and now it was Monday. She had called him when they had come to the bank to collect her. He had instructed her to say nothing and sign nothing, and told her he would meet her at the Special Prosecutor's office. She would have preferred him to come to the bank first, but of course there was no need for that. All the same, it would have been comforting to have an ally, someone at her side, as two police officers escorted her from the bank, the entire contents of her office following behind them, stacked on a pallet. She could sense the eyes of every one of her colleagues resting on her and was sure she heard someone whisper *'About time!'* as the lift door slid shut behind them.

She had known for a long time that this day would come, it had just been a question of when. But that didn't make it any less uncomfortable, especially as it was happening just as she was changing her legal representation. She had toyed with the idea of dropping the new lawyer and calling Jóhann and asking to continue to use his legal team, but she decided against it. It was time to draw a line.

Now in the Prosecutor's office she found herself so agitated that she could hardly sit still; her feet shifted constantly under the table and she didn't know what to do with her hands, repeatedly twisting and untwisting her scarf. It would destroy the fine silk, but she didn't care. One silk scarf wasn't something to be worrying about at such a moment.

When her lawyer entered the room, he was accompanied by Jón Jónsson, the investigator, and María, the specialist in economic crime. They had met several times when Agla's statements had been taken. Behind them came Ólafur, the Special Prosecutor, in person. He took a seat in the corner of the room while Jón and María sat at the table. Jón read from a sheet of paper, stiff and formal, informing Agla that her status was now that of suspect in the Special Prosecutor's investigation into deliberate market manipulation by certain of the bank's employees. Agla waited for him to add something, and when he didn't, she breathed more easily. That was as far as they had got, she thought. She took the sheet of paper stating that she understood her status and its implications, and handed it to the lawyer. He filled in his name in neat letters: Elvar Daggarson, lawyer. Once the prosecutor and his representatives had left the room, he opened his briefcase, took out a mobile phone and handed it to her.

'I've put my number in there and also the bank's number. You'll have to call them and let them know your status. I don't imagine they'll want you back at work for a while.'

Agla took the phone and nodded.

'If you want, I can get your phone from them so we can copy your numbers across to this one. I've no idea how long they'll want to hang onto yours.'

'No, thanks,' Agla said. She knew Sonja's number off by heart and there was nobody else she would want to call.

33

That morning it seemed to Bragi that the gloom was not just outdoors – it had also drifted inside and infected his colleagues. This was not unusual for the Monday following a staff party at the weekend. Some were despondent, maybe having overindulged and said things better left unsaid, or having made unwise romantic overtures to a colleague. There was also the sense of anti-climax now that something everyone had looked forward to was behind them and the next party wasn't in sight. Bragi had left the party early on the Saturday night and had been up to see Valdís first thing on Sunday morning, so now he was wide awake, sipping his coffee as he scrolled through the airport's CCTV feeds.

He had forgotten all about the fashions he had seen in the magazine and the beautiful lady who so often passed through the airport – that was until his eyes alighted on her in the departure lounge. Then it all came back to him. As always, she was impeccably dressed, but the screen wasn't clear enough for him to make out whether she had the grey or the beige coat neatly folded over her arm. She was waiting at check-in with an average-sized suitcase at her feet and a compact handbag on her shoulder. Bragi put down his mug, hurried out into the passage and went to the staff lift.

'Go and get yourself a cup of coffee,' he told the youngster who was checking boarding passes and passports at security. He was about to protest, but Bragi glared and waved him aside, and the young man admitted defeat and vanished. Bragi only had to wait a moment before the beautiful lady appeared, handing him her passport, open at the right place, along with her boarding pass. Everything was exactly as it should have been; everything about her was perfect. Bragi glanced at the passport and read the name; Sonja Gunnarsdóttir. He tapped the 'Iceland' button on the nationality screen, returned her boarding pass to its rightful place between the pages of her passport and handed it back to her. She smiled briefly, their eyes met, and for a moment Bragi doubted his own instincts. Her smile was shy and there was a sweetness in her eyes. This hunch of his about the way she dressed had to be nothing more than an old man getting the wrong end of the stick. Maybe he had it all wrong – it wasn't as if he had ever been anything of a specialist in female fashion matters. Were his instincts letting him down? Maybe it was time to pack the job in after all.

34

The thin cement surface of the steps seemed to crumble under her feet and the stairwell stank of piss. Sonja was on the point of turning around and calling Thorgeir to check if she was in the right place to collect the package. Until now she had met men in the lobbies of hotels and collected the shipments without exchanging a word. This was something new. Of course things would be different with big shipments, she should have known that. She would have to tough it out.

The flat was on the sixth floor. She could hear the music blaring through the door before she even knocked.

'Welcome, my darling!' exclaimed the tall man who opened the door to the flat; behind him she could see a table stacked with packages of cocaine.

'I'm here for the delivery,' Sonja said.

'Yeah, that's fine,' the man said, his accent thick and African. 'For my good friend Rikki in Iceland? No volcano now? We had a hell of a problem when Ey-fattila-kaka was pouring out its guts.'

Sonja had to smile at his pronunciation of Eyjafjallajökull, the volcano that had grounded air traffic across Europe. It had upset her own plans for a few weeks, and even now the regular arrival of yet more of the fine grey ash, carried over Reykjavík every time the wind turned east, had become an almost daily reminder of those weeks of turmoil and uncertainty.

'I'll get the bag for you,' the guy added, grinding his teeth so his jaws tightened. The darkness of his skin accentuated the white spittle that had collected on his lips. It was obvious that he had been diligently sampling his own merchandise.

Sonja stepped hesitatingly inside the flat, although she would have preferred to spin on her heels and run. She stared at the people in the living room and felt a deep desire to hide her face. It wasn't just that they had all seen her, but that the guy had announced in ringing tones that she was on her way back to Iceland. He had vanished into another room so Sonja took a seat, watching two skinny young women sitting at the table swallowing little packages of cocaine that two other men at the other side of the table were preparing. Sonja recognised one of them: an older man with cropped grey hair. She had once collected a kilo from him. He was filling the snipped-off fingers of rubber gloves with powder while a younger man with fair hair tied them shut with dental floss and dipped each package in a pot of thick, clear liquid.

'What's that you dip them in?' Sonja asked, for want of anything else to say.

'Wax,' the fair-haired man said. 'It protects the latex from stomach acid.'

Just as the tall man returned with a battered suitcase, the girl sitting at the table began to retch.

'No, no, no!' he yelped, dropping the suitcase and hurrying over to her. The three men jumped up, and the grey-haired man grabbed her head, pulling it back to stretch her throat.

'Breathe deep,' the fair-haired man advised. 'Just breathe and it'll pass.'

The girl did as she was told and took deep breaths, while her frame shook with spasms as she retched. Tears ran down her cheeks, and she gasped that she couldn't take any more.

'Everyone takes a half,' the dark man decreed. 'Everyone. No exceptions.'

Sonja took in the girl's bony figure and wondered how there could be room in her belly for half a kilo of little latex packets. She was probably no older than twenty – barely fully grown.

The dark guy took out a phial and used the long nail of his little finger to shovel powder into each of the girl's nostrils. 'Snort and you'll feel better.'

The girl sniffed and immediately stopped retching. As the grey-haired man let go of her head, she got quickly to her feet and took a few brisk steps across the living-room floor.

'Hey! Yeah!' crowed the dark man, and sniffed a nailful of powder up his own nose. 'This is pure stuff. There's no creatine in this, no caffeine, so no nausea and no headaches. Just clean Peruvian stuff.'

He cheerfully slapped Sonja on the back, opened the suitcase and began to drop packages from the table into it. The solid, half-kilo lumps clattered into the suitcase, each one loosely wrapped in a plastic bag. Sonja counted four, then five and finally six blocks.

'That's enough,' Sonja said. 'I was told it was going to be three kilos.'

'Four,' the man gabbled, this teeth chattering. 'Rikki told me four.' He added two more blocks. 'You don't want to turn up with less than I said I'd send, do you? He'll think you've stolen it.'

Sonja gulped. Of course she could not turn up with less than they had agreed, but she was furious. This was a typical snare tactic; saying one thing and the reality turning out to be something very different.

'Good girl,' the guy grinned and slapped her on the back as he handed her the suitcase. 'We look out for each other, don't we? Those of us who sell the pure gear, not that meow-meow, bath salts and all that cheap shit from China, that gives everyone bad comedowns and nosebleeds, and who knows what else a million times worse! We need to take care of each other, watch the quality and tell everyone about Peru! Peru's the place for quality. People need to recognise the best and say no to cheap imitations. We're thinking about the future, you see.'

As he rattled on, Sonja backed away towards the door, raised a hand in farewell, pushed it open and was gone. All the way down the filthy stairwell she wanted to yell, but decided to let that wait until Thorgeir could hear it. She'd make sure to let him have a piece of her mind for having sent her to that horrible place.

35

'I've just seen the paper. Why didn't you say anything when I called you last night?'

Sonja was on the gangway to the plane with a copy of *Morgunblaðið* in her hand. The news item about Agla being treated as a suspect was front-page news.

'I just wanted to put off you hearing about it as long as I could.'

'Why, Agla? This is just the kind of thing we ought to be telling each other.'

The stewardess stood in the doorway, her look sending a silent message to Sonja that it was time for her to get on board.

'I knew you'd hear about it sooner or later, but...'

'But, what?'

'I just wish you didn't have to.'

Sonja's eyes rested on the page; she felt a stab of anguish at seeing the photo of Agla being led away by two police officers.

'I know what you're being investigated for is serious. All the same, I do realise that sometimes we all end up doing all sorts of things. Things we think we have to do.'

Agla said nothing, so Sonja ended the call. She made her way onto the plane, much to the stewardess's relief, took her seat and fastened her seat belt. She was about to switch her phone off when she saw there was a message. She opened it, hoping it was from Agla. But she was disappointed. The first word she saw was *'Reunion!'* and she knew immediately where the message had come from. Libbý and the Sewing Circle had clearly made arrangements to meet. Sonja switched off her phone without reading any more. In a different life and at some other time it might have been a pleasure to meet the girls, knock back a few drinks and share some laughs about the old days.

But that life was somehow too far removed from the reality that was now hers.

36

'You ought to know who I am by now,' Agla said, but Inspector Jón Jónsson was unamused.

'It's an important formality,' he said. 'We have to have all the details right. Please state your name.'

'My name is Agla Margeirsdóttir; date of birth: 18th of January 1965. I'm the former head of the investment division.'

As on the previous day, in addition to Agla, Inspector Jón and María, Ólafur, the Special Prosecutor, sat on a chair placed behind them. Next to Agla sat Elvar, her lawyer, his hands trembling from a caffeine overdose. He had been awake for most of the last few days and nights going over the case.

'Before we begin the interrogation, we would like to inform you that you are charged with market manipulation, as is stated on this sheet,' Inspector Jón said, passing a piece of paper to Agla.

She looked at it, nodded and pushed it in Elvar's direction.

'You'll see that it is made clear that you are under no obligation to answer questions on the case in question, nor to explain pertinent circumstances, but if you choose to comment, you have an obligation to do so properly and truthfully.' As Inspector Jón intoned these standard phrases, it was obvious that he had done this many times before.

'Finally, here is a claim for damages from the bank's resolution committee, made against its former managers, which will be dealt with separately when the circumstances of the case are clear.' Another piece of paper made its way to Elvar via Agla.

She had read through the paperwork at home and this game of going through it all page by page was simply a matter of form. The atmosphere in the room, though, was more fraught than before; Agla could practically smell the electricity in the air.

'Let's start,' Inspector Jón declared, glancing at María, who opened a thick ring binder and extracted a sheet of paper.

'In co-operation with Interpol and several foreign investment funds,' María began, 'we have been investigating the ownership of those funds you used for the specific transactions in which we are interested.' María fell silent and looked Agla in the eye.

She stared back but said nothing. She was used to this treatment from María. The silence was a ploy to get her to talk. If she was made nervous by the quiet and said something just to fill it, there was a chance she might let slip some glaring mistake.

'If we start with this one, Avance Investment,' María resumed, 'we see that it is mainly owned by a Cayman Islands-registered company called AGK. After some considerable research, we have established that AGK is owned by you.'

María again sat silent and stared at Agla. Elvar shuffled through his papers, searching for information Agla knew wasn't there. This was something she had taken care not to inform him about.

The silence was abruptly broken by Inspector Jón hammering on the table with his fist and shooting to his feet. 'You lied to us about this in your statement!'

Agla was taken by surprise and for a moment wanted to turn her eyes away from her inquisitor's anger, beg for mercy, and run and hide.

'To keep quiet about something isn't the same as a falsehood,' she said pulling herself together. 'When Avance was mentioned, you asked about transactions through the fund, not about its ownership.'

'Let's paint a picture, shall we?' Jón suggested, sitting back down. 'Between October 2007 and February 2008, every week you trans-ferred between seven and nine hundred thousand dollars to overseas funds. Now it turns out that one of these is owned by you.'

'Mostly owned by me,' Agla said. 'Let's get it right.'

Jón got to his feet again, turned away and scratched his head so that his fair hair stood up in all directions.

'Are you trying to tell me,' he said, 'that you genuinely think we can't see through all this?'

'What opinion the suspect may or may not hold in regard to the prosecutor's astuteness is irrelevant, and she will not be answering this question,' Elvar said.

Jón continued as if he had not heard him. 'Hundreds of millions flowed along this route, via your overseas fund, which presumably invoiced the bank for its services. And you're seriously trying to tell me you didn't think this was worth mentioning?'

Jón paced back and forth as far as the limited space in the small room allowed. Finally he resumed his seat.

'What we're fishing for, Agla...' María continued placidly, '...what we're looking for is confirmation of what we already know: that this money went round in a circle. These amounts from the bank went to an offshore investment fund, but were in reality used to invest in the bank itself. This cash went on a world tour, just so it could come back here to lift the share price of a failed bank.'

'I can't confirm what I don't know,' Agla replied.

'We know this, Agla. We have all the documentation here,' María said gently, patting the ring binder with her hand. 'We know you're a crook.'

The insult was somehow sharper when delivered in such a mild manner. Their theories were entirely right. This had been exactly the route the money had taken. But there was no paper trail linking Agla to the purchase of shares in the bank. They would need witnesses to implicate her, and that was where the overriding uncertainty over her relationship with Jóhann and Adam came into the picture. The only consolation was that, by hanging her out to dry, they would be putting nooses around their own necks. All she could do now was keep her cool and allow the prosecutor's staff to muddle their way through everything piece by piece, hoping all the while they didn't ask the right questions; the questions they mustn't ask.

37

Sonja had never before had such an overwhelming urge to break into a run along the walkway at Keflavík airport. Her heart hammered in her chest, telling her to move herself as fast as the blood that it pumped through her veins. But there was no question of hurrying or showing any sign of agitation. She had to remain calm and self-contained until she had collected the case of goodies from the carousel. She reminded herself of the cameras that could peer into every corner of the terminal building and walked slowly but with purpose, without looking around her, down the steps and into the duty-free shop. She picked up a bag of sweets that would make Tómas happy, and a bottle of cognac that would please Agla just as much, and stood in the line to pay. Just as she reached the checkout, she saw the carousel for the London flight jerk into motion. Her heart lurched and fluttered.

While Sonja waited by the carousel for her case to appear, she ran through all the facts about the alter ego she had created: she was a software developer at SG Software; she was a company director; she was immersed in business and she travelled for work.

When the case finally appeared, Sonja had to force herself not to run around the carousel to snatch it up. She watched as it approached, at what seemed to be a snail's pace, wondering if the customs officers would appear as soon as she lifted the case off the conveyor belt, or if they would wait until she went through customs to take her aside. She tried to persuade herself that there was no chance they would touch her. Her precautions had been too elaborate. She had bought a vacuum-packing machine in London and had spent hours packing the blocks in layer after layer of plastic. She had then packed each one in a cocoon of coffee and vacuum-packed them a second time, before washing each pack in strong soap and packing them in yet another layer. That should be enough to fool the scanners and it was fairly certain that the sniffer dogs would be nowhere to be seen. It would have to be an unfortunate coincidence – a random check – that made them take her aside now. And she hoped that any spare manpower they had would be occupied looking for the decoy at Reykjavík's domestic airport that she had asked Thorgeir to set up.

Sonja lifted the case from the conveyor, trying not to make it obvious that it was heavy. She extended the handle and set off for the customs gate, walking briskly but steadily, the sound of her footsteps accompanying the beating of her heart, which made an occasional wild surge. The further she went along the passage, the more she longed to run, but she kept herself in check until she had passed through the arrivals lounge and was out in the car park. Then she allowed herself the luxury of letting go and jogging with the case behind her the short distance to the long-term car park where her car waited for her.

The car was frosted with a covering of ice, but she didn't have the patience to look for the scraper and instead fished a debit card out of her handbag and used it to clear enough of the windscreen so that she could see the road ahead. The rest of the ice would clear once the car and the heater had been running for a few minutes. She got in the car and started the engine, her breath forming clouds in the frosty air.

She felt the rush of her own blood so clearly that she could almost hear it as her car hurtled along Reykjanesbraut as if its wheels were barely touching the tarmac. She wanted to yell with relief.

Calm down, take it easy, she told herself. There was no need to pick up a speeding ticket just after successfully making her way through customs with four kilos of cocaine.

As she approached the city, she wondered whether or not to call Agla. She decided that she wouldn't; she'd go straight to her place instead. The case could wait in the car overnight. Sonja could feel her body bursting with energy, and she needed Agla – right away.

Agla answered the door wearing a creased suit.

'I must have fallen asleep on the sofa,' she mumbled, rubbing her eyes.

Sonja swept her into her arms and kissed her hard on the mouth. She didn't mind the smell of booze; if anything, it added to her excitement.

'You're in the mood, aren't you?' Agla said, suddenly wide awake.

'I am,' Sonja said. 'Come to bed.'

She stripped off in the darkness and pulled off Agla's tights, hearing that she too was beginning to breathe hard and fast.

38

Flat on her back, Agla stared at the bedroom ceiling. The glow from the street lamp outside shone on the light fitting in the bedroom so that the dead fly in the cover that had bothered her for weeks could be seen clearly. She didn't notice the corpse of the fly during the day, when she would actually be in the mood to get up on a chair and remove it; she was only reminded of its presence when she lay awake in bed, worrying, and the rays of the street lamp outside shone in, picking the fly out in perfect detail.

That morning's interrogation had taken her by surprise. Of course she had been well aware that sooner or later the pressure would be stepped up, but the investigators had seemed to have suddenly become more aggressive. Perhaps, as her new lawyer was still not fully up to speed, the Special Prosecutor's team were making the most of the opportunity, or maybe these were the usual tactics with someone who had become an official suspect in a case – they deliberately changed their attitude. Or it could be that they had some information they felt gave them licence to behave in such a discourteous manner. Had Adam or Jóhann given them some titbit of information that was to her disadvantage?

Agla could feel the weight of Sonja's head on her shoulder and her breathing slowed and calmed until her body rose and fell rhythmically with the breaths of the sleeping woman beside her. It was as if they were one, glued together by each other's sweat, and every tiny movement of her fingers on Sonja's skin sent an electric charge of sheer joy along her arm and deep into her heart. Her fingertips traced onto Sonja's naked skin the words that belonged there, but which would sound so awkward when spoken out loud.

My heart, my beloved, my sweet, my love, she wrote.

There was something so wonderful about letting her fingers express to the sleeping body next to her the words that she would never be able to articulate.

39

Bragi had just poured his first mug of coffee of his shift and made himself comfortable in front of the window overlooking arrivals when Atli Thór appeared, slapping his back so that a few drops of coffee spilled into a greyish puddle on the carpet.

'Guess what? I was asked to have a chat with you about retirement!' Atli Thór said, roaring with laughter.

'That was Hrafn, I suppose?'

'Yes. I told him I'd give it a try, but wouldn't get anywhere.'

Atli Thór pulled a few paper towels from the holder by the sink and wiped up the spilt coffee.

'Tell him that I said I'm staying on until I'm ninety, and I'll see him in court if I have to,' Bragi said with a smile.

Atli Thór grinned back at him. 'I'll look forward to passing that on to him,' he said, again patting Bragi on the back, but more gently this time, with no risk to the coffee in his hand. 'Hey,' he added. 'There was an arrest yesterday, two hundred grams of coke, heavily cut, at the domestic airport.'

'Really?'

Bragi's heart skipped a beat, and it was a moment before he worked out why. Two hundred grams was nothing special, but it could be an indicator of something bigger somewhere else. It was certainly suspicious that it had come in through the domestic Reykjavík airport, where only a few overseas flights landed, rather than the international airport at Keflavík.

'He'd travelled from Copenhagen via the Faroes. A proper junkie, shivering like hell.'

'And has he spilled his guts?' Bragi put his coffee mug aside, his thoughts focusing on a picture that was becoming steadily clearer in his mind.

'Well, he said some guy in Copenhagen got him to take it through. Said he doesn't know who it was – doesn't even know his name.'

'So that's the story.' Bragi caught Atli Thór's eye. 'And would I be right in guessing that he was picked up on the basis of an anonymous tip-off?'

'That sounds about right.' Atli Thór's voice was laden with curiosity. 'A decoy? Is that what you're thinking?'

'I reckon it's too obvious for words.'

'Shall I have a word with the analysts?'

'Let's wait a bit before we do that,' Bragi said, his hand on the door handle. There was a strong sense of competition between the analysts and the uniformed officers, and all too frequently the analysts were able to reap the rewards of work that the uniformed branch had as good as handed them on a silver platter. 'Watch the window, will you?'

Without even waiting for a reply, he hurried along the corridor, past reception and into the computer room. He sat at a screen and felt his hands shaking as he punched in the codes to retrieve the previous day's CCTV of the arrivals area.

40

Sonja stepped lightly out to the car park in front of Agla's house. Her car chirped in welcome as she pressed the button on her key fob. Of course it was almost unforgivable carelessness to leave a suitcase with four kilos of cocaine in the car overnight, but she felt that something inside her had changed. All those little security measures she had taken when she was travelling with just a kilo at a time now seemed slightly quaint. She was still dazed at how easy it had been to bring in such a substantial amount in one go and she felt buoyed up by last night's feeling of triumph. She felt strong and smart, and not even the thought of having to meet Ríkharður was enough to bring her down.

Getting into the car she turned the heater up to clear the wind-screen of the fog that had collected overnight. She switched on her pay-as-you-go mobile and reported in with a text message. Ríkharður answered as she pulled out onto the road, suggesting the Grandi dock. Stopping at a red light, she keyed in a reply: *'OK. Right now.'*

She had no reason to wait this time. The cocaine was in blocks, so there was no way she could shave anything off without it being visible. Another of her security steps – hiding it for Ríkharður to collect – now seemed childish. Now she was playing with the big boys, as Thorgeir had put it. Now she would have to play it as coolly as she could and hope that her interests and theirs would coincide.

The single question mark in Ríkharður's next text message indicated that he had expected the usual few hours' notice. But Sonja repeated that the handover had to take place right away and drove directly to the dock. She stood there by her car and breathed in the mixed aroma of oily waste and seaweed until Ríkharður appeared.

Ríkharður got out of his car with another man, someone Sonja had never seen before. This one was much the same as all the others, a smartly turned-out young guy with the look of hours spent in the gym about him. He kept his eyes on Ríkharður, as if determined to copy his every move. Sonja opened the boot and lifted out the case, but instead of putting it down and pulling it behind her, she held on to it as Ríkharður approached, and then offered it to him.

'All yours,' she said, meeting his gaze.

Ríkharður took it with one finger, as if it weighed nothing, then handed it to the young man at his side. He took the case and placed it on the back seat of their car before taking a seat in the front.

'No hide-and-seek this time?' Ríkharður asked, taking a step closer to Sonja. She wanted to take to her heels, but stood still. 'What's different?'

'At last I'm pretty sure that you're not fucking me about,' Sonja said.

Ríkharður took another step closer, grabbing her so quickly that she could not escape his grasp. He held her so tightly, she felt like a help-less animal caught in a trap. His hands were more steel than flesh, not giving an inch in spite of her best efforts to pull away. He shot a hand down the waistband of her trousers, slid it into her pants and squeezed so hard that Sonja saw black dots dance in front of her eyes.

He put his mouth close to her ear and hissed, 'Don't you be too sure that we're not fucking with you.'

41

The computer room was filled with the blue glow from the screen – Bragi had switched off the lights so he could see the screen more clearly. He sat in the blue twilight, searching the footage for a face he recognised; someone familiar, a face that rang all his warning bells. He started with the first arrivals of the day and skimmed through them quickly. These early flights were mainly from America; the arrivals hall filled with people still half asleep, lugging heavy cases. He fast-forwarded over the charter flights from the Czech Republic and Poland – none of the passengers looked likely, all of them looking to be honest tourists under the leadership of tour guides. Then there were the midday flights from Europe and among the passengers was a character he was sure he recognised from an old case. He switched to the customs corridor and zoomed in on the man's face. But he saw he had made a mistake. It was not the same person.

Bragi continued his search, skating rapidly over the afternoon charter flight arrivals, then slowing down for the evening flights. First there was Amsterdam, then Copenhagen, an extra Paris flight that had been added to the schedule, and then the London flight. Bragi paused the replay and zoomed in on the carousel with the baggage from London.

There she was: the beautiful lady in the overcoat. Sonja Gunnarsdóttir, who always looked like a film star.

He rewound and replayed the recording from the moment she appeared at the top of the escalator. She moved so completely in time with the people around her that he hadn't noticed her before. It was as

if she floated along on the tide of people without the slightest movement that might attract attention. Bragi kept his eyes locked on her as
she went to the duty-free shop and came out again with a shopping bag
in her hand. He zoomed in closer as she took her place by the carousel. She stood completely still, watching the conveyor belt pass before
her. But then a sudden, almost invisible shudder ran the length of her
body. It was so subtle that if Bragi had not been concentrating on her, it
would have passed him by. He watched on until she reached for a dark
case on the carousel. Then he rewound to watch her standing still, and
then suddenly shaking. It fitted perfectly. It would have been hardly
noticeable if he hadn't been looking for it, but she definitely shivered
involuntarily, precisely at the moment her case emerged through the
hatch on the carousel. Again he watched her reach for the case and
lift it off the belt. There was clearly some weight to it, but she acted as
if it was of no consequence, extending the handle and setting off at a
measured, steady pace with the case at her heels.

Bragi noted the exact time she had left the arrivals hall and then
switched to the customs corridor view. Nothing was happening there.
A river of people flowed through the narrow passage without a customs
official to be seen anywhere. He noted the minute she left the terminal
building and switched next to the same time on the car park camera. He
stared irritably, fretting at the coaches that seemed to always fill the foreground, blocking the cameras closest to the terminal. He had to wait for
a while before she appeared. He saw her walk at the same brisk, steady
pace away from the building, until she took to her heels and ran the last
stretch out of the airport car park, over the road and into the long-term
car park. He rewound the footage, back to where she walked from the
terminal before breaking into a gallop. It was as if she had been holding
in all that excess energy until she could burn it off in the fresh air. Bragi
was about to switch off when he noticed a man hurrying behind her on
the way to the long-term car park. He didn't follow her all the way there.
Instead, he got into a dark Mercedes sports 4x4 and drove away. The
man was of average height, but his thick legs gave him a rolling gait. This
time Bragi again switched cameras, shifting to a view over the entrance

next to the terminal and scrolling to find the right moment. He could see the open area between the terminal and the coaches, and watched the woman come out and head directly for the car park. He could now see, too, that the man was leaning against a wall until she appeared, at which point he took out a phone, punched in a number and held it to his ear. Then he set off after her towards the car park.

This was someone Bragi recognised: Ríkharður Rúnarsson, a well-known thug and dealer. He had often been linked to trafficking, but nothing could ever be made to stick; the drugs mules were invariably too frightened of him to say a word.

Bragi rewound the footage one more time and was zooming in on the man's face to make completely sure that it was Ríkharður when the computer suite door opened and Atli Thór's face appeared.

'Cuba Libre's dead,' he said, his voice shaking with emotion. 'It looks like poison.'

Bragi stood up. 'What? When?'

'Yesterday. Poor thing. I thought you'd want to know.'

Bragi sat back down in his chair and gathered his thoughts: first an anonymous tip-off that a shipment could be coming through Reykjavík domestic airport, just as Ríkharður Rúnarsson was seen at Keflavík, shadowing a mysterious woman as she arrived from overseas. On top of that, a sniffer dog was now also dead. He replayed the sequence once again, watching the woman gallop to the car park. He was sure now that all his instincts were right. His hands had stopped shaking and he was swept away with a warm glow of certainty.

This woman was no small fry. She was a big fish.

42

'And this?' María asked, pointing at a long printout of transactions. 'Was all this also routine business?'

Agla put on her reading glasses and peered at the list. 'No. Those are just trades in Greek securities.'

There was silence until Inspector Jón spoke up. 'Would you like to explain further?'

'Sure.' Agla sat up in her chair and reached out to the computer. She navigated to the Greek market and selected the shares in question. 'These ones in green are the government bonds, so we avoid them. They never drop,' she said, selecting a filter so the government bonds disappeared. 'That leaves loans that can drop significantly in value if that country's credit rating drops. These are what you buy, but it has to be a stack of them in one go. As you can see, we bought these in partnership with bigger German funds, as you have to establish a dominant position.'

'And?' María stared at her in excitement.

Jón's fingers drummed on the table and Elvar shifted awkwardly in his chair, but Agla knew there was nothing to worry about. This was something they could question her about to their heart's delight.

'In basic terms,' Agla continued, 'we bought at thirty per cent of the value, as far as I remember. Then it was the usual waiting game. When the Greek government wants to do a deal, there's a demand to pay out a hundred per cent of the value of those loans. And if the hedge funds have a dominant position, then the state has no choice but to pay up.'

'And you took part in this?' María's question sounded naïve, considering Agla was explaining the bank's role in this business, but her tone of voice demonstrated what María really wanted to convey: disgust.

'Everyone did it,' Agla said. 'We only took part on a relatively modest scale, but the German banks were massive in this. It's a recognised trade.'

'A trade built around bankrupting a whole country?' María's jaw tightened as she spat out the words.

'That's life,' Agla replied. 'I can't change that. Big players swallow little ones. That's nature.'

'What a delightful point of view,' María sneered, and stood up.

'It's the same as being happy to see lamb on your dinner plate. I'm sure you do that occasionally. We're all predators, whatever we like to pretend we are.'

Agla had hardly finished speaking when María spoke up again, her voice as cold as ice. 'How did we get from trading Greek securities to comparisons with lamb? And you can sit there and talk about this as cool as you like?'

'There's nothing illegal about it,' Agla shot back. 'You'll have to search for a long time before you'll find anything you can pin on us.'

'Nothing illegal, no.' María stood still for a moment, her mouth open as if waiting for more words to come to her. Then she snapped her teeth hard together and quickly left the room.

The door had hardly shut behind her when she rushed back in and dropped back into the chair opposite Agla. 'So who's the next victim? Denmark? Holland? Who?'

'No,' Agla answered coolly. 'Portugal. Then France and then the euro.'

She was about to launch into an explanation of why and how the volume of government bonds had to be so high that it could threaten the credit rating, and then you needed to buy just as things were starting, before the full weight of a recession could hit. But she didn't get that far – Elvar's elbow jabbed her in the ribs, giving her a warning that she should keep quiet, as María again rushed from the room.

43

'It's a sensitive subject,' Elvar told her, standing awkwardly on the icy pavement outside the Special Prosecutor's office.

Agla couldn't see that it made any difference. The Greek trade had nothing to do with market manipulation, and there was nothing illegal about it whatsoever. But it was as well to spin them a line, lead the Prosecutor's investigators off track with a few decoys.

'Don't worry about it, Elvar,' she said, patting his shoulder.

'It's maybe ... err...' He was casting around for the right words. 'It's maybe as well not to tell them too much about ... let's call them things that could influence their opinion of you.'

'And why should the Greek model influence their opinion of me?' Agla snorted. 'They were all doing it until just a few months ago. The German banks still are.'

'Like I said, it's sensitive,' he said placidly. 'You played those tricks on Greece, and now we, the Icelanders, are having to watch foreign investment funds playing the same tricks on us.'

Agla looked into his eyes and for a moment was astonished to see hurt in them. 'It's what happens, Elvar. Countries in recession are victims of hedge funds. Vultures sniff out corpses to feast on.'

'True,' Elvar agreed. 'But people probably didn't expect quite so many would jump on the bandwagon and end up sinking us.'

'These people can smell trouble a mile off and they simply gamble on it being serious enough for them to make a killing.'

'It just comes as a shock when we're talking about a whole country – a nation, and nobody is prepared to help out.'

'Iceland is just a pawn, Elvar. On a global scale, Iceland is just a village, like Kópasker or some other forgettable little northern village with a hundred inhabitants. How much interest would you have in helping Kópasker stay afloat?'

Elvar thought in silence. He shrugged and turned round. 'I suppose it depends on whether or not I lived in Kópasker,' he said as he walked away, leaving Agla dissatisfied.

This was a discussion with him that she would come back to. She found this over-sensitivity in the debate about the assault on the króna and the Icelandic state childish. It was naïve to see it as treason. It didn't require any deep insight to foresee the future of this tiny country, which had been playing at being a free and independent state these past few years. Aside from all the overblown rhetoric about culture, history and language, a century in the future, Iceland would never be much more than a remote outpost.

44

As she got out of her car outside Thorgeir's office, Sonja popped a piece of chewing gum into her mouth. She had thrown up on the dock once Ríkharður had driven away, and the terror that had held her in its grasp since their first meeting had gripped her with renewed strength. She was not just convinced now of how dangerous Ríkharður was, she sensed it with every fibre of her body. His presence had always disgusted her – goose pimples and cold sweat down her back were an inevitable part of meeting him – but it had been a long time since she had felt so physically sick.

On her way up the stairs inside the office building, a man hurrying the other way narrowly missed running into her.

'Sorry,' he muttered without looking at her.

It wasn't until the man had disappeared down the steps and out of the door that Sonja realised who he was: Húni Thór Gunnarsson, MP and friend of her former husband, Adam. They had often met at dinners and receptions, so if he had paused long enough to look at her face he would undoubtedly have recognised her. Perhaps not, she thought. Her looks were probably ordinary enough for her face to be easily forgotten, whereas he was in the media every week, so anyone who made a point of following the news would know who he was.

'Do you know Húni Thór?' Sonja asked, as soon as she had set foot in Thorgeir's office.

'Well, I do and I don't. I've managed his campaign fund for him.' Thorgeir said, immediately starting the business of opening the safe behind his desk. He knew that Sonja didn't care for small talk or anything that would keep her there long.

'If I was ever tempted to vote for him, that temptation has now gone,' Sonja said.

Thorgeir turned his chair round and faced her. 'What do you mean?' he asked, his tone unusually sharp.

Thorgeir's reaction to her remark took Sonja by surprise. She must have touched a nerve. She decided to cut things short. 'Precisely what I say,' she replied.

'I do all the usual legitimate legal work as well, you know,' Thorgeir said, turning back to the safe and taking three bundles of notes from it. This time they were pretty thick ones.

Sonja packed them away in her bag and watched Thorgeir's slim fingers tapping at the keyboard as he transferred a further decent amount to SG Software's account. She filled in an invoice form with the right numbers and passed it to him.

'Render unto Caesar that which is Caesar's,' she said, and he nodded.

With this payment she had enough of 'legal' income to be able to take out a loan for a small apartment, and there was enough in her safe deposit box for a deposit. But before she could even think of starting a custody battle with Adam she would have to get herself out of the snare. She would have to be completely free before she could take Tómas back; but that possibility was approaching rapidly.

'I don't want to meet Ríkharður again,' she said.

Thorgeir looked up from the computer. 'That's not up to you,' he said. 'We do things our own way.'

'Then I'll have to get a bodyguard to protect me from him. Which will mean there's a loose end in all this. I'm sure none of us wants that, but I'll need to do it if I'm supposed to deliver to him again. He's been threatening me.'

'I'll have a word and ask him to back off,' Thorgeir said, smiling as if it was something that tickled his sense of humour.

'Not good enough,' Sonja retorted. 'I've caused no trouble. I haven't made any demands, but still he sends me pictures of himself with my son and comes out with all sorts of crap every time I make a delivery. I want to deliver to someone else if I'm going to do any more trips.'

'You'll do as many trips as we tell you to, darling,' Thorgeir growled, his eyes cold.

Sonja sighed and didn't reply. He was right – she was in no position to dictate terms. She had been trapped. She saw there was no point now in telling him that she hadn't liked the London pickup point.

'We'll sort something out,' Thorgeir added in a gentler voice, as if he wanted to soften the harsh tone of a moment before. 'We like to keep the staff happy.'

'I'm not staff,' Sonja said over her shoulder on the way out. 'I'm a slave.'

45

The rest of his shift colleagues had gone home long ago and the night staff had taken over. It was now past midnight, but Bragi was still absorbed in CCTV recordings, going back through the archive. He had his schedule of shifts for the last month by his side, and tried to recall on which days he had seen the woman in the overcoat arrive in Iceland. There were two, or even three, occasions in the last month when he'd noticed her, and, if he remembered correctly, she had always arrived on a European flight from Paris, London or some such place. Now that he knew her name, he could have requested the passenger lists, but that would have meant providing an explanation that might lead to the case being taken out of his hands.

He fast-forwarded through images on two screens at once. At last he hit the jackpot – there she was. He noted down the date he saw her go past and called up recordings from all the terminal's cameras so he could follow her from the gangway all the way out to the car park. It was an evening recording, a flight that had arrived from Copenhagen. The woman appeared almost severe – definitely too formal for a flight at that time of day. Everything about her indicated that she was on the way out of the country to some important meeting or conference; not on the way home to Iceland at the end of a business trip. Normally people relaxed towards the end of such trips and there was a levity to them as they stepped on home soil once more after a long journey. She looked stiff, although there was nothing else about her that attracted attention. Bragi trailed her from camera to camera all the way out of the building, but when he switched to the car park she was nowhere to be seen. He went to the camera showing the entrance and the side of the terminal and tracked her down there. She had come out of the left-hand entrance, looked around and hurried to the other entrance, setting off after a couple who were about to cross the road. She stopped the couple, and a conversation seemed to take place, then the two women swapped what looked like identical cases. Bragi rewound back to the baggage carousels, but was unable to see anything, as the woman had taken a position at the end of the baggage hall where the view was obscured by a horde of travellers and their baggage.

It could have been a coincidence; the two women could really have taken the wrong cases, only discovering the mistake once they had left the terminal building. But Bragi didn't believe in coincidences. He was convinced that this Sonja Gunnarsdóttir knew exactly what she had been doing.

46

Agla had meant to sit in the chair on the balcony, but decided against it when she saw the thick layer of ash that had collected there. The ash was everywhere, brought every time the wind blew from the volcanic region to the east. Once it had fallen, though, it didn't blow away again, instead becoming sticky, clinging to whatever surface it had landed on.

Instead she stayed standing and took breaths of the chilly outdoor air. The big tree in the garden was bare and seemed to shiver in the cold. Every once in a while the idea came to her of buying a house and moving, but there was some comfort in having people living both above and below her. There were parts of Reykjavík she liked better, and some that were less windy than it was here, in the western part of town, but the dark, gloomy buildings of the area seemed friendly in a familiar way.

This was the moment when she would have lit a cigarette, if she had had one to light. Her overwhelming instinctive feeling was that this island had become a sinking ship and there was no sense in anything other than trying to save herself from going down with it. The government stubbornly continued to try to reach agreements, making efforts to keep everyone happy without any real idea about the enemy it was dealing with. They didn't realise that power was no longer in their hands and that everything was going to hell. The big international hedge funds and their pals would turn up right behind the IMF and snap up anything that had even the slightest value.

The doorbell buzzing startled her, as if she had been caught smoking. It was a moment before she realised that it must be her brother Elías, who had called and invited himself round. Neither he nor her other three brothers had much contact with her unless there was a good reason for it, so he had to be in a bad way.

'Hello,' he said, greeting her with a dry kiss on the cheek.

Agla took his coat and ushered him towards a chair in the kitchen.

His hair was shot with silver. He had been the darkest of the family, but was the first to start turning grey even though he was the youngest but one.

'Beer?' she asked and he shook his head. 'Coffee?'

'No, not for me. Don't go to any trouble.'

That meant a short visit; this had to be something other than a courtesy call.

'How are the kids?' Agla asked, taking a seat across the kitchen table.

Elías had three children and her other brothers had two each, so she had a respectable horde of nieces and nephews. She usually saw them at the family Christmas gathering and heard from them when they called to thank her for the birthday cash she made a point of sending them. She always remembered birthdays – she was able to recall practically every date of birth ever mentioned to her.

'They're doing fine. Magnús is doing well in his first year at college and you can expect an invitation to Katrín's graduation party in the spring.'

'Time flies, doesn't it?'

'You could say that.'

'True.'

Agla lapsed into silence and watched her brother twisting his fingers. He was tanned to the colour of coffee, just back from a break in Spain, the tan highlighting the white scar on the back of his hand. That was the scar left by the fork she had jabbed into his hand when she was ten years old.

'The news doesn't look good,' he said, and Agla knew he wasn't referring to the country's plunging credit rating, the droves of redundancies or the lines at food banks. He meant her. 'I was wondering...' he said, hesitating. 'You see, we boys were wondering if there's any reason to be worried about the house in Spain...'

Agla sighed. So that was what it was all about – the house in Spain she had given to their parents a few years before they had passed away, and which they had inherited between them and which the brothers had used frequently ever since.

'We own it outright, as you well know,' she said.

'It's just that, because of what we saw in the papers, we were wondering if there might be a demand for damages from the resolution committee...'

'You're frightened that the committee might find out I own one fifth of a house in Spain?' she said. 'The house I gave our parents.'

Elías smiled awkwardly but said nothing.

Agla stood up, a signal that it was time for him to be on his way. 'I'll make sure the house is entirely in your names,' she told him, handing him his coat.

'That wasn't what I meant...'

'I don't care,' Agla said. 'It's all yours. I never use the place.'

'Of course you could use it even if it's in our names.'

'If I want a house in Spain, then I'll buy one,' Agla snapped. 'Say hi to the kids for me.'

She shut the door behind him and for a moment she would have been only too happy to stick another fork deep into the back of his hand.

47

'Don't let the boys see you cry,' her mother had said, fetching cotton wool to stop her nose from bleeding. 'If you start out letting boys stop you doing things, letting them tell you that you can't do this or that, then it'll never end. It'll be that way your whole life.'

Agla had gone straight back out to the playground, fought her way back into the football game and hadn't held back, even though she never got the ball for long. She was a skinny girl, and the boys and their friends were all robust youngsters, but even though, before the week was out, a black eye had been added to the nosebleed, she could feel that they were no longer so keen to tackle her. They didn't go in full pelt anymore and it wasn't because they wanted to go easy on her but because they were a tiny bit scared of her.

'You're a beast, little mouse!' her older brother Jói had said with a laugh after an energetic session on the pitch.

She took it as a compliment. Mice could jump and bite back, and most people were frightened of them. That was the week she had conquered her fear of pain and no longer expected the boys to behave in any special way around her just because she was a girl and the baby of the family. Instead she made every effort to learn from the boys, behaving as they did. It would all help her in later life.

So when she stuck her fork in the back of Elías's hand when he tried to sneak a meatball from her plate, she felt both an instinctive remorse and a kind of pride – especially when their mother gave her a sympathetic wink as she wrapped Elías's injured hand in a cloth while he squealed like a stuck pig.

48

Tómas woke to the sound of voices. He lay still in the dark and tried to work out whose they were. He made out his father's bass tone and the piercing laughter of Dísa, his dad's girlfriend, and one more voice he didn't recognise, so they must have a visitor. Dad didn't like it when Tómas appeared while they had guests, but he could say he was going for a drink of water and that way he could see who had come to visit.

He tiptoed along the corridor and into the living room. There were candles flickering on the table, and Dad and Dísa sat on the sofa. The visitor was Dad's friend, Sponge. He lay back in a leather armchair with one leg hooked over the armrest and a bottle of beer nestling between his legs.

'Hey, ma man. Five!' Sponge burst out as Tómas appeared, holding out a fist. Normally there was something creepy about grown-ups behaving like that, but Sponge was pretty cool. There was something genuine about a fist bump with a guy like Sponge, so Tómas bunched his fist and gave Sponge a knock on the knuckles.

'Hi, Sponge.'

'What's the matter, Tómas?' Dad asked. 'You should have been asleep ages ago.'

'I was asleep,' Tómas said. 'I woke up and thought I'd get a drink of water.'

'Get yourself some milk instead and you'll sleep better.'

Tómas opened the fridge, poured milk into a glass and drank it down in one.

'You've got a milk moustache, sweetheart,' Dísa said as he went back to the living room. Tómas wiped it off with the sleeve of his pyjama top.

'Are you going to make pancakes tomorrow morning?' he asked.

Dísa nodded. 'Of course, sweetheart, if you like.'

Dísa winked and he winked back, even though he knew he couldn't do it properly. She laughed as he pulled a face trying.

'Good night, Tómas,' Dad called after him as he went back to his room.

'Good night, Dad,' Tómas replied. 'Good night, Dísa. Good night, Sponge.'

49

Would you like to elope abroad with me and stay there for as long as we live?

That was what Agla really wanted to say when she called Sonja that evening. Instead she managed to say practically nothing.

'How are you feeling?' Sonja asked, but Agla had no idea how to reply. There was no scale she could refer to in giving an answer.

'Not so bad,' she said at last.

Sonja persisted, offering to come to her place and stay the night. But Agla was too overcome with shame to accept. It wasn't just the usual shame for the normal dirty thoughts and lusts; it was a different kind of shame. She felt she had to be less of a person in Sonja's eyes, now that she had been publicly outed as a criminal. So she said little, letting Sonja do all the talking, revelling in the joy of hearing her rattle on about what the day had brought her.

Sonja said she had met a foul man who had once groped her, had an argument with her boss and finally had a big invoice paid, so she had celebrated by buying herself a new dress.

Agla could imagine Sonja wearing the dress, which sparked a new train of thought and she started to regret turning down the offer of having her come for the night. Then she remembered that tomorrow was another day with the Special Prosecutor's team; it would be as well to be on her toes. She would have to be cold and hard, not the soft, tender and shamefaced person she would be after a night with Sonja.

'Tell me a Sapphic secret,' she said, and heard Sonja laugh.

'What is it with you and Sapphic secrets?'

'I just find this whole world fascinating,' she replied. 'Tell me something I don't know.'

'This world...' Sonja said, still laughing. 'This world is just the same as the one that everyone else lives in. You know I'm only telling you tales to cheer you up.'

'I know,' Agla said. 'Tell me some Sapphic secret to cheer me up.'

'OK,' Sonja said and thought for a moment. 'Listen, here's one. Did you know that we believe Dolly's one of the sisterhood?'

'Dolly? The country singer?'

'That's the one, our woman in cowboy country,' Sonja said, laughing quietly as if it were a joke. 'There's been loads in the press about it. She's denied it, of course.'

'It's hard to believe she is.'

'Why?' She could hear the teasing scratch in Sonja's voice.

'She's hardly the type.'

'Hardly the type? You mean she's too girly?'

'Yes, sort of. I just don't get the feeling she's that way inclined.'

'Well, my dear. Maybe you ought to take a good look at your own prejudices. Exactly what is it that rules out Dolly being queer?'

Agla knew that once again she had taken the bait and given Sonja an opportunity to make fun of her. All the same, it was a relief, leading her thoughts away from the shame, the Prosecutor, the endless wondering just how long the investigation was going to take, from the fear that the whole thing was going to blow up in their faces in the worst possible way.

'You and your type!' she snapped. 'You're always imagining that the rest of us think the way you do. Not everyone's queer, even though you seem to think they are.'

'Good night, Agla,' Sonja said, and she could hear her making an effort not to laugh.

50

Bragi kissed Valdís tenderly on the cheek, and she briefly leaned close and rested her head on his shoulder. He breathed deep and allowed himself to enjoy the moment, memories of love and closeness flooding him. He had arrived early enough at the care home to help her out of bed, something he sometimes did when he had a day off. This was partly because he wanted her to remain accustomed to him helping her, touching and looking after her, partly so he could check for bruises. She had been there for almost a year when he noticed the dark imprint of a hand on her arm and a group of small bruises on her back, which he had seen when he had helped her undress. The manager had asked the staff about them, but nobody was able to recall Valdís suffering a fall or needing to be helped to her feet in such a way that could leave a mark. Since then there had been two more occasions when she had been badly bruised, but there was no point in asking her how they had got there.

Bragi led Valdís into the dining room for breakfast and helped her over to her usual place. He went to the sideboard, but there was only muesli and yoghurt to be seen.

'Is the porridge on its way?' Bragi asked the girl who was adding cornflakes to the selection on the sideboard.

'There's no porridge today,' she said. 'Just muesli and cornflakes.'

'Could you do some porridge for Valdís?' he asked. 'She struggles with dry food these days.'

'There's yoghurt,' the girl said, pointing to the carton. She was distant, and Bragi wondered if she might be the type who could be heavy-handed with an old woman; heavy-handed enough to leave a bruise.

'Yoghurt's bad for her stomach.'

'OK, I'll ask,' the girl replied and disappeared.

Bragi took a seat next to Valdís. She looked at him and he at her. Sometimes they could spend a long time looking into each other's eyes, and it was as if time ceased to have any meaning for Valdís; Bragi felt that this brought him closer to her.

'Here you go. There's only instant porridge,' the girl said, dropping a packet of dried food onto the table. 'Just pour hot water from the kettle over it and stir.'

Bragi followed her instructions, and once he had poured hot water over the contents of the packet there was something in the bowl that resembled porridge. It wasn't appetising, but Valdís wasn't going to complain. He glanced around, reached for the sugar bowl and poured a hefty amount into the porridge. The staff frowned on that kind of thing, running the place with a strict emphasis on healthy eating, although Bragi failed to understand why people who had so little time left in this world shouldn't enjoy whatever they felt like eating.

Valdís had developed a sweet tooth as she had become increasingly ill, so she ate the porridge happily. Bragi wiped her mouth with a bib that today was decorated with ducklings.

'Soon, my love,' he whispered and stroked her hair – as soft as silk – as he said goodbye. He had a long day ahead of him, starting with a visit to the police station.

'Do an old man a favour, would you?' he said a little while later, dropping heavily into the shabby visitor's chair in Inspector Hallgrímur's office. 'Can you let me know where a certain Ríkharður Rúnarsson hangs out these days?'

'Rich Rikki?' Hallgrímur asked in surprise. 'What do you want to know about him for?'

He and Hallgrímur got on well together, but each of them made a point of never bothering with a greeting or a goodbye, or asking each other courteous questions about how they were doing.

'People like him never live at their registered legal residence,' Bragi said. 'I've already checked that out.'

'But why do you want to know about him?' Hallgrímur repeated, staring at him over his reading glasses.

'Let's call it an old man's hunch; a gut feeling, you know. The kind of hunch you have to follow up.'

Bragi held Hallgrímur's gaze and was sure he could hear the cogs ticking over in his head.

'Is this something that your analysts should be dealing with?'

Bragi shrugged. 'Ach, a body has to have something to look into to keep the grey matter busy. I'll hand it all over to the analysts if it turns out there's anything in it. So just do me a favour on this, would you?'

'Two conditions,' Hallgrímur said, picking up the phone. 'One, you let me know if there's anything to this hunch of yours; and two, you don't go anywhere near the man.'

'Promise,' Bragi said.

'Cross your heart and hope to die?' Hallgrímur asked with a sardonic smile. 'You won't try to ask him about anything or do anything that might alert him to your presence? He's broken noses for less.' Staring over the top of his glasses, Hallgrímur kept his gaze steady until Bragi lifted his hands in agreement.

Five minutes later he drove away from the police station with an address on a little yellow post-it note.

51

Agla sat at the table in the interview room at the Prosecutor's offices, flicking through the internet while the investigators were downstairs in the canteen having lunch. The computer was new, a replacement for the one the Prosecutor's team had seized, and it was already getting on her nerves. It was as if the software designers felt they had some kind of a duty to change the interface with every new generation, simply to infuriate their customers.

Elvar had offered to fetch her soup or a salad, or even a burger from the kiosk next door, but she replied that if there was nothing he could bring her that contained alcohol, then he could forget it. Knocking back a double or two would certainly have dispersed the gloom created by two days of interrogations, but, naturally, she had been joking. The lawyer's expression indicated that he hadn't seen the funny side.

So far, it had been another day of silence. Elvar had made her promise not to answer anything directly. He only wanted her to reply to those questions he repeated and asked for her response on. But that morning there had not been a single one of these. He had sat and written everything down, answering the investigators by saying that Agla would respond in due course. By midday the dry-as-dust session had become so monotonous that Agla allowed her mind to wander, and as usual, it found Sonja. Sonja who loved to tease. It was as if she set out to provoke Agla until she had to snap out a response. But this annoying habit did nothing to cool Agla's longing for her – quite the opposite, it fanned the flames. Maybe that was part of Sonja's magic, part of the web of demands Agla was caught up in.

She took out her phone and keyed in a text message: '*Are you thinking about me?*'

The reply came back straight away: '*Yes, my love. Always.*'

Agla smiled to herself and erased the messages, as she had made a habit of doing. She had been relieved about that when the Prosecutor had seized her old phone.

'*My love*'. Sonja would sometimes call her '*my love*'. There was something so wonderful in those words, something that brought with it the comfort of the familiar. Hearing those words would always set her on edge, though, but they would also gladden her heart, even though she knew perfectly well how naïve it was to imagine that a couple of words could have any real meaning in a relationship that could never last for long.

In spite of her instructions, Elvar brought her a carton of salad and a can of Coke. Inspector Jón and María followed him into the room and Agla closed her laptop. She had no intention of letting them see that she had been searching for Dolly.

52

Ríkharður Rúnarsson, known to the police as Rich Rikki, lived in one of the sprawling blocks at Krummahólar in the upper end of Breiðholt, the northern suburb on the hill overlooking Reykjavík. Built in the sixties as a joint effort between unions and the government to try to provide housing for the poorest people, these flats had been on the open market for years and had gathered a colourful collection of inhabitants.

Rikki lived here with his girlfriend, or so Hallgrímur's source said. The girl had been handed a sentence a couple of years ago for trying to smuggle narcotics so there was no doubt that she was one of Ríkharður's mules. She had a flat supplied by social services and, according to the officer Hallgrímur had spoken to, he was able to live there most of the time, provided there was no trouble and as long as he didn't stay there permanently.

Bragi parked in the car park some distance from the block but close enough to see the entrance and to keep track of the cars coming and going. He was well prepared, with buttered rye bread in a paper bag and a flask of coffee. He switched on the radio and listened to the morning news bulletin as one by one the block's inhabitants left for work. Some had parked their cars in the indoor basement car park and were able to get straight into warm cars, while others had to scrape snow from windscreens, most of them with their bare hands. It hadn't snowed enough to make it worth getting out a scraper; just a light dusting that would be gone in a few hours as the weather promised to turn damp.

The thought of the rye bread was becoming increasingly tempting when Bragi saw Ríkharður saunter out of the block with a sports bag over one shoulder. He went straight down into the car park, and a moment later the Mercedes 4x4 that Bragi had seen on the airport CCTV hurtled past. Bragi started his car and had to rev the engine to keep up, staying close behind the 4x4 down the slope at Breiðholt. Once they were passing Mjódd, though, he let the gap widen, allowing a couple of cars between them.

Ríkharður parked outside the gym next to the Laugardalur swimming pool and got out of the car, bag in hand. This took Bragi by surprise. He had been sure that someone like Ríkharður would have trained at a dubious boxing club where steroids were the order of the day, rather than at a respectable place like this where his tattoos would undoubtedly cause a few raised eyebrows.

Bragi waited a while for Ríkharður to disappear through the doors before following him into the entrance lobby. He asked if he could use the gents and the receptionist pointed them out. On the way back he slipped past the glass doors and looked into the training room. Ríkharður was on one of the benches with two young men loading weights onto the bar. Ríkharður was clearly telling them to keep putting them on while they laughed at his bravado.

It was strange, Bragi thought, how men such as Ríkharður always seemed to have a posse of young men around them.

53

Bragi was about to wash the last of his rye bread down with some coffee when Ríkharður appeared through the doors of the gym. His face was flushed and it seemed to Bragi that he was even more bulky than when he went in. He got in his car and drove off, with Bragi following at a careful distance. This journey turned out to be only a few hundred metres long, though, as Ríkharður pulled into a space outside the health-food bar next to the Listhús gallery. Bragi parked as well, far enough away to have a view of the entrance. Soon enough he saw Ríkharður show up with a plate in his hand, taking a seat by the window.

Bragi poured what was left of his coffee into the cap of the flask and drank it as he watched Ríkharður eat a healthy, post-workout breakfast. He reflected that a more optimistic man would imagine that Ríkharður had turned over a new leaf and was now firmly on the straight and narrow. But Bragi's long experience told him that men such as Ríkharður never change. He sipped his coffee and shook his head at the stark contrast between a man taking such care of his own health when his living depended on wrecking other people's.

Once Ríkharður had finished his meal, there was another short drive, this time up to Lágmúli, where he parked his car and went into the office block next door to the chemist's shop. With no parking spaces to be had, Bragi left his car across the street and walked over to the building – a typical, shabby office block with a glass-fronted lobby. Inside was an old lift that would hardly meet modern standards, and a scruffy staircase. Next to the lift was a list of the various activities taking place in the building, including a travel agency, a dentist and three legal practices.

Bragi's eyes stopped at the name of one of the lawyers: Thorgeir Als. He stared at the name. In a culture that used patronyms in place of family names, seeing one of the latter was unusual, and this wasn't one that was easily forgotten; he wasn't sure where he had seen it before, though. Walking back to his car, he called the police station and asked for Hallgrímur.

'Thorgeir Als. What do we know about him?' he said as soon as Hallgrímur answered.

'He defends mules in court,' Hallgrímur replied. 'Why do you ask?'

'Ach. Nothing special,' Bragi said, and ended the call. After all, it wasn't as if he had any evidence to present to Hallgrímur, or that he was even after it. For the moment, Bragi had seen enough. And he was pretty close to knowing just what he needed to.

54

Sonja stood in front of the mirror, with the new dress in her hands. She pulled it on and examined herself, wondering whether or not to take it back to the shop. Until now, the cash her travels had earned her had gone on essentials – food and rent, businesslike clothes for travelling, some presents for Tómas, and not least the fund that was building up in the deposit box, which she would need to get her life back on track. She didn't need a new dress, she had just wanted it. But somehow it felt wrong now to be using the smuggling money for luxury stuff.

The phone rang, interrupting her thoughts. She stared at the screen in astonishment. She and Adam had not spoken for months. Text messages had been enough to organise Tómas's comings and goings.

The first thing that entered her head was that something could have happened to Tómas. 'Hello?' she said, not able to disguise the fear in her voice.

'Hi. It's Adam.' His stiff tone was a relief. That meant nothing was wrong.

'Hello, Adam,' she said. She almost added something friendly – *How are you?* or *Good to hear from you* – but stopped herself.

Adam got straight to the point. 'I'm not happy that you've given Tómas some kind of expectation that he can spend Christmas with you.'

'We haven't talked about Christmas or how we're going to arrange it,' Sonja said, in the faint hope that Adam would take the bait and that Christmas might be open to negotiation.

'There's nothing to discuss,' Adam said, strangling her dream. 'He spent last Christmas with you, so he spends this next one with me. That's clear in the terms of the agreement.'

'An agreement only has to be as binding as we want it to be,' Sonja protested, with no real hope that her words would have any effect.

'I'm not happy that you have access to him at all, but I have to accept it as it's in the agreement. If you don't want to stick to the terms, then that works both ways.'

'Calm down, Adam,' Sonja said, using the persuasive tone that had often worked so well while they had lived together. 'Let's try and remember that this is about Tómas's welfare—'

She didn't manage to finish the sentence before Adam cut in. 'Tómas's welfare, yes.' There was a chill in his voice. 'It's clear that being around you does nothing to contribute to his welfare. The boy's a fucking wreck every time he spends a weekend with his mother.'

Sonja had only just put the phone down when it rang again. This time it was Agla, calling to tell her that all that stuff about Dolly was bullshit – she had looked it up on the internet. Just because Dolly's husband lived in another state was no reason to cast aspersions and make up lies about innocent people. This woman Dolly lived with was her personal assistant and if they shared a room on the road, it had to be because Dolly needed constant assistance; with her costumes. And the hair.

December 2010 to January 2011

55

Regent Street's Christmas lights looked inadequate compared with the ones that festooned this elegant house. Sonja had taken a cab to Sloane Square and walked from there in the cold. This was her third large shipment. The previous one had been nothing special. She had met a grey-haired man at a railway station, where they had switched cases. Back home in Reykjavík she had made the delivery, telling Ríkharður to collect the case from her unlocked car parked in the centre of town while she watched from the safe distance of a coffee shop. Thorgeir and Ríkharður had been unhappy with the arrangement, but it had worked out well.

This time she was making the collection from another new place. This area was very different from the mouldy tower block where she had made the November pickup. Sonja went up the steps and peered through the foliage decorating the doorway, hoping to find a doorbell somewhere among all the baubles and angels hanging in the greenery. In the end she decided to knock. The door was heavy mahogany and its hinges squeaked as a pale servant opened it with a wordless invitation to come inside. She couldn't tell if it was the shock of leaving the chill outside, or if the house's heating had been turned up too high, but she immediately felt herself beginning to sweat.

The servant led her through a wide hall that opened up to the floor above, a sweeping staircase curving up to a landing and two doors. This was a staircase straight out of an old-fashioned movie, perfect for a film heroine in a long dress to make her entrance on. But the man who emerged from one of the rooms and came down the stairs without acknowledging Sonja's presence was far from a film-star ideal. He was muscular with South American features – broad and tanned, looking to be somewhere between forty and fifty. His head had been shaved so close, there was only a glitter of stubble, and he was dressed in shorts and a singlet so that the skulls, saints and flowers adorning his skin were thrown into sharp relief.

'Mr José,' the pale servant announced, as if he were calling out the name of a dinner guest at a royal banquet.

'Señora,' the man said, extending a hand to Sonja. As she reached to take it, he bowed and kissed the back of hers as if she were a duchess. Both his hands and his face were wet with perspiration. 'José. At your service.'

The greeting took Sonja so much by surprise that she unconsciously bent a knee in a brief curtsey.

'Come in,' he said, indicating that she should go ahead of him into the room on the left of the hall. 'Dinner is served.'

Sonja was so startled by the growl that greeted her as she entered the room that she took a step back and fell against José. He grabbed her with his sweaty hands and pushed her further into the room. The growl came from a full-grown tiger that stalked from end to end of a large iron cage in the middle of the room. Sonja stared as if mesmerised, her eyes locked on the restless animal, before José finally led her by the arm to the dinner table, helping her into a chair.

Only when she was seated did she manage to drag her gaze away from the huge beast and notice the sobbing man tied to an office chair in one corner of the room. She tried to open her mouth to ask what was going on, but the words refused to form and only one made it out of her mouth: 'What...?'

'I trust nobody until we have eaten together,' José said, taking a seat at the other end of the table. Sonja now realised it was laid for only two – a healthy helping of some kind of stew on the plates and a little dish of salad beside each serving. 'And my tiger always eats when I do,' he announced, and snapped his fingers.

On this prompt, the pale servant wheeled the man tied to the office chair towards the cage. The tiger stretched out a paw, trying to reach him through the bars.

'No! No! Please!' The man wailed every time the paw came close.

'I don't need to introduce you,' José said. 'You've already met.'

Sonja stared at the man's face. It was so distorted with fear, it was a long time before she recognised him. He was the tall man she had collected a case from in the shabby block of flats, back in November. He was in no state now to pat anyone on the back and mispronounce Eyjafjallajökull. Instead he wept and begged, his dark skin running with sweat and his teeth chattering.

'The thing is,' José said, forking up the stew and speaking as he chewed. 'I came to Europe to make the most of the opportunities here. All my accounts in the States have been frozen, so there isn't much I can do there right now, but in Europe prices are good and people have an appetite. Europe is the land of opportunities!'

He stuffed more food into his mouth, and this time he chewed and swallowed before continuing.

'So where are my problems? Not with customs; the Europeans aren't a problem and even those fucking Colombians keep their word. No. It's Africa.'

José pushed his plate away and reached for a dish, which Sonja now saw was piled high with cocaine. He took a cigarette from a packet in his waistband and rolled it between his fingers until the tobacco loosened and trickled out. He then used his knife to fill the cigarette with cocaine and then plugged the end with the tobacco.

'Dessert?' he offered politely, pushing the dish of cocaine towards Sonja.

She shook her head. Every rumble from the tiger's throat sent prickles of fear over her skin. Each time it thrust its paw through the bars she twitched, and her mind was so numbed, she was frozen, hardly even able to wonder if there was a chance she could stand up and leave. She sat, fixed to her chair, and stared as the man lit his cocaine cigarette, drawing the smoke deep into his lungs.

'For some reason, every shipment seems to get twenty per cent smaller between Lagos and London, all because Amadou here can't withstand the temptation to swindle people who have a lighter skin than his.'

José got to his feet, walked over to the weeping man and looked down at him.

'Amadou, up to now you've swindled white people, because they're stupid. But now you've made a mistake, because I'm not a white man. I'm Mexican. And so that you'll remember for ever that it doesn't pay to swindle Mexicans, my tiger is going to take a bite out of you.'

Sonja heard the patter of liquid falling to the floor; the trembling man in the chair was pissing himself with fear. The stream spread across the floor, but José acted as if he hadn't seen it, or heard the entreaties of the man, who was begging him for mercy.

'A hand or a foot, Amadou?' José said. 'A hand or a foot?'

56

'Now we have eaten together,' José said. 'I don't need to worry about you, do I?'

Sonja could barely shake her head. Her body didn't seem like her own, and José's words sounded as if they came from somewhere in the distance, while in the foreground her mind was filled with the repulsive cracking sound of the tiger chewing its way through the man's arm. Somehow the animal's gnawing at its meal was louder than the howls the victim made as the servant dragged him away, leaving a river of blood flowing across the floor.

Sonja tried to keep her eyes away from the dark pools now forming around the cage and the scatter of drops that had sprayed out of the man's severed arm and now trickled down the opposite wall. Instead she stared at José as he spooned cocaine onto a fifty-pound note and folded it into a neat package.

'A tip for you,' he said, handing Sonja the package. 'You can pick up the case at the door on the way out.'

Sonja nodded, managing to stand up and take a few backward steps, away from this man and the tiger that now lay licking the blood from its lips. She snatched up the red sports bag by the door and looked inside. It contained the usual bags of powder, but she didn't bother to count them in her hurry to escape this dreadful house that again echoed with the tiger's loud growls.

She was almost at the southern end of Hyde Park when she realised that she was running. She slowed down to catch her breath. She wiped the tears from her eyes, but it made no difference as they continued to run freely down her cheeks. This had to be her last trip. She couldn't do this anymore.

57

Elvar the lawyer arrived with a pizza in a box and placed it in front of Agla, handing her a serviette to use as a plate.

'You have to eat,' he said. 'Nobody can stay on top of their game if they don't eat.'

Agla bit obediently into the slice of pizza, but felt the need for something to wash it down with and fetched two beers from the fridge. She had suggested that he come to her place so they could prepare themselves, the whole office environment having become too overwhelming after days of questioning.

They ate in silence, after which Elvar stood up, cleared away the remains of their meal and took a folder and two stacks of papers from his briefcase, spreading them out over the table.

'Now, we ought to go over what we can expect next,' he said. His tone of voice was warm and infused with concern. Agla wondered how such a young man had come to be so responsible.

'Do you have children, Elvar?' she asked.

He shook his head. 'And you?'

Agla shook her head in turn, deciding it was best to concentrate on work. She laid a hand on one of the two piles of documents. 'You ask and I'll answer?' she suggested.

Elvar looked at her wearily. 'You have to tell me the complete truth,' he said. 'I'm bound by an obligation of confidentiality, so you need to tell me everything so that I'm able to defend you. I can't have the Prosecutor taking me by surprise with something unexpected.'

'Sure,' she agreed. 'I'll do my best.'

She looked into his eyes and smiled to conceal the lie. Telling him everything was out of the question. She would tell him only what he needed to know. If she were to tell him the whole story, he would, without a shadow of doubt, get to his feet and walk out.

'I'll keep working on the affidavit to the regional court concerning the resolution committee's claim for damages, as we have to be prepared to deal with that at the same time as everything else,' he said.

Agla nodded her agreement. He was entirely right, and this was precisely where he was going to be useful. A verdict was one thing – it was unavoidable, but a demand for damages from the resolution committee was another – the claim could be sidestepped.

'I'll be found guilty of market manipulation,' she said, 'I'm completely prepared for that.'

'I mentioned the claim for damages just so you're forewarned,' he said. 'There's no reason to be pessimistic.'

Agla smiled. She wasn't being pessimistic – quite the opposite. She would be fortunate to come away from all this with nothing more than a conviction for market manipulation.

58

It was well past midnight when Agla left the bathroom to find Elvar asleep on the sofa. They had drunk a few beers over the documents, and, as always when she had been drinking, she began to feel tender, her thoughts inevitably turning to Sonja. She had locked herself away, perched on the edge of the bathtub and tried to call her. There was no reply, so Agla left a voice message – several, in fact, asking her to call as soon as she could, night or day.

Careful not to wake him, Agla gingerly removed Elvar's glasses, laid them on the coffee table and spread a blanket over him. She was appreciative of the efforts he had made for her. Admittedly, she paid him well, but the thoughtfulness he was showing towards her was way beyond the call of duty. Then again, he was young and ambitious, and this serious case he was working on was a chance to prove himself, so it was no surprise that he was making a big effort. But he was also a genuinely warm-hearted guy, and Agla was thankful for that. She fervently hoped that, if things turned out for the worst, she wouldn't end up dragging him down with her.

Once she was in bed she tried again to call Sonja. It irked her that she wasn't picking up and dark thoughts began to appear in the back of her mind. Sonja had to be working – yet another trip abroad for her computer business, whatever that was all about. Agla felt a stab of conscience. Sonja had no need to work. Agla could give her everything she could ever want, if only she would accept it. Agla had frequently offered to pay for things to lighten her load, but there was always the same reaction. She had offered to find her a better place to live, but Sonja had refused – angrily – saying that she could support herself and that she wasn't for sale.

Maybe Sonja wasn't answering the phone tonight because she had found a new woman to make love to. Lesbians were supposed to be like that – happy to chop and change. And there was no doubt that Sonja was a lesbian, one who had been with many women. Agla on the other hand had never before been aware of having any of the feelings that had burst out when she met Sonja.

Sonja was the exception to everything in her life, and maybe it was this that made her so unbearable but at the same time so unutterably precious. Agla closed her eyes and recalled Sonja's aroma, the heat of her under the bedclothes, her thoughts carrying her into a dream of delight. Then Adam suddenly appeared in her mind, as vivid as if he were there in person, the little boy's hand in his, both of them with horror splashed across their faces. Agla felt her face flush with shame in the gloom. She put the phone on the bedside table, sighed and stared at the light fitting. The light cast by the street lamp outside made the silhouette of the dead fly so sharp she was sure that it was staring at her. This was going to be a night that was short on sleep.

59

Bragi took the letter, crushed it into a ball and sent it flying into the bin. An end-of-service interview. He had never heard such bullshit. It had never been customary in the past to send out written invitations to be pressured into leaving your job. There had to be some hungry youngster knocking at the door, in need of a senior post. But they would have to try harder than that to get rid of him. He wasn't going to be frightened by a letter.

'I told Hrafn it would end up in the bin,' Atli Thór laughed.

'What would?' Bragi asked, feigning innocence. 'Oh, you mean the letter? I thought it was some kind of scam.'

'Too late to worry about it now,' Atli Thór said. 'It's already been binned.' He took the filter from the coffee machine and dropped it into the bin, splattering the contents with cold coffee grounds.

Bragi smiled. It was good to have a colleague like Atli Thór. He put on his jacket and examined himself in the mirror. That was something else he'd miss – the uniform. The two bars and the star symbolised the time and energy he had put into the job over the years, and Valdís had always said that it suited him, that he looked good in uniform.

'The passenger list from the analysts,' Atli Thór said, handing Bragi the list.

Bragi took it and ran a finger down the list of names. He always made a point of checking the passenger lists, both at the start of a shift and again before he went home. He had an arrangement with the boys in the analyst team. They highlighted the names they were interested in, and he'd normally add a few suggestions of his own. The shift that relieved them was generally happy to get the list, as it was run by a young chief inspector who still hadn't developed a close enough rapport with the analyst team.

As the number of tourists had increased, so the passenger lists had become much longer. Bragi scanned this one quickly, paying attention only to the Icelandic names. There was nothing special there for the night shift to worry about, but the next day's list was another matter. His finger halted by one name, listed to land on one of the next day's evening flights. He would be on duty to meet her: Sonja Gunnarsdóttir.

60

Having carried the vacuum packer from her left-luggage locker back to the hotel Sonja's back ached. This was the last time she would be doing this; she would be carrying no more shipments. It seemed that this business was becoming increasingly insane. The sound of the tiger gnawing through Amadou's arm still echoed in her ears, his screams still chilled her bones, and the sight of his blood shooting across the room would stay with her forever. She couldn't take any more. She had made her decision: once she was home she'd set in progress the plan that she had been working on for months; the plan that would free her from the snare.

There were eight missed calls from Agla on her phone. She ignored them. She was used to this by now – the high number of calls simply meant that Agla had been drinking, and was desperate to know what she was doing, with whom and what she was thinking about it all. Then she'd want to hear some lesbian secret that would then infuriate her.

Sonja couldn't deny that she relished teasing Agla, prodding at her prejudices, but she also knew that it was a relief for Agla to have something to take her mind away from the investigation, and from the prosecution that was hanging over her head. Sonja would call her as soon as she landed in Iceland. Right now she needed to get all this powder packed up.

She started by wrapping each of the ten packets in plastic and running them through the machine. Each one became flattened as the air was sucked from it, which also made them easier to pack in her case. Then she took the packages to the bathroom, put them in the tub, turned on the cold tap and poured half a bottle of paraffin into the bath. While the packages soaked, she cleaned the machine with alcohol and then undressed, crushing her clothes into the bag the shipment had come in. She put the sports bag in a black rubbish sack, tied up the top and put it out in the corridor, where the night porter could dispose of it.

Then Sonja drained the bathtub, placed the packages on a towel on the floor and got into the shower herself, before stepping out onto the towel and drying both herself and the vacuum-packed packets. She then carried them back into the bedroom for the next step of the packing process. She was so hot that she didn't bother to dress, instead standing there naked as she put each packet into another plastic envelope and through the machine for a second time. Then she took them all back to the bathroom, washed each one again, in the sink this time, dried them with a fresh towel and took everything back to the bedroom.

The next stage was to put each packet in a larger plastic sleeve and pour coffee on top so that each one was cocooned in its own layer of coffee. This would mask the scent of the cocaine inside. Then there was a final vacuum packing, before she washed each one and her own hands yet again in alcohol. She lined them up on the bed, where she sat for an hour wrapping each one in Christmas paper decorated with a plump Santa Claus.

Finally she took her brand-new blue suitcase, slit the bottom with a carpet knife and arranged the packages under the board at the bottom. To finish off, she dipped a corner of a towel in paraffin and wiped it over the outside of the case. Not many people knew this trick, but by taking care and doing things right, both the scanners and the sniffer dogs could be fooled.

61

Inspector Jón leaned back in his chair, his face set for an argument. At his side María smiled sweetly, but Agla had already learned that this could mean anything. At any moment María could drop a razor-sharp comment but in such an innocent voice it could take a second for the meaning to sink in. It was astonishing just how much we understood other people through their body language, Agla thought. María seemed adept at saying one thing out loud while her manner said something entirely different.

'What you're telling us, Agla, is complete bullshit,' Jón said. 'All this was organised.'

'When you're supplying services it's difficult to keep track of every penny,' Agla replied.

'Because there are no direct costs,' María said, with an even more impenetrable smile. 'And that's what makes this a perfect vehicle for laundering cash.'

Agla was startled. 'I thought this was an investigation into market manipulation,' she said, forcing herself to smile back. She kicked Elvar under the table; he looked up and asked for a coffee break.

Agla went straight out into the harsh wind and marched over the street to a filling station, where she bought a packet of Winstons and a lighter.

Walking back, she keyed Jóhann's number into her phone.

'There's trouble in paradise,' she said as soon as he answered. 'We need to meet.'

Jóhann gave an anguished sigh. 'OK,' he said. 'I'll let Adam know.'

Back outside the Prosecutor's office Agla extracted a cigarette from the packet, lit up and dragged the smoke in deep. It was a long time since she had last smoked and it made her head swim; it wasn't as great as she remembered it being.

'Careful on the phone,' Elvar said when she met him on the stairs.

'What?'

'I saw you go outside and make a call,' he said in a low voice. 'Be careful what you say on the phone, both to me and other people.' He jerked a thumb at the door to the Prosecutor's office.

'You mean my phone's being tapped? The new one?'

'I can't be sure,' he said. 'Let's just say I have my suspicions.'

Agla felt her heart pound as she thought back to all the calls she'd made to Jóhann and his lawyer, and to Elvar. She was sure there was nothing said that could be used against her. But she felt her face flush as the familiar shame lodged itself firmly in her mind. There were other calls that she hoped no one else would have listened to.

'Are you ready to carry on?' María asked, her head appearing round the door on the landing above.

'Ready,' Agla replied, already on the way up. 'I really needed to smoke all of a sudden.'

'Hope you enjoyed it,' María said, again with the same inscrutable smile.

62

Agla sat in her car outside Reykjavík's Free Church and looked out over the city's lake. The water reflected the grey sky above, snatching at it and scattering it among the wavelets. The wind had dropped during the day, but it was still bitterly cold, with frost expected. She had spent the rest of that morning's session trying to gauge from the expressions on María's and Jón's faces whether or not they had listened in to her conversations with Sonja. She hoped they hadn't. She had no desire for people to look at her through a filter that coloured their opinions and feelings about 'those sorts of people'. She didn't want to be 'that sort of person'. She wanted to be what she had always been.

She got out of the car as she saw Jóhann walk over the narrow bridge by the City Hall. From a distance he still had that familiar dashing-banker look about him. He was wrapped in a thick wool overcoat and a scarf, a more sensible choice for this weather than the skirt and tights she had worn for the meeting at the Prosecutor's centrally heated offices.

They met outside Iðnó, where the birds immediately began to gather around them, geese, swans and ducks clambering up the bank in the expectation that bread crusts would come their way.

'Is Adam coming?' Agla asked. The words were hardly out of her mouth when he appeared around the corner, looking smart in a suit and coat, a woollen hat on his head.

'What's happening?' he asked abruptly.

'They're on our trail. By accident, I think.'

Agla avoided looking at Adam, fixing her eyes on Jóhann instead, as if he were some kind of intermediary between them. She had met Adam several times since that fateful day when he had walked in on her with Sonja, but she still felt deeply uncomfortable near him.

'It makes no difference if it's accidental or not,' Jóhann said. 'This is an investigation into market manipulation, so if they want to go in some other direction, then they'll have to start from scratch – new warrants, declaration of status, gathering material. They're not going to be too excited about that if there's something juicier within reach,' Jóhann continued, his eyes on Agla.

She knew what Jóhann was thinking, she just hadn't wanted to be the first to mention it. 'You mean if they start to make progress on the market manipulation case, then that's where they'll focus their attention?' she said with a sigh.

'We have to do everything – and I mean everything – to throw them off the scent,' Adam said. 'We can't afford to lose any more money. These aren't people who will be satisfied with whatever they can get out of the resolution process. They'll want to claw back every single penny. And we've already agreed that it's my job to see that they're satisfied.'

So that was it. Agla would be sacrificed. 'So you're exempt,' she said. 'And they already have their hooks into Jóhann. That just leaves me.'

'You owe me,' Adam retorted, and they both knew he didn't mean money.

63

Sonja was surprised by how little she was shocked now that reality had finally caught up with her. Perhaps it was because she had always known that this would happen one day.

She stared, speechless, at the grey-haired customs officer who seemed to have appeared from nowhere as she stood at the carousel. She hadn't noticed him, and now he was taking the case from her hand.

'This is yours?' he asked.

She nodded, her power of speech having completely failed her.

'It's not labelled. Are you sure it's your case?'

'I'm sure,' Sonja said, finding her voice.

He indicated that she was to follow him through a side door in the arrivals hall and she dutifully obeyed.

Inside the small room was a luggage scanner. He lifted the case onto it and watched the screen as it went through.

'It looks like there's some organic material in there,' he said, stopping the belt and staring at the screen, which showed the contents of her case in shades of blue-green and pink. He told her to place her hand baggage on the scanner and again she obeyed, her thoughts frozen and her heart hammering so loud that she was sure the customs officer could hear it.

It made no difference that she had mentally prepared herself for this moment and thought she knew exactly how she would react. Now it was as if her body was running on instinct alone, drawing all the energy from her mind and routing it instead to the pounding in her chest.

The customs officer lifted the case from the belt and took it to a table where he opened it.

'Can you tell me a few of the items that are in here?' he asked.

Sonja's eyebrows lifted in question.

'So I can be sure it's your case,' he explained.

She swore silently to herself; this meant that the man must be aware of her trick of switching luggage.

'Of course it's my case,' she said, trying to maintain at least the pretence of complete surprise. 'There's the usual stuff in there – clothes, a make-up case, some Christmas presents.'

'Could you be more precise?' he asked, looking at her over the lid of the case.

Sonja tried to concentrate on remembering what she had packed, but the image that filled her mind was the tiger – the big, powerful beast, trapped in its cage, ready to snap its jaws closed on any hand that went near it. It was as if seeing it was what this whole trip had been about. As if that had been her warning, right there: a wild animal in a cage in front of her in the big, elegant house in London – a cruel, living sign of a coming disaster. And she had been too blind to see it.

The customs officer widened his eyes, waiting for her reply.

'There's one black plastic make-up case with perfume, powder, mascara and some other stuff,' she stammered out. 'There's a sponge bag made from red flannel with nail clippers, a nail file, two small bottles of shampoo, and a hairbrush, some conditioner and toothpaste. Oh, and a toothbrush. A pink toothbrush.'

The customs officer opened the case and the bag one after the other, nodding when he saw the contents. There was a satisfied expression on his face now that he was convinced it was her case.

'My name's Bragi,' he said. 'I'm Chief Inspector here at Keflavík Airport. Now I want you to come with me to the examination room.'

He closed her case and lifted it as if it were weightless.

The examination room gave Sonja a crushing, helpless feeling. This amiable but strict grey-haired gentleman in his black uniform showed her to a chair near the table in the middle of the room. He took everything out of the case, arranging each item on the tabletop. Sonja tried to sit still and remain calm, making an effort not to sink into despair, even though she felt that she was being stripped naked as the uniformed man handled her underwear and make-up things.

'Could I go to the toilet?' she asked, suddenly desperate, her mind going back to her college years when the stress of an approaching exam normally hit her bladder. It was years since stress alone had left her desperate to pee.

'Of course,' the customs officer said, taking a walkie-talkie from his belt. 'Female escort to the bathroom!' he called into it.

If it hadn't been for the pounding in her chest and the ache that was spreading from her jaw through her whole head, she would have laughed. There was something so ridiculous about how he pressed the walkie-talkie's buttons and then yelled into it, as if he didn't really trust the technology to carry his voice.

The door swung open and a young woman, also in customs-officer uniform, came in, announcing that she was Sonja's escort to the toilet.

In the room she showed Sonja into, there was no toilet; instead there was a chair with a toilet seat and a washing-up bowl beneath it.

'You really expect me to pee in that?' Sonja asked in amazement.

'Yep,' the woman said, and smiled as if it was the most natural thing imaginable.

Sonja looked at her, but she made no move to leave the room.

'I won't be long.'

'I have to stay here with you,' the girl said as her smile changed to a look of apology. 'I'll turn the other way while you do your business.'

She spun on her heel and stood facing the corner, standing to attention as if she were at the head of a troop of scouts.

Sonja shook her head at the strange combination of tub and chair. 'I don't think I need to go after all.'

64

Bragi was more than astonished. He was dumbfounded. He had been through the contents of the case, but there was nothing suspect in it. He'd twice put it through the scanner but with no result. He had taken out the lining and the base, leaving nothing but the cloth and the frame itself, in which he had drilled a hole. There was no question – there was nothing illegal in the case. While the woman was escorted to the bathroom, he had opened the three Christmas presents and was again disappointed. There was an iPad in the first one

– the latest thing the younger generation demanded; the second held a Lego book; and in the third was one of those monster figures that boys played with these days, with a human body and the face of an animal. When she came back, all that was left to check were the two packets of coffee, which were presumably the organic material the scanner had picked up.

'I'm going to have to open these,' he said.

She nodded as she took a seat. She appeared relaxed, but as she avoided meeting his eye, he was unable to tell from her expression how she was really feeling.

He took out a carpet knife and sliced into the packet of coffee, emptying it into a plastic bag. There was nothing but coffee to be seen; the aroma that filled the room reminded him of the fresh coffee he had ground for his grandmother using the little mill that he had thought was so clever.

'You're bringing coffee into the country?'

'Yes,' she replied. 'I really like this dark-roasted coffee, so sometimes I buy some to bring home with me, for that first cup in the morning.'

She smiled briefly, and Bragi was assailed by doubt. It was the same feeling he'd experienced when she had smiled at him before at the security point when he had checked her passport. The feeling that struck him was that he was wrong, that he was wrongly accusing her, that he was losing his touch. To reassure himself he fetched the handheld analyser and stirred the coffee with the probe, but there was no reading. He swept the analyser through the case, over the clothes and the cosmetics: nothing. This didn't add up. He couldn't accept that for the first time in thirty years he had backed the wrong horse. She had to have the dope either on her person or internally.

'Well,' he said and sighed. 'I'll have to ask you to accompany me to the hospital in Keflavík. You can either go with me as escort and I arrest you as a formality, or else I call the police and they'll take you, which means a formal arrest and more paperwork.'

'Let's just do it the easy way,' the woman decided.

65

Sonja had time to think as she waited in the corridor at Keflavík's hospital with customs tape wrapped around her trouser legs. A doctor had been alerted to carry out a physical search and she expected to be x-rayed.

The grey-haired officer sat at her side, breathing noisily through his nose. 'You were in Copenhagen, you said? Or was it London?'

It was the third time he had asked the same question.

'Like I told you, London, Copenhagen, home. A meeting in both places. You can ask as often as you like, the answer's going to be the same.'

Sonja was gradually reclaiming her self-confidence, and the blinding headache that had suddenly struck her was receding. As far as she was concerned, they could x-ray her as much as they liked. That wasn't a problem. What was worrying were the endless questions concerning where she had been, which indicated that they had been tracking her movements. That was disturbing. Being on a customs black list wasn't good.

'So why did you stop me?' she asked.

He shrugged his shoulders. 'Just a routine check,' he said.

Sonja did not believe that. A routine check didn't end up in front of an x-ray machine. It was as well that this was her last trip.

Her phone buzzed and she looked at the screen to check the message. It was the latest one from Libbý, repeating the *reunion* announcement, with the emphasis on how much the girls in the Sewing Circle were hoping that she would be able to join them in the first week in January. Libbý suggested that she jump on a flight to the north. Sonja had a sudden overwhelming feeling that it was all a dream, that the last two years had been some kind of mirage that had deposited her here in this clinic, and that before long she would wake up and life would be just as it had been. Or maybe these messages from Libbý were a symbol of the new direction her life was about to take? Once she was free she would be able to return to some kind of normal life, one that would give her opportunities for things like taking a quick flight north to see the Sewing Circle. In the aftermath of the divorce she had wriggled out of turning up to their gatherings using a series of white lies: she was too busy; Tómas was unwell; that sort of thing. The truth of it was that when Tómas was with her for a weekend, they ate at IKEA because children could eat for nothing, and in the wake of the crash there was no way that she could think of shelling out for a flight to Akureyri and going clubbing with the Sewing Circle.

She slipped back into a trance, still thinking of her old friends in the north, and realised that it was her former life that had been the dream world, a nebulous existence in which she had drifted with the tide. Two years ago she had woken from the dream – with a shock. And now she existed in the real world – a place where she had witnessed a man mauled by a tiger.

The clinic door opened and a woman in a white coat stepped out. 'Sonja?'

66

Tómas watched impatiently as his father made his snack with painful slowness. It was as if he had decided that morning, the last day before the Christmas holidays, when he was already unusually late, to take extra care to make sure that both pieces of bread were buttered precisely and all the way to the edges.

'Hurry up, Dad,' he said. 'School starts at ten past eight.'

After school he'd come home, have a shower and change his clothes, and then his mother would come to fetch him. They were going to have a Christmassy time together, she had told him. His bag was packed and ready under his bed, with all the usual stuff he took with him: a board game he was going to teach her to play, a change of clothes and his passport, just as she always wanted. There was also a present in the bag for her, something he had made at school. It was a breadboard he had sawn, sandpapered and branded with both their initials. His and his mother's.

'What's it like when you're with your mother? Does she feed you properly?' his father asked, slowly slicing the cheese as if he needed to take extra care with it.

Tómas nodded. 'Yeah. Brilliant food.'

'What sort of thing?'

'All sorts. Meatballs. Spaghetti. And salad, you know, like Mum makes.'

'Does she often have parties, your mother?'

'Parties?'

'Yes, like dinner parties. Does she get a lot of visitors?'

'No, not much. Sometimes. Just a few.'

That wasn't true. Tómas had never seen anyone at Mum's place, but he didn't want his father to think that she had no friends. That would be unfair, seeing as there were so many visitors at Dad's place.

'And *her*? Is *she* there sometimes?'

Tómas shook his head. He knew who his father meant: his mother's girlfriend.

'No,' he replied. 'She's never there. I'm going to be late, Dad.'

'You're sure?' his father asked, finally finishing making the sandwich. 'Hasn't *she* ever dropped by?'

'No,' Tómas said and this time he was telling the truth. But even if he had seen *her* at his mother's place, he would never tell his father. He knew perfectly well that his father didn't like *her*, and he understood why, even though he was just a child. The way he saw it, though, it was his father's fault that Mum had found herself a girlfriend; she wouldn't have done it if he'd been nicer to her.

'If you ever see *her* at your mother's place,' his father said as he wrapped the sandwich in foil, 'you'll tell me, won't you?'

'Sure,' Tómas said, snatching the sandwich and stuffing it into his schoolbag.

67

The dead fly, jet black in the rays from the street lamp, didn't inspire any new ideas that night – no more than it had any other night. She felt that she had become the central point of a circle of thoughts that spiralled inward, collapsing into itself. Adam's suggestion was the only option. She would have to sacrifice herself. There was too much at stake for any other course of action. They couldn't dare leave the Special Prosecutor to continue to dig randomly; they would have to steer the investigation in the right direction.

It was up to her to take the initiative. Agla got out of bed. She was still tired and both her body and her mind cried out to be allowed to rest, but it was a relief to get out of the tumbled sheets. In the shower she thought about the boys who had offered to help. There were three of them, all middle-level managers at the bank, young men the financial crash had left with crushing debts and who would be happy to take a rap for the right amount. Of the three of them, two were worth considering as they had both worked in financing, under Adam.

While Agla brushed her teeth and applied her make-up she considered these two, compared each one's pros and cons, and decided on the guy she liked the least: Davíð. He was a smug bastard who had brown-nosed Jóhann and the other senior people at the bank on his way up, and then went out of his way to snub them now they were in trouble. He was also one of those men who hated to have a woman among the heavyweight players. There had been a few people like that at the bank before the crash. It had irritated her to never be invited on their boys' weekends to Amsterdam or Florida, although there was one big advantage to being absent: she was the only one Jóhann hadn't videoed in some compromising situation. That left her as the only one with a free choice to say yes or no to whatever Jóhann and the board had proposed in the days before the bank came tumbling down.

'It's Agla. Café París?' she said as soon as Davíð answered the phone.

This was undoubtedly a call he had long been hoping for. He instantly agreed to the meeting.

She put on a grey jumpsuit with a black shirt, sprayed on plenty of hairspray and picked up her bag from the kitchen table. Night had almost completely retreated by the time she opened the door onto the outside steps. She blinked furiously. There was a dry wind from the east, and the volcanic dust clung to her eyeballs, leaving them dry. At least it meant she had a good excuse for constantly using eye drops; given the present conditions, everyone understood, which meant it wasn't so obvious that she had been lying awake for nights on end, staring at the corpse of the fly in the light fitting.

Of course it was shit; she would have preferred to be free of the whole thing and able to disappear from the country. But with things as they were, there was no other choice than to do what needed to be done.

68

As Agla walked into the coffee house she saw Davíð standing up, waving to her. He was his usual self, his blond curls untamed and his face red. If she hadn't known exactly what kind of a man he could be, she would have judged him to be a perfect angel; an oversized, over-friendly angel. But some of the arrogance seemed to have been knocked out of him. He extended a hand and held on to hers for a long moment.

'Good to see you,' he said in a low voice, and the words sounded sincere as he looked into her eyes.

She was his lifeline. She knew what kind of a burden he was carrying and how crucial it was for him to find an escape route. The self-confidence of a lot of the young guys had been hit hard by the financial crash, as if their fundamental beliefs in the rules of existence had turned to dust and they were ready to snatch at any straw. They had undoubtedly all changed in the wake of the crisis.

Agla ordered coffee, and Davíð did the same, then they sat and admired the city centre's Christmas lights outside for a moment. The city was coming to life – shops opening up for the day and the streets already busy.

Once the waiter had brought their coffee, Agla straightened her back. 'We need to get Adam out of some difficulties. Are you in?'

Davíð's cup clattered onto the table so quickly that some of the froth spilled onto his hand. Flustered, he snatched up a serviette, wiping himself as he nodded energetically. 'Absolutely. Just tell me what needs to be done.'

Agla smiled. She had known he would grab the lifeline that was being offered to him, but she couldn't help enjoying seeing him humbled. It was a complete change from the days when he had looked through her as if she had been invisible and had sniggered during board meetings when she spoke, as if anything she could put on the table was somehow lightweight and laughable.

'You could get two years inside,' she said.

Davíð nodded again. 'It's an opportunity. Two years is nothing compared to the life sentence I'm under at the moment.'

'OK,' Agla said. 'We'll find a way to transfer your debts over to a holding company overseas, and they can sit there for good. You'd better go home and figure out what you need in cash. And don't be shy. We want you to know that we appreciate this.'

'Agla ... you don't know what this means to me. You've no idea how important this is.'

'That's good,' she said quickly. She had no intention of listening to this angelic-looking figure weeping tears of gratitude. It wasn't as if she was doing some kind of charity work; this was a lousy business from start to finish.

'We need to admit to having accepted payments from overseas accounts, which you then used to buy shares in the bank, on Jóhann's instructions and with my knowledge.'

'OK,' Davíð agreed, his curls nodding in time with his head.

'And what needs to be crystal clear is that all three of us excluded Adam from this. This might mean you'll have to confess to forging his signature a couple of times.'

'OK, no problem,' Davíð said, as if they were discussing some trivial matter. But then a questioning look appeared on his face. 'Everyone knows that Jóhann's in the shit already, but you? Why do you want me to say you knew about it?'

'Let's just say it's a question of choosing which is the least bad pile of shit to be in,' Agla said. 'It's a strategy to focus the Prosecutor's attention in the most convenient direction.'

'...Because things would be a lot worse if the investigation were to look elsewhere,' Davíð nodded understandingly.

'Exactly,' Agla said, getting to her feet. 'My lawyer will be in touch with the paperwork and he'll go through it all with you.'

Davíð stood up too and shook her hand earnestly.

'Have a good Christmas,' Agla said, then turned and walked out of the café.

Outside on the pavement she took out her phone and stopped the recording. If there was one thing she had learned from Jóhann, it was that a tape of a conversation could always come in useful. She was about to call Elvar, but decided against it. What she had to say was best discussed face to face.

69

'Come on, now, Tómas,' Sonja frowned, turning around to face him in the back of the car.

'It's no fun waiting in the car,' he mumbled, unwilling to give way. For some reason, she was sure that it was safer if he were to wait in the car.

'I'm just going to run inside, collect my case, and come out again. I'm not stopping.'

'Who are they?'

'Just some really sweet, helpful young people who were good enough to take my case home for me because they were on a weekend break in London, and I had too much baggage and had to go via Copenhagen.'

'Why can't I come in and see them?'

'Tómas, please. Don't be like that. I'm going to knock on the door, get my case and go. And you shouldn't forget that your Christmas presents are in this case.'

'All right, then,' he said, reluctantly.

Sonja hurried up to the house. Halfway there, she turned and waved encouragement to Tómas. The entrance was at the side of the house, up a couple of steps, and he could still see her from the car, so she hoped that would be enough to keep him in his seat. The outside light was switched off, so Sonja had to peer to see the doorbell. She pressed the button and was startled as it chimed just the other side of the door.

She was ready to run, down the steps and around the corner, suddenly certain that something was wrong, that these people had opened the case and seen the contents; that she was about to walk into the arms of the police who were waiting for her inside. But it was too late – she could hear footsteps approaching the door and a shadow fell on the glass.

'Hi,' said the young man who opened the door. 'How was your flight?'

Sonja nodded and smiled. 'Fine, thanks,' she said. 'It all worked out in the end, and, thanks to you, I got home with all my baggage.'

'No problem,' the young man said. 'Happy to help.'

'You're a lifesaver,' Sonja told him, taking the blue case as he handed it to her.

'Coming in for a coffee?'

'Thanks, but I mustn't,' Sonja said. 'My little boy's waiting in the car.'

She could feel the man's eyes on the back of her neck as she went down the steps.

'Happy Christmas!' he called as she reached the bottom.

She turned and gave him a cheerful wave, then pressed the key fob to open the boot of the car, dropped the case inside, then got into the car and started the engine.

'Was I quick?' she asked Tómas, looking at him in the mirror.

He nodded agreement. 'Can we go to the pictures now?' he asked. 'Jói and his mum were going to be there early so we could buy our popcorn before the adverts start.'

70

'Soon, my love,' Bragi whispered in Valdís's ear and, as always when he spoke these words to her, she looked at him with a mysterious smile. Bragi was certain she understood. This was their secret. He had read some newspaper articles out loud for her -- the news he had now become used to since the crash: cuts in health provision and the redundancies that were part of it; the lines for food banks becoming steadily longer; Iceland's credit rating falling; snowfall from a roof that had smothered a child in north Iceland.

That last item seemed to have sparked some interest, maybe because it was something that had a conclusion; a positive ending. A neighbour who chanced to see the snow fall from the roof had immediately run over and dug out the little girl, who had emerged from the incident unscathed. Valdís kept her eyes on Bragi while he read this news item and he decided that from now on he would seek out good-news stories to read for her.

He reflected that everyone had probably seen enough bad news, and maybe Valdís had as well. Even if she did not fully understand the content, the anger and sorrow that seemed to have gripped this once optimistic and wealthy nation had permeated the whole media, and this could hardly have a positive effect on her.

The good-news stories on the other hand might trigger some memories; stories like the one about the child in the snow.

Valdís had always loved it when the streets and houses turned white in winter. When the children had been little they had often played together in the snow for hours at a time. There weren't many housewives who were happy to forget the housework, pull on wool socks and mittens and go and play with their children outside in the fresh, newly fallen snow as Valdís had done.

Bragi took the hairbrush from the bedside table and carefully brushed her grey hair. It billowed down her back as he ran the brush through it again and again until it was as smooth as silk. He parted her hair in the centre and measured each side against the other. They were equally long, which was the way it should be. Valdís had taught him that when he had asked if he could comb her hair. They had been young, and she was delighted that he was so struck by her hair. She had been blonde back then, and the first time he had offered to comb it had been on a late honeymoon in Italy, the sun shining through the window, making it gleam like gold as she loosened her plaits. Now the gold had become silver, but the waves in her hair after the plaits were undone still captivated him, as did the silky feel to it once it had been combed for long enough. He was halfway through braiding the first plait when one of the staff appeared.

'You needn't bother with that,' the man said. 'It's her bath time.'

This man clearly didn't understand Valdís, or else he didn't care. Bragi glanced at her face and sure enough, there were tears in her eyes.

'No bath,' she croaked.

Bragi wiped away the tears that were running down her cheeks. 'I thought it was bath day tomorrow,' he said.

The man shrugged and muttered something about the shifts being rescheduled around Christmas.

There was a crudeness to the man's attitude, or simply a lack of consideration. Bragi felt the usual suspicions awaken in his mind; maybe this man was behind the bruises.

'No bath,' Valdís said, as the man took her by the arm and made her go with him along the corridor.

'Gently,' Bragi said in reproof, taking Valdís's other arm. 'You have to be gentle with her.'

'You ought to be off,' the man said. 'This always goes so much better when you're not here.'

Bragi knew there was no point arguing, even though he had to swallow back the lump in his throat. He couldn't deal with yet another touchy-feely talk with the social adviser who talked about the importance of letting go the reins where sick loved ones were concerned.

He gradually slackened his grip on her arm, leaned close and whispered to her again.

'Soon, my love. It'll soon be over.'

71

This was where Sonja would have chosen to live, the Fossvogur valley to the south of the capital. This was a sheltered district with mostly two-storey concrete houses, built in a modern Scandinavian style, with plenty of mature trees, all situated around an area at the bottom of the valley where people jogged or cycled in summer and pulled children behind them on sledges during the winter. Living in one of these smart houses at the lower end of Fossvogur was the ideal of a happy family life; unless you had a neighbour like Thorgeir, of course.

The pounding music could be heard from the end of the street; she had no choice but to park here, there were so many cars outside the house. The house itself was festooned with Christmas lights and in front stood a pair of illuminated reindeer that flashed in time to the music that blared from the open front door. 'Father Christmas is coming tonight!' a ragged choir belted out inside.

After ringing the bell several times without getting a response, Sonja hesitantly stepped inside.

There were people everywhere; she scanned their faces for a sight of Thorgeir, holding the handle of the blue suitcase in an iron grip. Two women were deep in a private conversation in the kitchen, and in the hall a man was sitting, talking on the phone, which Sonja couldn't fathom, as she could hardly hear herself think for the music.

The real fun was taking place in the living room, a large space stretching the length of the house, with the whole wall facing the valley taken up by one wide window. Not that the party guests were interested in the view, they were too busy clapping and hooting at a bare-chested man with a Father Christmas hat on his head dancing on the table.

'Father Christmas is coming tonight!'

Ríkharður was reclining on a leather sofa with a young girl on each arm. Sonja could not resist giving him the finger when their eyes met. Ríkharður scowled at her in response, then turned to one of the two girls and pushed his tongue deep into her mouth.

'Sonja! Hello!' Thorgeir yelled, jumping out from among the group around the table and hugging her as if she were an old friend. 'What do you think of our MP now?' he asked with a laugh, jerking a thumb at the dancing man, who now turned towards Sonja so she could make out his face. Although Húni Thór Gunnarsson was certainly in the more awkward situation, it was Sonja who quickly looked away, instinct telling her that she had no desire for anyone there to recognise her. She hauled Thorgeir with her into the hall and handed him the case.

'I'm not putting myself on the line bringing this shit into the country just to have to hand it over at a party in front of a bunch of people,' she hissed at him.

But he seemed impervious to her anger. 'Take it easy, will you? Christmas is almost here!'

He opened the case, ripped out the base, extracted one of the packets and disappeared into the kitchen, returning with a knife and a spoon. Sonja followed him back into the living room, where he slashed the packet lengthways and stuck the dessert spoon into the contents, dumping the packet onto the table so that a mist of powder filled the air above it.

'Christmas buffet! Help yourselves!' he yelled.

Sonja turned on her heel and hurried up the stairs. She quickly looked around, glancing into every room to memorise the layout. In the bathroom there was a toilet with a cistern that could be opened. In one bedroom there was a floor-to-ceiling wardrobe, and in the other room she managed to see a ventilation grille, before she backed out so as not to interrupt the couple engrossed in each other on the bed. There was a trapdoor in the ceiling in the upstairs hall with a cord hanging from it; that meant a set of steps could be pulled down to reach the attic. On the way back downstairs she saw a vast chandelier suspended over the landing. Looking upwards she saw that it was attached to a hollow, cylindrical, patterned cupola. That would do. Now she knew all she needed to know. She sighed with relief once she was back outside in the street. The frosty air mixed with volcanic dust was as good as a breath of really fresh air after the sweaty atmosphere inside.

She glanced at her watch. It was time to collect Tómas from the cinema.

72

Bragi filled the coffee maker with water and dosed it generously for his coffee-loving sister.

'I don't have anything to serve with it,' he apologised.

She shook her head and patted her belly, which had grown considerably in the last few years. 'Just as well!' she said. 'It's a relief not to have cakes in front of me, and you know I can't not eat them if they're there. And Christmas is coming!'

'Well, then,' Bragi said, relieved. There had been little baking done in his house since Valdís had been taken ill.

He stretched out an arm for the packages on the kitchen windowsill, square and neat, wrapped by the bookshop. After Valdís had dropped out of normal life, he had taken to going to the bookshop with a list that the staff dealt with, packing and labelling every one for him. His sister took the packages and handed him a bag.

'I didn't know what we should give Valdís,' she said. 'I tried to remember what she always liked, and ended up with cognac and chocolate.'

Bragi smiled. 'Good thinking,' he said. 'I'll smuggle it in for her.'

'Is it really that strict there?' she asked, standing up and helping herself to coffee in the face of her brother's poor hospitality skills.

'They like to keep things in order,' he said. 'I don't blame them. They mean well, but I don't see why people with not long to live shouldn't be allowed a luxury or two now and then.'

'I don't know,' she said, shaking her head before sipping her coffee. 'Did anything come of your complaint about the bruises?'

'Nothing,' Bragi replied. 'You just hit a wall. They say that the blood-thinning drugs mean that she bruises very easily, but I'm not so sure.'

His sister added milk to her coffee. 'It's terribly empty here, dear boy,' she observed, looking around.

'I know,' Bragi said. 'Things are going to change.'

He got to his feet and poured himself coffee. It was heart-warming when his sister came for a visit. They had always been close, and Bragi had always known that she was his ally in life. It was cosy now, being able to sit in the corner of the kitchen and talk things over just as they would have done if Valdís had been here as well.

'How are the kids?'

'The same as usual. I had an invitation, but I'm not sure if I feel up to another trip to Australia. And it would feel wrong to be away from Valdís at this time of year.'

'Neither of them is likely to come home for Christmas?'

'No,' Bragi replied. 'They don't seem to have much interest in Iceland anymore. They're too busy putting down new roots over there.'

'Life's easier there.'

'Yes,' Bragi said. 'Very true.'

73

'Wasn't it really expensive, Mum?'

Tómas sat by the Christmas tree, a worried look on his face and the new tablet computer in his hands.

'I bought it abroad, sweetheart. So it was much cheaper than here. This one's the latest thing, everyone's getting these.'

'I know.' He turned it over a couple of times in his hands, as if wondering what to do with it.

'Tómas, the money side of things is better now. It's all going in the right direction. Now I can afford to give you proper presents.'

'But wouldn't it be better to save up, you know, for a better house or something, so that I can be with you?'

'I'm doing that as well.'

Sonja moved from the sofa to the floor, and sat stroking his hair. 'One part of showing that you can support a family is to be able to buy some cool presents. So it's good that you get such a nice gift.'

'Really?'

'Really.' Sonja kissed the top of his head and took a deep breath of the aroma of his hair.

They had decided to have a pyjama party starting the day before Christmas Eve. She had been up early, putting on a CD of Christmas songs and lighting candles all over the apartment before she woke him with a mug of cocoa. They had spent a wonderful time together over the presents, and he had been delighted with her pleasure at the breadboard he had made for her at school. They had giggled together all morning, right up until he came to the tablet. It was as if all his worries alighted at that moment on his young shoulders. Sonja would have given anything – literally paid any price – to lighten his burden. It wasn't healthy for such a young child to be so fearful of the future.

'Wouldn't you like to try the tablet while I get lunch ready for us?'

Tómas nodded and settled himself on the sofa with his present.

Once Sonja had placed the smoked lamb on a dish, warmed the peas, sugar-browned the potatoes and made the white sauce, the last touches to the traditional Christmas meal were ready, and she finally decided it was time to open the parcel from her mother.

There was no sender's address on the package, but the Akureyri postmark left her in no doubt who it was from. She used the bread knife to cut open the box, and inside found a soft package with Tómas's name on it and a large tin decorated with Christmas scenes. Her eyes filled with tears when she opened the tin and saw the traditional deep-fried, hand-decorated 'snowflake' bread inside. The sight of the layers of patterned flatbread, carefully cut and plaited, took her back to her childhood, to the smell of frying in her mother's kitchen, to a long-lost world that had been so much safer than the one she lived in now. From the back of her mind, where it had lurked since she'd seen it in London, the tiger paced forward, growling, its jaws dripping blood.

She shook her head, trying to rid herself of the image.

'Thanks for the parcel, Mum,' she said as soon as her mother answered the phone.

'It's not for you so you don't have to thank me. I didn't want Tómas to have a Christmas without any snowflake bread.'

So that was it. The snowflake bread hadn't been for her at all. It had been too much to hope that her mother might have been sending her something.

'In that case, thank you on his behalf. I'll give him your best wishes. Happy Christmas.' Sonja put the phone straight down and took a few deep breaths. She had no intention of letting Tómas see her weeping, least of all over her own mother. She had shed enough tears over her to last a lifetime.

The doorbell rang just as Sonja had put the food on the table.

'I've come to collect Tómas. Send him down, will you?' Adam's voice ordered through the intercom.

'You're too early. We're just about to eat...'

'And that's my problem? You got to have him longer than you were supposed to and now I've come to get him.'

The rage surged through her, along with the violent urge to break something – anything that she could hurl against the wall, but her fury evaporated when she saw Tómas appear with a downcast look on his face. He was already dressed and had packed his Christmas presents in his bag. Tears streamed down his face and he made no effort to wipe them away.

'I have to go, don't I?' he asked and Sonja nodded.

'Just think of New Year's Eve,' she whispered. 'We'll have a four whole days together at New Year. Just look forward to that.' She hugged the boy tight and smothered him with kisses. 'Don't let your father see you crying,' she said, wiping his cheeks with her sleeve.

She stood frozen, waiting until she heard the outside door downstairs slam shut, then she crumpled to the floor with her back to the door and cried.

A knock took her by surprise, and for a moment there was a spark of hope that Adam had changed his mind and that Tómas was back, but then she heard her neighbour's voice.

'Are you all right?' she called.

The sound of her sobbing had obviously carried out into the corridor. Sonja got to her feet and opened the door to see her neighbour there in her usual uniform: a housecoat and her hair in curlers.

'Just a disagreement with Tómas's father,' she said apologetically.

'It's tough being without your kids,' the neighbour sympathised, handing her a carton with a clear lid through which she could see layers of snowflake bread. 'Just a thank-you for all the help with the computer,' she said.

Sonja took the box gratefully and could feel a new flood of tears on her cheeks. This was snowflake bread she would gladly eat.

74

Agla felt her breath leave her lungs when Sonja opened the door. She was so beautiful, it was almost painful. She was dressed in a dark-blue dress and heels, her hair piled high, and there was a smile in her eyes that told Agla how welcome she was. That first moment their eyes met after any period apart was always so intense it threw Agla so off balance, she was sure she was set for a tumble. The animation in Sonja's eyes as she looked at her was accompanied every time by that unique feeling – the knowledge that they were linked together in a way that excluded everyone else; it was a connection that could not be put into words. There was nothing in the world like the feeling of being able to set light to someone's eyes simply by being there, by standing there on the landing with a Christmas parcel in one hand and a bunch of flowers in the other.

All the same, this was almost a step too far for Agla. Spending Christmas Eve together was practically a declaration that they were a couple – a real couple. Next they would be holding hands in the street, then yelling about human rights while they marched under a rainbow banner. But Sonja hadn't brooked any opposition, muttering that it was ridiculous that they should each be alone on Christmas Eve. She'd demanded to cook a Christmas dinner for them and finally threatened to invite someone else if Agla didn't take up the offer herself.

So she had given in. Now that she was here and placed a hand on the thin silk covering Sonja's back as she stirred the red-wine sauce to go with the goose, her heart overflowed with gratitude, and ten thousand butterflies fluttered in her belly as she looked forward to the evening ahead of them.

After dinner and a couple of glasses of red wine they gave each other presents, each accompanied by a long kiss. Agla had bought Sonja a white-gold necklace set with a single diamond. She would have loved to shower Sonja with diamonds, but was sure that she would resent her going too far. Agla was struggling to cope with the hairline gap between a gift that would truly gladden Sonja's heart, and one that she would take as an economic slight. Sonja gave her a shawl and some perfume, and when they had kissed again, she whispered that there was another present.

The parcel contained a small card with a heart on.

'I'm sorry I can't run to anything genuinely classy, but this is the one thing I really want to give you.'

Agla opened the card and read the inscription: *I love you.*

Seeing the words written down made her shiver. Their impact was so different spelled out than whispered over the phone or in the heat of passion. Agla could feel the irritation rising inside her and turning rapidly into anger.

'Perfume is more than enough,' she snapped. 'And I wish you would stop harping on about me being so rich and upper class.'

'Don't you like it?' Sonja asked. 'Don't you like what it says?'

'I'm not comfortable with that kind of thing.'

'What kind of thing?' Sonja stroked her cheek, but Agla got to her feet.

'This need to define everything. Why do you need to attach a label to everything and analyse every little bit of human feeling to death?'

'So you don't like me saying it?'

'No, I don't like it!' Suddenly her voice had risen to a shout. She felt the blood rushing to her face and the overwhelming shame returning so powerfully that she could hardly breathe. She knew that she would never be able to hold her head up in public if anyone were to know all the nonsense that went on between her and Sonja. A torrent of anger focused on Sonja swept through her. If it hadn't been for her, then she would never have been in this position and wouldn't have to feel like this.

'You're going?' Sonja asked in a low voice as Agla shrugged on her coat, her eyes wide and questioning. But her downcast expression showed her question needed no reply.

Agla knew she was leaving Sonja upset, but she had to escape. She had to get away from those tender eyes that were so easily hurt, escape from these ridiculous demands that Sonja made on her, get away from this love that had brought such turmoil into her life.

The street was completely deserted and the sharp east wind found its way through her clothes. The air was damp and the temperature remained close to freezing. She should never have agreed to go to Sonja's for Christmas; it was always going to end up in disaster. She fumbled in her bag for car keys, and came away empty-handed. She realised that she must have put them on the sideboard by the door, or on the kitchen worktop instead of putting them in her bag. Agla dropped a couple of well-chosen curses, growling like a caged dog.

Now she would have to walk back along the street in this freezing wind, look again into Sonja's eyes, search for her car keys, apologise for coming back and then say sorry for her angry outburst, walk again along the ice-cold street, and then get in the car and drive home to her empty apartment where she knew she would immediately start to pine for Sonja. However often she left her, her addiction to Sonja was so great, she would always instantly miss her.

Agla shivered with cold as she knocked on the door. Sonja answered, as beautiful as ever, but with the make-up around her eyes smudged by tears. Around her neck was Agla's necklace.

'All right, then,' Agla said. 'I do like you saying it. Just don't write it down.'

75

'Tell me a Sapphic secret,' Agla whispered the next morning. It was daylight, so it had to be close to midday. They had lain awake side by side for a long time without saying anything.

'You mean, Happy Christmas.'

'Happy Christmas. Now tell me a Sapphic secret.'

'No, I'm not telling you any more secrets,' Sonja said, sitting up and swinging her legs out of bed. 'You never believe them.'

'Tell me something I'll believe,' Agla said, pulling her back down onto the bed. 'Something that's fun to know.'

'Something that's fun to know,' Sonja repeated, and pondered for a moment before a thought came to her. 'Eating pineapple makes you taste sweet down there...'

'Sweet? How so?'

'It'll taste sweet and delicious.'

That was all that was needed. Agla was on her feet and picking her clothes up from the floor. Sonja watched her with a smile on her face. She felt sorry for her, but couldn't resist the temptation when Agla practically asked to be teased. She had her own set of rules governing what could be said and what should be left out, but seemed to desire nothing more than Sonja break those rules.

'Shall I make coffee,' she called out to Agla, who was now in the bathroom. There was no reply. 'I said, would you like some coffee?' Sonja repeated.

Agla appeared in the doorway and shook her head. 'No. I have to go.'

Sonja got to her feet, but not quickly enough. By the time she reached the hall the door had already clicked shut behind Agla.

Sonja turned to the kitchen, where she filled the coffee machine and switched it on. As it bubbled, she spread butter thickly on a slice of her neighbour's snowflake bread. She had just swallowed the last mouthful, washing it down with fresh coffee, when Agla called.

'What you said about pineapple...' she heard Agla whisper into the phone, followed by a long pause.

'Yes?' Sonja said, waiting for a reaction. Maybe she had searched online and found all kinds of theories about the effects of fruit on female physiology, or it could just be that she wanted to tell her off for talking about such things on Christmas morning. She hated anything that could be construed as vulgar. Except when they were making love, of course, caught up in a tornado of lust in the dark. Agla said nothing, so Sonja broke the silence.

'You mean about pineapple making you taste sweet? Is that what you mean?'

'Yes,' Agla said and coughed. 'Does it work with tinned pineapple as well?'

76

Every twenty minutes Bragi started the engine and let it run for five minutes, enough to keep both it and him warm. He had been sitting here since early that morning, coming straight from visiting Valdís. By now the little daylight Reykjavík enjoyed at this time of year was starting to fade. He had moved the car a few times so as to not be too noticeable, each time taking care to keep the lights off.

He knew that this was a hopeless task – this occasional monitoring would not give him anything by way of evidence, but he needed to do something that would help him feel that he was useful. He had been forced to take time off over Christmas – a time of year when it was more difficult than ever to be alone. But he simply couldn't stand being at home. The place felt empty, its soul ripped out, even though the only thing missing was Valdís. He had unpacked their little plastic Christmas tree that had always stood in the dining room and decorated it with lights and baubles, but that had made his situation even less bearable. Why should an old man, alone in the house, be bothering with a Christmas tree? Christmas was something to celebrate with other people.

He had spent as long as he was able with Valdís at the care home and taken what part he could in the Christmas celebrations there – if they could be called celebrations. But Valdís now slept for hours during the day, and he was unable to explain why he would prefer to sit and watch her sleep than 'be free to enjoy Christmas' as one of the staff had put it.

So here he was instead, keeping watch on a shabby block of flats in the hope that Sonja Gunnarsdóttir would show her face. There had been nothing to be seen all morning. The people who had turned up here had clearly been on their way to Christmas gatherings: men in polished shoes and women in stockings with smartly dressed children in tow. He had seen only one person leave the block – a tall, middle-aged woman he recognised from the news, but he dismissed any thought that she was important. It seemed unlikely that the main suspect in the major banking scandal that currently filled the papers could live in this building or have been an overnight guest there. It seemed even less likely that this woman could have anything to do with Sonja Gunnarsdóttir.

Bragi glanced at his watch. It was getting on for four o'clock, so he reached for the coffee flask and the slice of Danish pastry he had bought. It reminded him of the pastries that Valdís had always baked for Christmas. He sliced a piece of the pastry using his pocket knife and was about to pour himself some coffee when Sonja appeared at the door, dressed in jeans and a down anorak, and with a black woollen hat on her head. Even though these clothes were very different from the outfits he saw her in at the airports, he recognised her instantly.

77

Thorgeir stared, scowling in disbelief.

'You've got a mouth on you!' he said, but still reached into the safe behind him for a bundle of notes. 'I suppose you deserve this as a Christmas bonus,' he said, handing them to Sonja.

'Not a Christmas bonus,' Sonja said. 'A retirement bonus.'

She kept her eyes fixed on Thorgeir's face as he stared back at her, and she could see he was thinking over what she had just said.

'I quit,' she added. 'No more trips. I won't see you again, and certainly not Ríkharður either. We can all forget that I ever had anything to do with this business.'

Now Thorgeir's mouth was open and he leaned back in his chair. 'Really?'

'Really.'

'You're sure about that?'

'Very sure,' Sonja repeated. 'There's a kilo stashed somewhere in your house.'

'What are you talking about?' Thorgeir laughed as if she had told him a joke. 'If you mean the party the other night, then that shipment's all gone. Do you really think I'm so stupid as to keep stuff at my house?'

'I mean the kilo I hid in your house,' Sonja said, enjoying seeing the superior look on his face change to one of disbelief and then finally to fear. 'I found a fantastic hiding place, though I do say it myself. You can spend time figuring out whether it's in the ventilation system, the cistern, up in the attic, or somewhere in the kitchen cupboards. You can try your damnedest to find it, but the drug squad will find it quicker; especially if someone tells them where it is.'

'You wouldn't dare...'

'Oh, yes I would,' Sonja said firmly. 'And that's exactly what'll happen if you or Ríkharður come anywhere near me or my son again.'

The tiger, which for all these weeks had terrorised her dreams, now felt like it was giving her a dangerous strength, baring its teeth in a threatening snarl.

78

Bragi had all the evidence he needed to show that Sonja was linked to Rich Rikki. It hadn't been a coincidence that Ríkharður had been waiting at the airport when she arrived in Iceland, as Bragi had seen in the CCTV recording. He was in no doubt that he had been there to make sure she had got through, which meant that she had been bringing in something big.

Bragi followed her from her home and when she turned into Lágmúli, he knew immediately where she was going. It needed no stretch of his imagination to guess that she was heading for Thorgeir Als's office, where Ríkharður was also a regular visitor.

Bragi parked his car outside the chemist's and watched Sonja disappear inside the office building next door. He checked the time.

Exactly a quarter of an hour later she reappeared and drove off. Bragi wanted to follow her, but there was no reason to do so. He had made the connection between her and Ríkharður. Now it would be a better use of his efforts to go back to the recordings at the airport and try and figure out how she had managed to bring the goods into the country. He turned the car around, drove up Lágmúli and set his course for the Reykjanes peninsula.

Exactly two hours later Bragi was sitting in the darkened computer room, watching the fifth recording of Sonja Gunnarsdóttir arriving in Iceland. He examined her every movement from the second she left the aircraft until she vanished from view outside the terminal. In particular he concentrated on her behaviour at the baggage carousel. He couldn't see anything she did that attracted attention, though; she never behaved in exactly the same way every time. That in itself was grounds for suspicion. Most people stuck to the same habits, but she always varied them. She never stood at the same place by the carousel twice; and sometimes she went into the duty-free shop and other times she didn't. Sometimes she appeared to be in a hurry and other times not.

Bragi stopped the recording and was about to choose the sixth and last one that he had been able to find, when the door opened and Hrafn, the senior customs official, came in. Bragi swore under his breath, knowing that this time he was cornered and there was no escaping the conversation he had been avoiding for weeks.

'What are you doing here on Christmas Day?' he asked Hrafn.

'I could ask you the same thing,' Hrafn said, taking a seat beside him. Bragi sighed and waited.

'Retirement,' Hrafn continued. 'What do you reckon, Bragi? Haven't you started thinking about it?'

Bragi turned to face Hrafn. 'I understand that I have every right to work until I'm seventy.'

Hrafn looked at him wearily. 'Rights and more rights, Bragi, my friend. There are plenty who rattle on about the right to retire, while you talk about the right to put it off until it can't be avoided any longer.'

'Well, I enjoy my work,' Bragi said. 'And I've no idea what I'd do if I had to hang around at home all day long.'

'True,' Hrafn said with resignation. 'I'm aware of your circumstances. There can't be much to look forward to with Valdís as sick as she is.'

Bragi nodded. 'I'm not prepared to discuss retirement until I'm literally forced to go.'

Hrafn sighed. 'Fair enough, Bragi. So it's clear where we stand. We're looking at August, aren't we?'

'Yes,' Bragi confirmed. 'I'll be seventy on the second of August.'

79

Sonja felt an instant rush of adrenaline as the fist smashed into her face, but her fury focused not on her attacker, but on herself. She should have expected something like this. She should have known that Thorgeir would set Ríkharður on her. How could she be so stupid as not even to have thought of it. She had been certain that the threat of a visit from the drug squad would be enough and that she had nothing to fear. So when there had been a knock at the door, she had opened it, suspecting nothing. The punch to her face sent her flying back onto the floor. She lay there with black spots dancing before her eyes, amazed that Ríkharður was so quick on his feet as he grabbed her by one ankle, dragged her to the middle of the living-room floor and started lashing out with a series of kicks.

'Where the fuck did you stash the gear?' he yelled between strikes.

Sonja rolled herself into a ball, trying to protect her face and neck with her hands, thinking as quickly as she could. It was clear that they intended either to beat the information out of her or else shut her up for good.

'My lawyer has a letter,' she gasped. 'It'll go straight to the police if I die or get hurt.'

But her words seemed to have no effect on Ríkharður. He continued to kick her side and hips now that she had rolled onto her front. She tried to find some shelter by the sofa, something that would protect at least one side of her body, but Ríkharður grabbed a handful of her hair and hauled her to her feet. The pain sent cramps shooting through her body and her lungs refused to give her the air she needed to scream.

'Where did you hide it, you bitch?'

Sonja knew that if things looked black now, this was nothing to what would await her if she were to talk. Telling Ríkharður the truth would mean that any hopes of getting out of the snare would vanish. She had to convince them that she still had this hold over Thorgeir, that he was at her mercy, that in some way she could match his hold over her.

'Thorgeir's going crazy searching with all his people there, so you needn't think you'll get away with this,' Ríkharður snarled, both his hands on her throat tightening their grip.

Sonja fought back, but soon realised that this only made things worse; he gripped harder the more she struggled, so she tried to stay still, fighting for breath, telling herself that Ríkharður would stop short of murder, that he was trying to threaten her because at last she had some power.

The world was starting to go dark and she was about to pass out when the thought came to her of Thorgeir and all his accomplices frantically searching. It was a pleasant image somehow, and gave her a little strength. They wouldn't find any coke at Thorgeir's house, because she hadn't, in fact, hidden anything there.

80

'They don't have anything concrete,' Elvar said for the tenth time that morning.

'It'll count towards a reduced sentence, Elvar. Don't worry.'

'It's just your nerves,' he pleaded. 'Think it over for a few days.'

They had been round in circles as he did his best to persuade Agla out of her decision. To begin with he had been angry, then he had tried to argue it out, and finally he was begging.

'I want this to be over,' she said, hoping that the Prosecutor's staff would come back into the room so this disagreement with Elvar could come to an end.

'But this could drag the whole case out endlessly,' Elvar said, his voice hoarse. He had repeatedly described to her how the case might unfold – in one direction, if she were to confess, in another if she were to keep quiet.

She smiled apologetically yet again. 'This is the way I want it,' she said.

He sat down at last. He seemed worn out, his hair tousled and his face grey. 'Could it be, Agla, that you have a guilt complex?' His voice had dropped, his hand was on her arm and he leaned forward to look into her eyes. 'Don't you think it's worth waiting, just for a day or two, and maybe talking to someone?'

'Talk? Who to?'

'A psychologist, for instance.'

Agla smiled again and laid her hand on his, patting the back of his hand. She felt sorry for him; all this wasn't going to be good for his reputation, although in reality she was saving him from something much worse. Going down this route at least meant that she was able to steer the course of events and exercise some level of damage control.

She sighed with relief when María and Inspector Jón finally entered the room. They looked cheerful and relaxed. Jón had a cup of coffee in one hand and started by arranging papers on the table.

'We're waiting for Ólafur,' he said. 'He wants to keep an eye on all the major developments in the case.'

María perched on the edge of the table next to Agla, one leg swinging back and forth so that her skirt rode up a few centimetres and more of her leg became visible. Agla looked away, intending to shift her eyes to María's face, but instead found herself looking straight at her chest; it was uncomfortably close and her blouse was unbuttoned halfway down her cleavage.

'So you're ready to go for a deal, some run-to-the-courthouse kind of arrangement?' María asked with the mysterious smile that Agla had a sudden urge to smack off her face.

'Not until I've had some coffee,' she replied smartly, standing up and going to the coffee machine.

81

The woman at the refuge had been sincere and beautiful, and Sonja was grateful for her sympathy, even though it was misplaced. The cut in her forehead had been stitched, she had been thoroughly x-rayed and now she sat on the edge of the bed with an ice pack pressed to her side and a bandage over her eye. She wanted to go home.

'Most women hesitate to have the aggressor charged, co-dependent all the way. That doesn't make anything better, it just makes it worse.'

'Tell me about it,' said Sonja's neighbour, who had not left her side since she put every ounce of her strength into hitting Ríkharður on the head with a rolling pin, shooing him out of the building. A rolling pin and a few well-chosen words had done the trick, she said.

Sonja didn't want to think things through right now, but it was likely that her neighbour had saved her life. The last thing she remembered was Ríkharður's hands on her throat, the pressure increasing until everything went black. Then she had woken up here, in the emergency department of the hospital. Both her neighbour and the emergency staff had seemed to take it for granted that it was a boyfriend who had beaten her up and one of them had called the refuge.

'You're sure you wouldn't like to spend at least a night at the refuge?' the sweet lady asked, but Sonja shook her head. She longed for her own bed. She desperately wanted to crawl under the bedclothes and lick her wounds in peace – mull over her options and the future.

Because, now that she was free of the snare, she had a future again. Her plan really had been to hide a kilo in Thorgeir's house and tip off the drug squad where to look. But that would have had repercussions – she would have had to disappear from the country for a while until the dust had settled. Now she realised it had different consequences – it had been expensive to even threaten it. She'd know better than to open the door without checking first.

'Does he have a key to your place?' the woman from the refuge asked.

Sonja again shook her head. 'No,' she said. 'I was stupid enough to open the door.'

Her neighbour nodded and Sonja could almost hear her favourite phrase being repeated: *Tell me about it.*

'He'll be back and he'll tell you how much he loves you. But violence isn't love.' The expression on the woman's face was serious.

Sonja would have smiled back if her face hadn't been so sore. If one thing was certain, it was that Ríkharður would not be knocking on her door with an outpouring of affection on his lips.

'Liquid sustenance for the next few days,' said the young doctor, coming into the treatment room. 'Because of the mandible fracture.' He pointed to his chin, and Sonja knew that he meant her broken jaw. 'There's nothing we can do about the broken nose,' he added, handing her a sheet of paper with guidelines for making an appointment. 'I've put the prescription for painkillers into the system.'

Her neighbour drove her home, and after wincing with pain as she got out of the car and pulled herself up the stairs, Sonja struggled to get her key in the lock. With one eye under a patch, her sense of depth was all wrong. The neighbour took the key from her, opened the door and followed her to the bedroom.

'It's as well the little one wasn't here,' she said, taking the duvet from the bed and shaking it out.

Sonja realised that she thought Ríkharður was Tómas's father. If she hadn't been so tired, she might have corrected that misconception, or maybe not. A misunderstanding isn't always a bad thing, she decided, reflecting that it would be harder to explain that the beating had been all about cocaine smuggling and not a love affair gone sour.

Sonja crawled into bed and curled up on the side that was less sore as her neighbour spread the duvet over her. Sonja wanted to ask her name, but it seemed discourteous to be asking at just this moment; it was something she ought to have known but couldn't put her finger on. She'd check the name on the mail box when she next had a chance.

'I'll keep hold of your key and check on you tonight, like the doctor said.' The neighbour's voice was firm – there was no point arguing with her. 'If you need me, just shout loud enough and I'll hear you,' she said, shutting the bedroom door as Sonja slipped into sleep, knowing her dreams would be spent dodging massive paws and vicious, blood-stained teeth.

82

Sonja sounded the horn outside the white house in Vesturgata in Akranes and waited for Tómas to come running. The low fence they had put up when Tómas had been small was gone, and the tubs she had planted with summer flowers every spring had also vanished. The end of the garden nearest the street had been filled in with pale gravel, leaving only a single sad bush with drooping branches shivering in the wind. It had been their dream home, a roomy building with wide windows facing out over the back garden where she would watch Tómas run around with his ball.

She had been so fond of this house. Tómas had lived here since he had been three days old, and although she longed for him to be with her, she found reassurance in knowing he was still here. Not that it was the same house as she had lived in; according to Tómas, Adam had stripped everything out and replaced it with new furnishings.

Sonja sounded the horn again and checked her face in the mirror. She felt better having slept for two days and eaten a diet of chicken soup, courtesy of her neighbour, who never tired of telling her how she had clouted Ríkharður on the head with her rolling pin and called an ambulance. But her appearance hadn't improved. The swelling had subsided, leaving just a bag under her black eye and a bruise that had blossomed into a full palette of colours make-up could not hope to hide.

She was startled by a tap on the window. It was Adam. She wound down the window.

'Problem? Isn't Tómas coming?' she asked, ready to be disappointed. Adam leaned over to inspect her face.

'Yeah. He's coming. I just wanted to see you.'

Sonja thought there was a grin on his face as he walked away, but she could not be certain. Why on earth had he come out to the car to see her? Normally he did his best to avoid meeting her. Could he have seen from the window of the house that she had been in the wars? Why hadn't he asked what had happened to her?

Her thoughts were interrupted by a wild whoop from Tómas as he got into the car; his cry of pleasure turned into a wail as soon as he saw her. She took his face and held it in her hands.

'I fell down the stairs, Tómas. It's all right. It looks bad but it won't be for long. It's all right.'

83

Agla had behaved oddly all evening. She had been fine with Tómas, not making anything of the fact that she hadn't known he was going to be there when she arrived. She joked with him and talked about football, and they had played rummy while Sonja washed up. But her attitude towards Sonja had been strange. Now that Tómas had fallen asleep, Sonja was almost nervous about going back to the living room. It could hardly be Tómas who had upset Agla; therefore it had to be the state of her face. She had given Agla the same explanation she had given Tómas – that she had tumbled down the stairs. When she had been here yesterday, she had seemed to accept this. But this evening she had been strange – cold and distant.

'Sorry it had to be soup for dinner,' Sonja said when she came back to the living room. 'I know you'd have preferred meat, but I still can't chew anything.'

'Dinner was fine,' Agla said, sipping her glass of wine. Sonja wondered how many she had knocked back while she had been putting Tómas to bed.

'What's the matter?' Sonja asked, sitting next to Agla on the sofa. 'Am I ugly? You don't like my new look? You don't think it's smart to have one eye blue?'

Agla surveyed her face with a shadow of a smile. Sonja would have gladly kissed that faint smile if her lips hadn't been so sore, but then it vanished from Agla's face and the moment had passed. Agla stretched and moved away slightly, creating a distance between them.

'It's probably not a great idea to bring the lad into this...' Agla said haltingly, searching for the right words. 'Into our relationship, I mean.'

So that was it. Tómas had been the reason behind Agla's coldness all evening.

'Why not, Agla?' Sonja reached out and stroked her arm tenderly. 'You saw how happy he was. He's so sweet and he was so pleased to have someone new to play with.'

'The boy isn't the problem, Sonja. Please understand that.'

'If we continue to see each other, Agla, then sooner or later Tómas is going to be part of our lives. You know I'm aiming at having him with me permanently.'

'I've been happy with things as they have been,' Agla said, reaching for her glass. She took a gulp of wine. 'I'm not sure the time's right to be taking this to another level.'

Sonja felt the anger start to boil deep inside her, as if it was emerging from some deep well in her belly, rising gradually to her head.

'Another level means we take more of a part in each other's lives. That's what happens when people have been sleeping together for a while,' Sonja said. 'That's how relationships develop.'

'You're always talking about love,' Agla said. 'I'm not ready for that kind of commitment.'

'You're being outed as a "bankster" in every single newspaper, yet you're ashamed of being in love?'

'I'm not sure it's going to make the headlines any better. Do you want to be next to me on the front pages?' Agla drained her glass and put it on the table.

The rage that a moment before seemed about to burst in Sonja's head now seemed to settle into a cold wind that blew through her mind. Suddenly everything was so much clearer than it had been for a long time.

'Now you had better go, Agla,' she said, rising to her feet. 'You had better go and not come back. I can't do this anymore.'

Agla stood up and Sonja went wordlessly with her to the door. Once she had closed it behind her, she leaned up against it and waited to burst into tears, waited for the sorrow to overwhelm her. But something else filled her heart instead. It took her a while to identify what emotion it was. It was freedom, a painful, hellish freedom.

84

Sonja was no stranger to this kind of freedom; it was the same when she had told Adam that their relationship was over. He had been prepared to '*work things out*' and treated her affair with Agla as a mistake of some kind; but when Sonja told him that she was in love with Agla, and in any case, she was more attracted to women, he went berserk. Sonja could hardly blame him for that.

He yelled at her, something he had never done before, and while he went through the living room hurling every ornament he could lay hands on at the walls, Sonja realised that this was what she had always feared. There had always been the hint of a violent nature beneath Adam's exterior. There had been times when he would grind his teeth in fury and ball his fists, so that Sonja always backed off, whether the discussion had been about if she should go out to work part-time or have the Sewing Circle come to their house.

Soon after Tómas's birth she had given up arguing with him because she hated to see all that suppressed anger so close to the baby; it was as if she thought his deep-seated violence would one day break through the surface. She began to fall into a wheedling tone when there was a need to compromise or ask his permission for something. But the day his anger finally boiled over when she told him it was over, Sonja realised that the inner rage wasn't so dangerous after all. He could smash ornaments as much as he wanted and shout until his lungs ached. It was no longer a threat to her. She was free.

85

'Yes, please,' Sonja said when Libbý called to impress on her once again that 'all the girls' were hoping she would come up to Akureyri for the Sewing Circle's night out in the first week of January.

'Wo-onderful!' Libbý said, drawing the three syllables into four. 'It's so miserably dark and cold this month, and once all the fuss around Christmas is over you have to have something to look forward to so you don't die of depression. Wow ... the girls will be *sooo* pleased to hear you're coming.'

'I'll be up there as long as I can get away,' Sonja said. She could see no reason that might stop her from having a weekend in the north now that she was free and didn't have to worry about money.

'You know, I spent half of yesterday with your mother while she was making pancakes,' Libbý said, as if this was something to be happy about. 'When I ran into her the other day on Glerártorg she said I ought to drop by one day for pancakes. She gave me a call and told me to pop right over, and it was like being treated like a proper celebrity – meringues, doughnuts and all the rest of it, just like your mother does best.'

'Really?' Sonja replied and scowled to herself. It was just like her mother to besiege Libbý with friendly overtures. She could imagine what they had talked about.

'And we talked about you!' Libbý laughed. Sonja waited for her to continue, knowing that sooner or later she would have more to say. 'She seems terribly sad that you and Adam split up,' she said.

Sonja sighed. 'Well, I always got the feeling she was more in love with Adam than I was,' she said.

Libbý giggled. 'Judging by what she has to say about him, that's probably not far from the truth.'

Libbý lapsed into silence and Sonja waited, this time through an unusually long pause.

'Er ... is it ... is it right what your mother says about you being gay?' The question was hesitating, almost doubtful. Sonja was still composing a reply when Libbý carried on. 'I'm just asking because I wasn't sure if she meant it or if she was just trying to say something bad about you.'

'Something bad?' Sonja asked.

Libbý was again thrown off balance. 'No! I mean ... I've nothing against that kind of people! Not at all. I'm not prejudiced, not in the least. It's just, well, I just ... I'm not prejudiced at all.'

'Well,' Sonja said. 'That's good.'

'That's right. My brother-in-law's *like that,* and we get on with him just fine. He lives with a guy who's a complete sweetie, and the kids just love him to bits. They call them both uncle and everything. And we're really pleased that the children are brought up seeing that it's normal and everything.'

'That sounds good to me,' Sonja said, and didn't know what she could add.

'So it's true?' Libbý asked.

'Yes.'

'And ... er ... you're with ... a woman?'

'No,' Sonja said. 'It didn't work out.'

'Oh,' Libbý replied.

'Well,' Sonja said, 'that's life.'

Now, the next time they gossiped over pancakes, Libbý could give her mother the news that what her mother called her *unnatural relationship* was over.

86

It was close to midnight when Agla left the Slipway Bar and headed for the city centre. She hadn't planned anything, but it had seemed too unbelievably lonely to stick around at home on New Year's Eve. The booze was practically finished; the dregs of a bottle of Campari and a six pack of beer weren't going to keep her going until midnight. She had found a hotel bar with a free table and sat there far into the evening with one drink after another. In between, the waiter brought her some kind of Christmas meal; she had told him to pick it for her from the menu of variations of grouse and smoked lamb.

At around eleven the dining room had started to empty, and the foreign tourists made their way to their sightseeing buses. For a moment it occurred to her to jump on one of them and pretend to be a tourist desperate to see the Northern Lights and the Icelandic mania for fireworks, but she dismissed the idea as quickly as it had popped into her head. Instead she went to the bar and asked for a bottle of champagne to be added to her bill.

She stuffed the bottle in her coat pocket, and outside in the street pulled on her leather gloves. It was a bitterly cold, clear, bright night and the city centre seemed strangely quiet. Most Icelanders were still at home watching the annual comedy revue on TV while the tourists were on their way up to the wooded Öskjuhlíð hillsides for a night-time view of the city. Walking past the darkened windows of the shops in the Kvosin district, the weird thought came to her that she was dead, wandering in a dimension that only she inhabited, and that these empty streets were in reality thronged with people she had been irrevocably cut off from hearing, seeing or touching.

Her foot slipped on the icy pavement and she put out a hand to steady herself against a wall, just as a firework exploded over the distant roofs of the Rock Village district, lighting up the sky with its glittering silver sparkle. It was a relief that there were people alive somewhere, although that just emphasised her loneliness. Whoever had set off the firework was undoubtedly in a garden behind one of the little wooden houses, welcoming the New Year in the steadfast hope that it would be an improvement on the old one.

On Austurvöllur Square Agla opened the champagne, splashed a decent drink on the pedestal of the statue of Jón Sigurðsson, the hero of Iceland's independence movement, and took a long swig. The square was deserted and the weathered black stone of the Parliament building made it look more like a prison than the cradle of democracy. This whole fucking country was one big prison now, she told herself.

She walked along the bank of the lake towards the Hljómskála-garður park, which, at any other time of year, would be home to brass bands and vibrant flower beds. By the time she reached the gardens the air was filling with fireworks, their cracking reports and many-coloured displays mirrored in the waters of the lake. The steps down into the gardens were caked with ice, so Agla sat on a bench, pulled off her shoes and socks and put the shoes on again with her socks over the top. It was a good way to cope with the treacherous ice underfoot, although the socks would end up shredded. She gulped more champagne from the bottle, stood up and carried on into the gloom of the park from where she would be able to see the New Year's fireworks overhead as she walked home.

Just at the point where two paths crossed a sudden nausea took hold of her. She leaned forward to vomit. Once her stomach had settled, she spat, then took a swig of champagne as a mouthwash. She felt dizzy now, and leaned against the grey metal of a nearby electrical enclosure, taking another pull at the champagne bottle.

As she finished the last drop of the champagne, the bells began to ring. She couldn't make out exactly where they were coming from, as it seemed as if the bells from the cathedral and those from the churches on each side of the lake – one in each district – all blended into a single medley that echoed over the placid waters, competing with the thunder of fireworks above.

Unable to keep her eyes open, she decided to close them for a moment. But as she did, she felt her legs give way and she slid on her bottom down the face of the electrical enclosure until she was sitting on the ground. It was a relief to relax to the crackle of exploding fireworks overhead. She didn't feel the cold and there was a moment of peace deep in her heart.

She was startled by a warm hand settling on her cheek. A beautifully dressed woman was looking down at her, ordering her to wake up.

Agla shook her head, pushing the woman away. She felt exhausted, her eyes as sore as if there were sand under her eyelids.

'You mustn't fall asleep here. You could die. It's a cold night.'

Agla waved the woman away, but felt a hand take her arm and lift her. When she opened her eyes she saw that the woman was not alone; she was surrounded by a horde of people who looked to be on their way to a fancy-dress party, each one of them in gold-embroidered clothes so bright that the sparkle of it hurt her eyes. She struggled to get away, determined to rest, but she had hardly closed her eyes when someone shook her awake. She peered from under half-open lids to see María and Inspector Jón standing in front of her. She was certain that they were threatening her with hell and high water if she didn't get to her feet. Across the lake, a firework exploded, illuminating everything around it. When the glare had faded, Jón and María had vanished too and Sonja was in front of her, gently telling her to come with her. She wore a blue dress with a gold belt and had a crown on her head. Agla longed to ask why she was done up in fancy dress, but somehow the words refused to take shape on her lips and instead she mumbled something.

'Shouldn't we call her a taxi?' asked a man's voice from somewhere behind Sonja, and then Agla realised the woman wasn't Sonja, but someone she was sure she knew but couldn't place.

'Where do you live?' the woman asked. 'You ought to go home. You'll freeze to death out here.'

'Let's leave her. Let the police know and they can pick her up.'

'Come on, everyone,' someone else said, and Agla again felt sick, crouching down on all fours to vomit.

When she looked up, the people had gone and the park was dark and silent.

'Elves,' she muttered to herself. 'Just some fucking elves.'

She scrambled to her feet and took cautious steps across the ice towards the university.

She remembered nothing more until she was at home and struggling to take off her shoes.

She went to the kitchen for a pair of scissors and cut away what was left of her socks, and as she did so, noticed a note by the front door. She picked it up and peered at Jóhann's handwriting.

'Hakuna matata! Damages case to be dismissed. Copper-bottomed. Happy New Year.'

87

It had turned into one of the most beautiful New Year's Eves Sonja could remember. The air remained sharp and still, so far at least. Soon enough the smoke and smell of gunpowder from the fireworks would carry through the air. Normally a breath of wind would have swept them away, the same east wind that brought the volcanic ash that polluted the city far more than the fireworks could. But tonight it was breathless.

She and Tómas had dressed in warm clothes and were out on the street early enough in the evening to see people making their way out of their houses just as the annual satirical review of the year's events on TV finished. Some people went no further than the steps of their houses, standing in doorways or on balconies with sparklers or bangers, which flashed blue or green. Other people were better prepared, setting themselves up with firing positions in the car parks in front of their blocks or on the pavements outside the detached houses – and on the other side of the road if they were setting off heavyweight fireworks, the kind that Sonja and Tómas were getting ready to light.

Sonja wondered if she had bought this arsenal of fireworks in some kind of competition with Adam. Tómas was due to go home at midday the next day and another firework display had been promised for the following night. It wasn't as if it mattered all that much. There was something about the combination of a small boy and fireworks, the glee in Tómas's eyes and the whoop of joy as yet another rocket shot skywards with a whoosh and exploded in an array of colours high over the roof of the block.

The neighbours all made their contributions and one explosion after another merged into one long barrage. The sky was filled with lights of every hue, painting a series of constantly changing patterns – flowers, hearts, trees in blossom and glittering waterfalls. Finally the sound of church bells could be heard through the din, and the sound of 'Auld Lang Syne' carried through windows and doorways.

Sonja reached for Tómas and hugged him close.

'Happy New Year, sweetheart,' she whispered in his ear. 'Let's hope next year will be a better one for us.'

88

Bragi sauntered along the terminal corridor. He was still feeling bloated after yesterday's New Year's roast dinner that he had managed to cook for himself.

He had seen her, Sonja Gunnarsdóttir, on the surveillance cameras, and now he wanted to pass the time of day with her, even though she was leaving the country. It was always worthwhile to remind people that he was there, apply a little pressure, give them a reason to be nervous. He wanted her to know that she was being watched. Sooner or later she would put a foot wrong.

'Hello there, Sonja,' Bragi said, as he approached where she sat in the corridor.

She turned and seemed to take a moment to recognise him, staring first at the uniform as if her eyes were glued to it. At the same moment he saw the state of her face – a black eye that stretched halfway down one cheek, stitches in one eyebrow, a lip that looked to have had the same treatment and a dark bruise across her nose. She was wearing a roll-necked sweater, so he guessed that there had to be some marks on her throat as well.

The thoughts flew thick and fast through his mind, but he managed to remain outwardly calm.

'Going abroad?' he asked.

'Yes,' she replied. 'A late winter holiday in Florida. For some sunshine, time to relax.'

'Have a good trip,' Bragi said and carried on as if he had merely stopped for a moment to say hello.

His feelings were pulling him apart inside, however. On the one hand he knew that she was a smart smuggler, on the other he felt deeply sorry for this petite, defenceless woman who sat there with bruises on her face. But her battered appearance only served to deepen his suspicions. It was more than likely that she had upset one of the trafficking fraternity; someone like Rich Rikki.

89

Sonja sighed with relief as the aircraft's engines powered it off the ground. A contentment that she had not felt for a long time flowed through her. For ten days nobody would be able to reach her, and there was nothing she needed to worry about. This was the rest that she had been longing for. Now she just had a gentle flight through the skies during which she could sleep like a rock. She was free of the snare. Thorgeir would not dare send her to fetch any more shipments and risk a visit from the drug squad; she had to be free.

All the same, it was certain that she would have to tread carefully for the next few months. She would take care not be out and about alone, and would fit a bolt to the door when she came home. But there would be no more trips. She wouldn't have to watch men pushing bundles of cocaine down the throats of tearful young women, and she'd never again have to watch as a tiger chewed off a man's arm. She was free. She had survived. She had won.

The aircraft took a long turn to the south-west over the Reykjanes peninsula far below; it looked like an abstract artwork, the jagged lava fields contrasting with the white blanket of snow that covered everything else. The road along the peninsula that connected Reykjavík to the airport at Keflavík a half-hour drive away looked like a grey snake stretching across country as far as the eye could see. There wasn't much traffic to be seen on New Year's Day; not that many people were travelling overseas or returning home. A plume of steam from the Svartsengi geothermal power plant rose vertically into the still, frozen air, and the bright blue of the lagoon beneath it was just a peculiar little dot from this height. The mountains along the south coast of the peninsula shrank as the aircraft climbed, turning into molehills as the landscape flattened out. Distance shrank everything, including the fear and helplessness Sonja felt she was finally leaving behind her, far away on the ground.

January to February 2011

90

'I thought I was going to be here for days,' Agla said when the cell doors swung open to reveal Elvar standing outside with the warden. She had been here a day and a night, let out as far as the passage and with only two half-hour spells of fresh air in the yard.

'That's what happens when you don't show up to make your statement,' Elvar said, a concerned frown on his face.

'I just overslept,' Agla snapped back at him.

She really had overslept, unintentionally losing track of time. She had taken a crate home with her from the off-licence and had sat drinking herself so deep into self-pity it had been hard to drag herself back out. This inner pain had grown larger recently and was showing no signs of abating; what other people called reality seemed to be remote from her present existence. If she fell asleep, she dreamed badly, having visions either of the Prosecutor's staff or of Sonja; and she always woke up with a start and a burning pain in her throat that only a few gulps from the Jägermeister bottle on the bedside table would extinguish. Sometimes she'd be able to get back to sleep, and sometimes she would lie still, her heart pounding, staring at the corpse of the fly in the light fitting that she still had not got round to removing.

'Most people don't oversleep for days on end,' Elvar said, the reproof on his face softening as Agla apologised. 'Let's say this is a sort of symbolic custody,' he said. 'Something for the press.'

Agla had certainly been aware of the media people and their cameras. There would be some magnificent pictures of her in handcuffs in the papers today.

The warder cleared his throat.

'Yes,' Elvar said. 'It's here. The indictment.'

The warder handed Agla a sheaf of papers stapled together in one corner and she read the first page.

From the Prosecutor of the Special State Prosecutor, according to law 135/2008:
Indictment at the Reykjavík Regional Court of:
Jóhann Jóhannsson, Managing Director, registered legal residence in Luxembourg; Davíð Muller, Director of Markets Division, registered legal residence in Reykjavík, and Agla Margeirsdóttir, Head of Investment, registered legal residence in Luxembourg, for the following offences in contravention of laws governing trading in shares:
For having conspired to manipulate markets in the shares issued by the bank over a period of 189 trading days from 1st March 2007 to 1st February 2008 on the Icelandic market using the NASDAQ OMX Iceland hf trading network (hereafter referred to as Kauphöllin), via the offshore entities Iceland Trading Ltd, ML Holding and Avance Investment, ensuring an abnormal price level, manipulation of share prices and providing or attempting to provide incorrect or misleading share price information.

The opening page was followed by pages of detail precisely outlining the indictments.

It was lousy, and her twenty-four-hour sojourn in a cell had been no better. Agla had no desire to serve her sentence once the verdict had been given. But that was the way it would be, the way it would have to be.

91

Bragi fought off his own nagging conscience as he examined every one of the woman's possessions. Sometimes he enjoyed this. He couldn't deny that on occasion he relished taking people's luggage and going through every single thing they carried, watching their frustration grow and grow. There were particular types he couldn't help enjoying handing out this kind of treatment to. But it was different with the unfortunate woman who seemed dazed as she sat in the white room's plastic chair awaiting her fate.

After he had seen her in the airport corridor he had found out when her return flight was, and had been waiting for her in the baggage hall when she disembarked. He was pulling the lining from the last of her cases when her phone rang.

'Can I answer this?' she asked, and Bragi nodded.

She put the phone to her ear, and he could hear a man's furious voice carrying all the way to where he stood at the inspection table.

'Is this going to have to wait until the spring?' he heard her ask. The response was clearly not what she had expected. 'I'm going to contest custody, so you won't need to worry about that,' she said, and he could hear that her words were not warmly received. It was clearly the father of her child on the line.

He felt deeply sorry for the poor woman, but all the same, there was something about her that had triggered his instincts, tugging at his gut feeling, telling him that she had something to hide. It was easiest to explain the feeling by saying that if he were a sniffer dog, he would go straight for her. Bragi finished examining her luggage and replaced everything in the cases. As usual, the stuff that came out wouldn't fit back in, so what was left over went into a plastic sack.

'It's not good for Tómas to live with a father who hates his mother,' she said, and the reply was upsetting enough for her to end the call and throw her phone into the handbag that Bragi placed before her. She breathed hard and fast, on the verge of sobbing.

'Are you all right?' Bragi asked, and she shook her head.

92

When Sonja looked back, she sometimes felt that the affair with Agla had been the result of her strained relationship with Adam, rather than the reason for it. She had already been tired of their marriage long before things started to spark with Agla. She and Adam had both been bored. He had taken to spending a couple of nights a week in town, and she didn't trouble to ask where he had spent them, simply assuming he slept on the sofa in his office at the bank. There was a shower and a wardrobe full of clean shirts there, which was convenient for both of them. He had no need to be irked by not getting the reception he would have liked when he came home, and she was free of any guilt at seeing the disappointment on his face. On occasions she missed her old companion – the young man with the bright face she had once trusted and adored. But that Adam was long gone. It was as if he had outgrown himself, and Sonja knew well that it was work at the bank that was behind it. It came with heavy responsibilities that she sometimes felt that Adam struggled to cope with, and on top of that he had taken to snorting during the week as well, even going for a lunchtime line that left him irritable and short-tempered.

She remembered wishing that they could turn back the clock, that they could again be the friends they had been when Tómas had been a baby, when they had laughed with joy at what a sweet child he was, when Adam had held her tight and told her what a lucky man he was. But she had made no attempt to rewind that tape, and at some point she had stopped wishing that it might happen. She had just gone with the flow, as she had done her whole life, and waited for something to happen. What had happened was Agla.

She had seen Agla a few times without noticing her particularly. What had struck her was that Agla was one of those people who are more beautiful when they don't smile than when they do. She had a long face, with a high forehead and a heavy upper lip, and somehow a serious expression suited these angular features better – she was most attractive when her expression was at its saddest. Sonja remembered that she had found her sulky and odd at the Easter party she and Adam had held for the bank's top brass; she seemed to be the only one who hadn't been cheered up by a line of coke. At the end of the party, as the laughing guests were getting into the taxis Adam had ordered to take them into town where they were going to continue the party, Agla had come hurrying back and Sonja thought at first that she had forgotten something.

'I just realised that you're not coming to town with us,' she said, out of breath.

'No, Tómas is staying with his friend next door, so I'd rather be here in case he wakes up and gets homesick.' Sonja wanted to justify herself further. She wanted to explain that she was a mother and her child took precedence over any party in town; that she didn't care that her coked-up husband was going out for the night without her. But Agla wasn't looking for an explanation.

'I just wanted to thank you for your hospitality and a lovely meal,' she said. 'It's wonderful to have home-cooked food; there's nothing that beats roast lamb with all the trimmings.'

She quickly hugged Sonja, turned on her heel and was gone, hurrying back to the taxi where the passengers were already singing. Sonja stood there with a lump in her throat. Agla had been the only guest who had bothered to thank her for the meal. After that she felt a warmth towards her whenever they met.

Whether it was the result of or the reason for the rift with Adam, her affair with Agla had not given him the exit she'd long thought he wanted. It turned out that Adam had been nursing the hope that they could start again and go back to when they had been happy together. Why else would he have been so implacably angry when everything was in ruins? She must have hurt him much more deeply than she could ever have imagined.

93

Agla found herself trembling as she walked back to her car. This was the third time she had rung Sonja's doorbell without success. She looked up and saw that the flat's windows were dark, as before; she had to be away. It was most likely she was on a work trip somewhere abroad. She sat in the car and stared at the building in front of her, regretting so much. She regretted never having asked Sonja about her work; she only knew that it was something to do with computers – she was selling computer systems; Agla had never paid much attention to Sonja's explanations about what these systems were for. In fact, they had never talked a great deal, and now she was overwhelmed by remorse.

As Agla sat brooding, a car drove up to the building and parked in a space in front of the entrance. It took her a while to realise that Sonja was behind the wheel. She was always changing cars. It was like a compulsion – constantly replacing whatever car she had with one that was just as lousy, and in between those she used hire cars. Now she was driving an old Ford with a dented bumper.

Sonja looked tired as she stepped out of the car and seemed to need every ounce of energy to open the boot and lift out her cases. She had two of them, plus a plastic sack full of more stuff, so she must have been away for a while. Agla was relieved that there was a reason Sonja had not been home and had not answered the phone. Of course, she had called a few times too – quite a few times. But if Sonja had been abroad it was understandable that she hadn't wanted to answer. She was always broke, poor thing, and it was expensive to use the phone abroad. At least, that was a more comfortable explanation than the possibility that Sonja had sincerely meant what she had said and no longer wanted to see her.

Her heart pounded as she fought back the desire to jump out of the car, run to Sonja and throw her arms around her, hold her tight and refuse to let go. After that she would help her carry the cases upstairs, crawl into bed with her and keep her in her arms all night. It was so tempting, such a normal train of thought – the usual conclusion following their arguments. They had decided to bring things to an end several times, had said hurtful things to each other, even screamed, but things had always worked out. They had almost automatically fallen back into hugs, giggles and kisses. But this time things were different. Agla didn't dare go to Sonja, trembling with desire, simply to be told once again that she couldn't do this, that she didn't want to see her again. Agla had no desire for this confirmation that everything between them was over.

Agla watched Sonja lug the cases inside, one after the other. An unfamiliar feeling seethed inside her, boiling all the way up to her throat. She swallowed a few times, but the burning sensation wouldn't go away. She started the car and drove off, and was almost home when she realised what the feeling was: she wanted to cry. She longed to relieve the pain in her throat and in her heart by opening her mouth wide and howling out loud. She considered the possibility for a moment, then dismissed such weakness. She refused to weep tears over the end of her relationship with this woman. She would never have any part in her life. Whatever her desires might be, that was the cold reality of the matter.

94

Sonja was exhausted by the time she had carried the last of the bags up onto the landing. She was just about to slot her key in the lock when she heard the door behind her open and her neighbour appeared.

'Thank God you're back!' she exclaimed. 'I've been having no end of problems with my computer.'

Sonja wanted to snap at her that there was no shortage of computer repair shops in town, but after the trip to hospital and the night that followed it, she could not bring herself to be anything other than polite.

'Just let me have it, and I'll take a look tomorrow,' Sonja said.

The woman hurried into her own flat and was back with the

computer in her hands just as Sonja's phone began to ring. She used it as an excuse, pointing at the phone and taking the computer, thankful not to have to listen to a list of the machine's shortcomings, which, as often as not, sounded like the antics of a strange beast.

As soon as she was inside the door, she answered the phone and heard Thorgeir on the line.

'I've searched the house high and low. There's no kilo hidden there,' he said. 'You're bluffing.'

'You're sure?' Sonja asked, relishing the thought that Thorgeir had spent two weeks searching every nook and cranny – two weeks that she had spent in the sunshine.

'Yes, it happens that I can be sure,' he said. 'I even got a sniffer dog to go over the whole house.'

'A sniffer dog?' Sonja asked in surprise.

'That's right,' Thorgeir replied. 'I had one brought in.'

'You brought in a coke hound?' Sonja could hardly conceal her astonishment. 'You bought it?'

'Let's say that I had assistance from friends overseas. Compared to coke, a dog's child's play to get past customs.'

'And you're going to tell me that a cheapskate like you stumped up for an expensive dog?'

'It's a worthwhile investment,' he said. 'If there are other fuckwits like you who get the same idea. Handy as well for searching out supplies that disappear. You can't imagine how many people try to cheat you in this business.'

'You don't say?' Sonja said, trying to sound sarcastic, but not succeeding now that her heart was hammering with fear.

'So now I know there's nothing at my place and your threats are empty. You're going to London this week to fetch a shipment. Just so you know.'

'Go fuck yourself,' Sonja answered and ended the call.

95

Tómas awoke, thinking that he could hear voices, and then realised that he badly needed the toilet. It had to be the pressure in his bladder that woke him, and the voices he was sure he had heard and that still echoed in his sleepy head had to be part of his dream. The babysitter who had been there that evening had allowed him two cans of fizzy drink, and now he could be thankful that he hadn't wet the bed, as had happened last time he had drunk so much just before going to sleep. He rubbed his eyes and went out into the passage. The night light he always plugged in before he went to sleep was on, but there was also light coming from the bathroom.

Tómas pushed the door open and for a moment the brightness blinded him.

'You can't help yourself!' he heard his father say in accusation. 'You never seem to know when to stop!'

He saw the blood on the sink and Dísa sitting in tears on the edge of the bathtub, bloodstains down her yellow dress. His father sat next to her, his face twisted with anger, holding a towel to Dísa's face. Tómas screeched in terror and felt the hot piss run down his leg, forming a pool on the bathroom floor.

He was sobbing by the time his father led him to the shower and washed him down. Dísa, still with the towel to her face, wiped clean the bathroom sink.

'Did you hit her, Daddy?' Tómas asked, hesitating.

His father shook his head. 'No, my love. Of course I didn't hit Dísa. She just had a terrible nosebleed.'

'It's just a nosebleed, sweetheart,' Dísa echoed.

'Why were you so angry?' Tómas asked.

His father wrapped him in a towel, picked him up as if he were a baby and carried him back to his bedroom.

'We were just having a little argument because Dísa can be a bit full-on and when she got a nosebleed I was a bit annoyed with her.'

Tómas wasn't sure what Dad meant when he said Dísa had been a bit full-on, and he didn't understand why his father was angry because she had had a nosebleed. He sometimes had nosebleeds and his father had never been angry and said he had been a bit full-on or anything like that. It wasn't as if you could help getting a nosebleed.

'You want the Superman pyjama bottoms?' his father asked.

Tómas nodded, even though he was sure they were too small for him and hardly reached his ankles. But that didn't matter now. He could still feel himself ready to sob, and could hear Dísa sniffling in the bathroom. But his father said he'd make hot chocolate for them both. It would calm them down, he said, leading Tómas to the kitchen and lifting him onto one of the barstools before he poured milk into a saucepan.

'We're going to make more of an effort, little one,' he said, and for a moment Tómas pitied his father. He looked so tired as he crumbled a slab of chocolate into the milk, his hands shaking and drops of blood on his shirt.

'It's about time Dísa and I stopped this crap.'

96

Sonja surveyed the young people absorbed in their computers and wished that her alter ego were real, that she really could be some kind of digital guru. They all seemed to be concentrating so hard, yet looked so relaxed, surrounded by wires, tools, cans of energy drink and piles of computer components.

'I don't know what's wrong with it,' she said in all honesty to the young man who took her neighbour's laptop. 'It would be great if you could give it a facelift.'

She had done what she normally did – restarted the computer and then used the vacuum cleaner to remove the dust from the keyboard and the air vents, but this time it didn't help. It would only get halfway through the start-up process.

'Shall I install some more memory?' the young man asked.

'Please do,' Sonja agreed, without any real idea of what she was agreeing to; more memory must be as good for computers as it was for people, surely? She took the pink receipt the man had scrawled a date on, and hoped that she could convince her neighbour that the repair could take a while this time.

Her musings about the computer were interrupted by her phone ringing. She felt a sudden burst of adrenaline as Adam's name appeared on the screen. Considering how their last conversation had ended, Sonja was in no mood for a screaming argument, so she declined the call.

It was followed by a text message that came through once she was outside in the car: '*Please, please call!*'

This didn't look like he was going to yell at her, so something had to be up. Sonja tapped Adam's number with a trembling finger.

He answered instantly. 'Tómas has disappeared,' he said, his voice hollow, as if he were about to burst into tears.

'Disappeared? What do you mean, "disappeared"?'

'He wasn't in his bed this morning,' Adam said. 'And it's a rule, one he knows not to break: he's not to leave the house without saying anything. And he's not at school.'

'And you don't know when he went?' Images of Tómas outside on a dark winter's night flashed through Sonja's mind. 'Yesterday evening? Or during the night? Have you called his friends?'

'I've called everywhere – schoolmates, the football lads, everyone I can think of. He's just disappeared!'

She heard Adam gasping, and she shivered at the sound. Adam wasn't the type to give in to fear. She had never even seen him shed a single tear.

'I'm going straight home,' Sonja said. 'In case he's on his way there. He has to be on the way to me. He'd never go anywhere without telling me.'

97

Sonja had been driving a few minutes when her phone pinged. She opened the message, stopped at the traffic lights by the Nóatún supermarket at the top end of Laugavegur. She stared for a moment at the poor-quality image on the screen, trying to understand what she was looking at, trying to figure out what had happened as the black dots again began to dance before her eyes.

He greatest fear had just come true. This was her worst nightmare. What she had hoped were empty threats were clearly nothing of the sort.

A horn sounding behind her startled her; she looked up and saw the green light, but failed to connect her thoughts with the everyday reality of Reykjavík's traffic; not now that her world was falling apart around her.

The picture showed a smiling Tómas with an ice cream in his hand. Next to him was Ríkharður, one arm firmly around the boy's shoulders. The horn sounded a second time, and she drove off much too fast, spun the car in a U-turn by the Hlemmur Bus Station then put her foot down hard to speed towards Thorgeir's office at Lágmúli. But the car slipped out of the grooves in the snow, stalled and she came to a halt in the slush by the roadside. As the car's engine stopped, Sonja realised that it was her own voice she could hear so clearly and loudly.

'*No, no, no, no!*'

This couldn't be happening. It wasn't possible that Tómas could be in danger.

She got out of the car, narrowly missing a car that shot by with its horn wailing as she opened the door. She looked around, but there was nobody who looked like they might stop and help her free the car from the snow.

She saw a filling station across the road, and a young man working in the kiosk. She waved until he saw her, then took the two rubber mats from the footwells and stuffed them behind the car's wheels. Getting back inside, as the lad approached she pointed to the front of the car, indicating that he should push. When he arrived, she started to reverse as slowly as she could, even though every fibre of her being demanded that she should hurry, putting her foot hard to the floor. But in the snow there was no point being in a hurry, she knew she had to take it gently, let the car rock back and forth until it had built up the momentum to free itself. The second the car was free, Sonja jerked it into drive and hurtled away, leaving the bemused pump attendant standing there with the two rubber mats in his hands.

Her thoughts were completely centred on Tómas and the danger he was in. The *no, no, no, no!* mantra echoed inside her head, that refusal that is the last straw everyone snatches at when they know their situation is hopeless.

No, no, no, no! repeated itself in her mind. This couldn't be happening.

98

There was no secretary at reception, so Sonja barged into Thorgeir's office with snow still on her boots.

He looked as if he had slept in his clothes, his shirt was crumpled and spotted, although this went with his lined face rather better than the immaculately pressed suit he usually wore.

'Where is he?' Sonja yelled, her emotions flashing from fury to fear and back again. She didn't know whether to fly at Thorgeir with her fists, or get down on her knees and beg, beseeching him to spare her child, to not do Tómas any harm.

'There's nothing wrong with him. He's in good hands and he'll be returned as soon as you arrive in London to pick up the shipment,' Thorgeir said amiably, as if he was chatting about nothing more remarkable than the weather. His eyes were wide and sincere.

Sonja stared at him, wondering how he could be so relaxed. 'And if I go to the police?' she said. 'If I give up and tell them everything about the whole operation?'

'You won't go to the police,' Thorgeir retorted. 'You're not that stupid. Ríkharður's quite capable of looking after children, but if he gets upset ... Well, I wouldn't guarantee anything.'

'You've no conscience.' Sonja's voice was shaking and she could feel the tears running down her cheeks.

'Don't talk such shit,' Thorgeir said laughing. 'Of course I have a conscience. I can just turn it off when I need to.'

'Where's the pickup?'

'The Thistle. In the lobby. Midnight tonight.'

'Don't hurt him, please,' she croaked. 'Don't let Ríkharður do him any harm.'

'Of course not,' Thorgeir said. 'He won't come to any harm as long as you behave and do as you're told.'

He looked hard at Sonja as she wiped her face with her sleeve.

'But if you try any stupid shit,' he continued, his eyes turning cold and hard. 'Then we'll do whatever we have to.'

Sonja fell to her knees, sobbing. There was no way out. She was still caught in the snare, and the vicious beast had her in its bloody jaws, ready to rip away the most important part of her.

99

Bragi drew a red ring round a name on the next day's passenger list.

'Get someone off the other shift to swap with me, will you?' he said to Atli Thór. 'There's someone here I've been keeping an eye on.'

'Shall I ask him to take your night shift next week?' Atli Thór asked, running a lint roller over his black sweater. This was on Bragi's instructions. Staff were expected to show respect for the uniform they wore. Ties should be knotted at the throat and in winter, when they wore black sweaters over their uniform shirts, they were to roller them before each shift and the tool belt was to lie over the top. According to Bragi, they were representatives of the Directorate of Customs; a carelessly buttoned shirt or a scruffy sweater over the tool belt were disrespectful of the authority they represented.

'That would do nicely,' Bragi said as Atli Thór sat at the computer to change the shift details.

'Aye, aye, Cap'n Ahab,' he said, saluting.

Bragi whacked him good-humouredly with the rolled-up passenger list.

He felt the old excitement as he walked out to his car. He knew in his gut that this time he would have her. She had flown that afternoon and was due back the following day; it was a typical pickup trip. All the same, it struck him as odd that she hadn't dropped out of sight after having been searched twice in a matter of only a couple of weeks. But then again he had never understood how smugglers thought. These people seemed to take risks that were far beyond the limits of anything sensible. Maybe she thought that, as she had been searched twice with no result, they wouldn't bother doing it a third time. If it was, though, she had another think coming. Bragi would be waiting, his tie knotted at his throat and his black sweater spotless, and there would be no mercy.

He took a deep lungful of the cold air that, because of the high wind that tugged at his hair, was free of the smell of aviation fuel. The brakes of a jet landing on the runway squealed, and the heavy drone as its flaps lifted blended with the crunch of ice underfoot.

In spite of everything, life was pretty good and soon it was going to get much, much better.

He was going to see Valdís on the way home.

100

When Sonja took her phone out of her bag to switch it off before take-off, she saw there were three messages from Adam. They would just have to wait. He would have to wait until she had landed in London. By now he must have called the police to report Tómas's disappearance, and she did feel sorry for him. He knew nothing, had no idea where Tómas could be. At least she knew that Tómas was with Ríkharður and could console herself with Thorgeir's promise that he wouldn't be harmed. She would do her utmost to ensure that he was returned home. She would make the pickup at the right time, and as soon as she had the goods, surely they would take Tómas home. The boy's explanations of where he had been would undoubtedly result in more questions, but that was a problem that could wait. If the police were involved, then this could all be linked to her, although that wasn't a certainty. A stranger who abducted a child sounded dubious and that might focus the police's attention elsewhere.

All Sonja could do was deal with the fallout tomorrow when she had arrived home with the shipment and Thorgeir was satisfied – or as satisfied as he could be after everything that had happened.

Sonja trembled as the aircraft accelerated, feeling her nerves jangling as it lifted off. She didn't experience the usual feeling of tranquillity once the wheels had left the ground. Now she longed to be able to make it fly quicker, or fast-forward so she could be in London already, ready to collect the goods earlier so Tómas would be free sooner. Free and safe.

101

It was always a surprise to Agla when someone rang her doorbell. This time she was astonished to see María, the economic crime specialist, standing outside.

'Could I have a word with you?' she asked, and Agla stepped aside to let her in.

She had started with a beer when she got home, followed by another, and then she had fallen asleep on the sofa. So she knew she wasn't looking her best, her blouse creased and her hair tousled. María, on the other hand, looked immaculate, not a hair out of place and her suit looking as if it had just been pressed.

Agla glanced at the clock. It was almost ten; presumably María had come straight from work. That was one thing that could be said for the Prosecutor's staff, they worked like galley slaves.

'Would you like a beer?' Agla asked, opening the fridge. 'Or water? That's all there is.'

'A beer would be fine,' María said.

Agla opened the bottle and handed it to her without asking if she wanted a glass. María didn't seem to notice and drank from the bottle. Agla waved her towards the living room and offered her a seat.

'Do I need to call Elvar?' she asked.

María shook her head as she sat down on the sofa. 'No,' she said. 'I have just one question and I wanted to ask it in private.'

Agla sat down in an armchair and waited. María cleared her throat, sipped her beer and leaned forwards, looking into Agla's eyes.

'Could it be the case...' she began in a low voice. 'Could it be that you're under pressure from Adam?'

María looked her so steadfastly in the eye, Agla had to force herself not to look away.

'I'm not sure I know what you mean,' she replied.

'I mean are you under some kind of pressure, or even duress?' María said, her face serious. There was no mysterious smile that hid something now, no ambush to watch out for. She seemed to be sincere.

'I'm not sure what kind of duress that could be,' Agla said, picking up her beer and taking a long drink from the bottle.

'One of our staff has been going through the tapes that were found among Jóhann's things,' María continued, and Agla began to understand where this was going. 'I was wondering if Jóhann or Adam might have a tape of you, or something else that might put you in a difficult position...'

'And that's why I'm shouldering all the responsibility?' Agla laughed. 'Do you think I was ever invited on any of those boys' jaunts?'

'So you knew about Jóhann's videos?'

'Didn't everyone?'

Agla saw that this took María by surprise. It was clear that they had only just stumbled across the recordings.

'It occurred to me that there might be more than the ones we seized. Or there might be some other material that shows you in a position that could put you at a disadvantage.'

'I can't imagine what could be so bad that it would induce me to take someone else's prison sentence,' Agla said, finishing her beer and getting to her feet to fetch another.

'Fear of embarrassment can make people do the strangest things,' María said as Agla sat down again.

'More than likely,' she agreed. 'There's a Polaroid of me somewhere with a rolled-up five-thousand note stuck up my nose. But that was how things were at the time. I wouldn't do prison time for someone else, if that's what you're driving at.'

'No. That's not what I mean. What I have in mind is ... some personal matter, possibly something that you're struggling with yourself, that could put you in a difficult position. Maybe your relationship with Sonja Gunnarsdóttir?'

Agla's heart lurched, and she felt her cheeks flush.

'Relationship?' she sneered. 'There's no relationship.'

She would have got to her feet and turned her back if she could have trusted her legs to keep her upright, but she felt drained of all energy suddenly, so remained sitting still, staring at the floor.

'Let's say your acquaintance with her, then,' María corrected herself. 'Sonja is Adam's former wife, so that could put you in an awkward position on a personal level? Maybe Adam or Jóhann could have something on you that you would take steps to keep discreet?'

They had clearly tapped her phone and heard everything – everything that had passed between her and Sonja, both the passionate whispers and the arguments. The shame engulfed Agla, as if it had been poured over her from a bucket. This was what she had feared all along, that at some point someone would sit opposite her, knowing everything about her and Sonja. But now it was a reality, she realised it changed nothing at all.

'There's nothing of that nature going on,' she said to the floor, then looked up at María, meeting her piercing gaze, which cut into her like a knife. This wasn't the usual inquisitorial look that María used at the office; there was sympathy in her eyes, but somehow Agla found that grated even more.

'You've misunderstood things,' she said. 'Sonja is ... She's an exception in my life, something unique. And not something permanent or ... what shall I say? ... At any rate, it's over. Completely finished, which is just as well. Because I'm not ... not that way inclined.'

'I see,' María said and got to her feet. 'I just wanted to be sure that you weren't being put under any pressure.'

María stood still, clearly waiting for Agla to stand up, but she remained seated. She didn't have the strength in her legs to carry her as far as the door and see María out.

102

Sonja felt as if she were suffocating. However hard she tried to fill her lungs, she felt unable to breathe properly. The feeling was the same as when Ríkharður had held her by the throat and squeezed, and indirectly, that was what he was still doing. The picture of him and Tómas was imprinted on her mind, and no matter how often she muttered to herself that everything would be fine, that it would all turn out for the best, she was unable to convince herself that that was true.

She had only just managed to catch the evening flight to London, had taken the tube directly into town and hurried to the hotel, arriving just in time for the grey-haired man to hand her the case containing the shipment.

She didn't have a hotel room booked, she had dumped the vacuum-packing machine after her last trip and she had no case of her own with her – she was as badly prepared as it was possible to be. Yet they wanted the delivery the next day. She'd have to come up with something, some smart idea she hadn't tried before, preferably one that meant she didn't have to carry the stuff into the country herself, because it was a certainty that this time customs would have her. The elderly officer seemed to be following her doggedly, and she was sure that he suspected something. He had clearly sniffed out that she was up to no good, but she couldn't work out what exactly had put him on her trail.

She paid for a room at the Thistle as she had no desire to be walking the streets of London with the goods in a sports bag, searching for some cheap place to stay.

Once in her room she called Adam.

'Is he home?' she asked, a tremor in her voice as soon as Adam answered.

'Yes, he was back right after dinner. He said he'd gone off on a hike with his pals. I told him he's never to do that again without telling us where he's going. I've been in touch with the police – told them that everything's OK. They said we don't need to bother them again.'

Sonja gulped. Tómas must have lied to his father about where he had been. Why he had done that was impossible to say. Maybe Ríkharður had threatened him, told him to stay silent.

'Can I talk to him?'

'Sonja, what planet are you on? It's gone midnight. He's asleep! First the boy disappears, then you lose your shit and disappear for hours on end. I've been on the verge of a breakdown while your phone has been switched off. Then you call after midnight and expect to talk to him. You're just not making sense.'

'Sorry,' Sonja sighed. 'I'm in London. It's a work thing.'

'You go running off to London just when your son disappears? And you say you want custody?' There was no mistaking the sarcasm in his tone.

'I had to, Adam. There's no way to explain it.'

'It's true,' he replied. 'There's a lot about you that can't be explained.'

Sonja stifled a sob. After the day's events she deserved that particular barb.

'Adam,' she said beseechingly. 'Look after him.'

Adam snorted and put the phone down. Sonja lay back on the bed and burst into tears. She struggled to replace the mental image of Tómas in Ríkharður's steely grip with one of him asleep at home, safe in the white house in Akranes village with his father close by.

103

Tómas buried his face in the dog's fur and breathed deeply. He loved the scent. He couldn't understand why some people said that dogs smell bad. This dog was clean and warm, and it was a pleasure to have him on his bed. Tómas stroked the black fur of his head and whispered 'good dog' to him.

The dog grunted, stood up and shook itself. This was fun. It was great to wake up with someone, and it was even better now that that someone was a dog. Dogs were so fascinated by people, looking so hard into your eyes, watching every movement, tail thumping, always ready to play. This dog was no exception; he was always desperate to play. They had played with a ball all evening in the garden. The dog didn't seem to care about the cold or the frozen ground beneath his paws; all he wanted to do was fetch the ball again and again, tussle for it and then be chased around in an endless game of hide-and-seek.

A dog had been Tómas's dream for a long time. He had always expected that when his father would finally give in, there would be a puppy, but when Dad had said yesterday that this dog needed a home, Tómas saw that it was even better to have a grown-up dog. They wouldn't need to toilet-train him or anything, and he could do all kinds of tricks at the drop of a hat. He would sit, roll over and play dead when he was told to. It was as if a dream had come true.

Tómas fought with the dog over an old sock, and when the dog won, they ended up in a furious pursuit around the house.

'Hey, hey! Tómas! Take it easy!' his father called from the kitchen, and Tómas whispered to the dog to calm down.

It was almost as good as having a brother. He was thinking of calling him Teddy.

104

That was the fourth shop that didn't have a vacuum-packing machine and Sonja was running out of time. It was already eleven and she had to be at Heathrow at two. She had booked a late checkout at the hotel and left the bag of drugs under the bed, with the do-not-disturb sign hanging on the door handle.

The taxi had taken her around the city, looking for the machine without success. Now she would have to find another way. She switched on her pay-as-you-go phone and called Thorgeir.

'What do you want?' he demanded.

She explained that she needed an extra day to pack the shipment properly to make sure it would get through safely.

'Forget it,' he said. Sonja could hear that he was buzzing – he sounded irritable, his temper on a knife-edge. And it was still early. It would be no fun trying to talk to him later in the day.

'Come on, Thorgeir. I'll bring it tomorrow.'

'If you don't shift your arse back here by tonight then Ríkharður will be going for another little drive with the boy, and this time it won't be ice cream he'll be getting.'

Sonja ended the call, feeling desperation put its cold hands on her heart. Before, Thorgeir had always been easy to deal with, and she had been allowed to do things her own way. Now that had all changed. It hadn't been such a great idea to threaten him. The image of the tiger switching its powerful tail back and forth sprung into her mind.

Sonja blinked, her eyes dry, and tried to think clearly. She had not slept a wink all night, instead she had lain awake while dark thoughts whirled through her mind and her body twitched with the tension. It was clear that she was more entangled than she had ever been before. She was like a fish caught in a net, desperately fighting to free itself, only to find that it was becoming ever more enmeshed. It had always been her fear that Thorgeir and Ríkharður would act on their threats against her son, but she had never truly believed that they would do it. She felt a surge of pain as she thought about how Tómas must have spent the whole day with Ríkharður, and then lied to his father about where he had been. She would probe him when she had the chance – gently, as that was the best approach with Tómas – to find out what had happened during the hours he had spent with Ríkharður. Then she would do everything in her power to ensure that this couldn't happen again. But the question was how? More pressing, though, was how to get the shipment home. She had only two hours to work it out. She had to find something, and fast.

She told the taxi driver to drop her off back at the hotel, and from there she jogged around the corner to a supermarket on Oxford Street. She went from aisle to aisle searching for something she could pack the cocaine in. Fortunately, it was in powder form this time, not the chunks she'd carried before, so she should be able to decant it into some kind of container.

She carefully checked out the coffee beans, but they were all in metal containers. A collection of cylinders in her baggage could look like an explosive device on the scanners, which would mean the case would be opened at Heathrow. She went past another row of shelves and found herself by the chilled cabinets, so she turned back, going deeper into the shop, scanning the shelves for anything that could suit her purpose. What would happen if she found nothing, was forced to travel with it badly packed, and the dope scanners pinged as they got to her case? Or what if she spent too long packing it and missed her flight? In either case Thórgeir would send Ríkharður to collect Tómas. Would they really punish her by harming him? Sonja fought for breath, the tension inside her preventing her from taking air into her lungs. She was sure she was about to faint.

'All right, are you, darling?' asked a middle-aged woman, lightly touching Sonja's arm.

Sonja started and managed to snatch a breath. She was so over-whelmed that she wanted to throw herself into the woman's arms. It was at that moment that she saw what she had been searching for.

'I'll be fine, thanks,' she gasped. 'I was just looking for this.' She pointed to a row of plastic tubs of waffle mix and dropped the whole lot in her basket.

The woman stared at her in astonishment. 'Well, you do like your waffles,' she said, walking away.

It was a relief to have found the right containers. Now all she needed were a few other items so she could pack the goods quickly and securely. She went through the shop, picking up clingfilm, plastic bags and disposable gloves, as well as a few packets of coffee, before heading for the checkout.

The queue was short, but it seemed to take an age. Sonja leaned forward to see what the problem was and saw that it was a self-service system. As always, one of the shop's staff went from one checkout to another helping people. It seemed that every single customer needed assistance. Sonja gritted her teeth and checked her watch. She had ninety minutes.

When it came to her turn, she rushed to the checkout, hurriedly scanned the waffle mixture bar codes, but when it came to the coffee the scanner refused to recognise what it saw. She smoothed the packet out and tried again, then tried a second packet, each time with the same result. The machine just emitted a dull tone instead of the happy ping it gave when it had successfully scanned something.

Sonja looked around for one of the assistants and saw that the man was busy at another checkout at the far end of the shop. For a moment Sonja toyed with the thought of packing everything in a bag without paying, to save herself some time. But that could mean an even longer delay; now was not the time to spend hours in a London police station explaining away a minor shoplifting offence. There was too much at stake.

She tried to scan the coffee again, but it wouldn't work. She decided to leave the coffee, scanned the other items, but then the machine declined to scan the latex gloves. They were essential. She suddenly found herself hyperventilating, the muscles in her chest fighting against her. She was sure she wasn't getting enough oxygen. Before she knew it, she had snarled in frustration and landed a kick on the check-out machine. The shop assistant hurried over, a security guard behind him, both asking her to calm down, otherwise she would be escorted out of the building.

'I'm sorry, I'm so sorry,' Sonja muttered again and again, trying to explain that she had a flight to catch.

The assistant scanned the coffee and the gloves for her, and took her through the payment process while the security guard watched through narrowed eyes, Sonja continuing to apologise the whole time.

She longed to explain to them the terror inside her, to tell them that if she didn't catch this flight, great danger was waiting for her son – her son who was her joy, her reason for living.

105

She wouldn't have a chance to switch cases, and there was no way she would be at the airport early enough to track down someone willing to check her case in for her. She had already thought of taking the evening flight instead, but it was fully booked, so she would have to stick with the afternoon one she had a ticket for. All she could do now was hope for the best and trust her luck. She knew it wasn't a smart way to operate. Luck was rarely there for people like her.

Back in the hotel room, Sonja emptied one waffle mix tub after another into the toilet, knowing all the while that she really wasn't thinking straight. One moment she wondered whether there really was a danger – was she simply being hysterical? Another moment, she knew it was insanity to be taking so much powder into Iceland with so little preparation. But she had to balance this against the risk of what Ríkharður would do to Tómas. She had no way of knowing if Thorgeir really meant what he said, whether or not Ríkharður would genuinely harm a child, but it wasn't a chance she dared take. Recalling vividly how Ríkharður had treated her, she preferred to risk prison rather than have him hand out the same treatment to Tómas.

Taking everything into consideration, though, if she did end up in jail it might be the best outcome for her son. Surely it was madness for her to have anything to do with the child while she was in this situation.

Drug running and bringing up a child didn't sit happily together, as the last twenty-four hours had demonstrated.

Sonja pulled off her clothes, piled them in a corner of the room and put on the gloves. She carefully decanted the cocaine powder into the eight waffle-mix tubs. The shortness of the time available to her was an advantage – the later the goods were packed, the smaller the chances were that the smell would work its way through. The smell of cocaine would eventually permeate every kind of plastic – enough to alert the sniffer dogs, at least, but it took time. If she were careful and ensured that there wasn't the slightest trace on the outside of the tubs, then it would take a good while for the smell from the contents to penetrate the thick plastic. And that was assuming the customs service had acquired new sniffer dogs.

She took the tubs with her to the shower, washed them carefully, then got out of the shower and put on fresh gloves to pack each one in a plastic bag. She strewed coffee in each bag and wrapped the whole lot up in clingfilm. She threw the pack of tubs into a tourist bag decorated with an image of Big Ben, packing a hotel towel and her coat on top.

It was almost one o'clock when she got in a cab to go to the station. She was going to be late, but it looked likely that she would catch her flight. She felt sick as the taxi moved off, so she wound down the window to take a breath of air. The aroma that swept in through the window was a mixture of food smells, exhaust fumes and an undertone of wet, rotting leaves, but beneath it all, on the cold air, she was able to make out a faint and hesitant hint of approaching spring.

106

Agla left all the talking to Elvar. She had nothing to say, in any case. María's visit the night before was still at the forefront of her thoughts, in particular the questions about her 'relationship' with Sonja, the piercing look of sympathy in her eyes, and the knowledge that María, and possibly others at the Special Prosecutor's office, had listened to her calls. When she thought back to all the times she had called Sonja drunk to alternately berate her and declare her love for her, Agla could feel the blood pounding in her face. She was sure it was bright red under her make-up.

Elvar sat behind a stack of documents, grown huge, now that they were close to the end of the long process. The investigation had been going on for many months and was now almost complete. Ahead was the Prosecutor's preparation for the indictment at the regional court. Elvar would see to preparing her defence.

Agla signed the papers Elvar passed to her, nodding in response to Inspector Jón's questions about whether or not she understood her status of defendant and all that it entailed. In fact, she didn't understand it all, but Elvar would explain the details later. She just wanted to get out as soon as possible and escape María's inquisitorial looks and the triumph on Inspector Jón's grinning face. Over the coming weeks there would be no statements to give, no questions to answer and no reports. On top of that, there was no need for her to go to work, plus there would be no Sonja to complicate life even more. It had been worth bringing that to an end before the whole world heard about it. Fortunately the Prosecutor's staff were bound by confidentiality rules regarding the status of the investigation, so nothing about her friendship with Sonja would find its way out.

To celebrate that there was nobody and nothing that she had to deal with anymore, and that there was little likelihood that anyone would have any business with her, she decided to stop off at the off-licence on the way home, stock up and shut herself away for a few days. She might even give Thorgeir's tame gorilla a call and get him to bring her something to toot. Her ego could do with something to give it a boost.

107

Bragi stood at the surveillance window and tightened the knot of his tie as he surveyed the escalators down to the arrivals hall. She had left the aircraft and he had watched her on CCTV as she walked along the corridor. She would appear on the escalator at any moment. He had been surprised to see that she was not as well dressed as usual – she was wearing jeans and flat shoes; and she had an air of urgency about her that he had not seen before. Having watched so many recordings of her arrivals in Iceland, he felt that by now he knew her well, and tonight there was definitely something unusual about her. She had pulled out her phone as soon as she was out of the aircraft and had taken the corridor almost at a run, moving noticeably faster than the other passengers. She had never done any of this before.

Bragi could feel his excitement building. The hairs rose on the back of his neck as she appeared on the stairs. It was time. Today was the day. Until now, he had fluctuated between a nagging conscience for having searched her so often, and his intuition that told him that this was a big fish. Now, though, that gut feeling, which he had thought was starting to fail him, was so strong, he no longer had any doubts. She was a serious player and it was time to catch her red-handed.

So as not to give her any opportunities for acrobatics with cases, he went out into the baggage hall and went straight towards her. She noticed him approaching when there were still a few steps between them; he saw her sigh, slumping like a punctured balloon. Her shoulders sagged and she dropped her handbag to the floor. She had clearly been expecting exactly this reception.

'Could I ask you to point out your case on the conveyor?' he asked, politely but firmly. Downcast, she acquiesced and pointed to an ugly sports bag emblazoned with London's most famous clock. Then she wordlessly followed him to the inspection room.

108

For some reason the officer wanted her to sit on the other side of the table this time. He made a meal of moving a chair to the other end of the room and placing it by the wall. Then he took up his position at the steel table, pulled on latex gloves and opened her handbag.

Sonja felt conflicting emotions. She was relieved that he started on the handbag instead of going straight for the sports bag, as that would delay for a few moments her inevitable crash landing; but she also wanted him to get it over with so that she could be released from this horrible tension. He was in no hurry, though; he took everything out of her bag and lined it all up on the table. He turned the bag upside down, shook it, unzipped the pocket on the outside and felt for anything that might be inside. Then he put everything back in the handbag, as unhurriedly as he had taken it all out, and put it to one side.

The sports bag was next. He glanced at her. Sonja was sure she could see the anticipation in his expression, as if he knew that this time he would pin her down. His expectation was well founded. For a customs officer, catching someone with six kilos of cocaine had to be like Christmas and a birthday rolled into one. He was an elderly man, the same one who had stopped her twice before. He had an air of discipline and a distant manner about him, but these were combined with a kindly face. He had to be close to retirement, Sonja thought, wondering if he had often caught people with this kind of quantity. He unzipped the sports bag, the cheap zip catching a couple of times so that he had to tug at it. Then he pulled it open and lifted her coat out.

'Coat,' he said, placing it on the table.

The hotel towel followed and joined the coat on the table.

'Towel,' he intoned in a voice so flat that Sonja wondered if they were being taped.

She looked around and saw a camera lens mounted in the ceiling directly opposite her. It struck her as strange that the officer stood with his back to the camera, blocking its line of sight to the bag and its contents. The officer peered into the bag where the tubs lay, carefully wrapped in plastic, lifting one of them out and holding it in a gloved hand.

'What do we have here?' he asked, without seeming to direct his question to Sonja; it was like he was talking to himself.

He took out a pocket knife and cut the plastic from one of the tubs.

His expression said that he had expected better of her, and Sonja had to admit that bringing in the powder in plastic tubs like any other hopeful coke-head was hardly something to be proud of.

This ugly sports bag with its picture of Big Ben would now undoubtedly be photographed from every possible angle both as evidence and as material for the TV news report. It was far from being her finest hour as a smuggler. The officer unscrewed the lid of the tub. He took a pinch of powder on the tip of his knife, took a plastic phial in the other hand, thumbed off the lid and tapped the powder from the knife into it. Then he squeezed the phial until a click was heard, shook it energetically and held it up to the light.

'Zero-zero-one says it's coke,' he said and looked at Sonja, who nodded in reply.

Her eyes widened as he wet the tip of a finger against his tongue, dipped it in the powder and put it in his mouth. She was sure officials weren't supposed to do that kind of thing. He rubbed the fingertip on the gum above his teeth and raised a questioning eyebrow.

'Pretty pure stuff, isn't it? I'm numb all the way up my nose.'

'Yes, it's not supposed to have been cut,' Sonja replied, and wondered when she should start asking to see a lawyer, and whether she should ask for Thorgeir or someone else.

'How much is there here?' the officer asked, putting on reading glasses to read the figures on the phial.

'Six kilos,' Sonja said.

'So you have the value of three or four city apartments here in this bag?'

'I suppose so. I've never thought of it like that.'

It was true. Sonja had never even wondered about the real street value of what she transported. She only thought of her share, never what happened to the drugs once she had delivered them.

The officer replaced the lid on the tub and put it back in the sports bag.

'Should I be asking for a lawyer now?' Sonja said, but he shook his head.

'Let's wait a moment,' he said. 'I want you to know, not that it matters all that much, that I'm doing this because I have to. Because my wife is seriously ill.'

He delved into his trouser pocket and handed her a folded sheet of paper. She took it and opened it out. It was a computer printout of a shift schedule with the name 'Bragi Smith' below the list of dates and times.

'You're Bragi Smith?' she asked, still unsure of what this all meant.

'I am,' he said. 'And I'm offering my services as a reception committee. In return for an acceptable slice of the cake.'

There was a long silence between them.

Sonja couldn't tell how long they stood without speaking in the inspection room, looking at each other. Both of them had doubt in their eyes, Sonja waiting for confirmation that she had misunderstood or misheard what he had said.

'What?' she said at last, simply because she was unable to find better words to express herself.

There was a rasping sound from the sports bag as he quickly zipped it closed. 'You're free to go,' he said, handing her the bag.

She took it, and waited, still unsure that she had heard correctly.

'Isn't there a recording of all this?' she whispered, pointing to the lens behind him.

'Not for long,' he said, going to the door and gesturing for her to come with him.

In a daze, Sonja followed him along the corridor, through a door and another room, and then through a second door, which led to the passage to the arrivals hall.

She was through, with all six kilos and with an open route into the country. She felt as if a gift had dropped into her lap.

She stopped outside the terminal building and drew a deep breath of chill air. She could feel an ache in her belly and her head felt numb.

109

'You'll have to pay him out of your cut,' Thorgeir repeated for the fourth time.

There was no doubt he was hung over, and the angry tone was the same as he had been using with her ever since she had threatened to bring the drug squad down on him.

'Don't you get how big this is?' Sonja hissed. 'There's an open route through Keflavík airport. I could bring in ten or fifteen kilos in a single trip.'

Thorgeir got to his feet and turned his back on her. He opened a small fridge in the corner of his office and took out a beer.

'What are we supposed to do with fifteen kilos all at once?' he demanded, still irritable.

'Well, why not? There seems to be plenty of demand.'

'That's exactly it,' Thorgeir replied. 'There isn't enough demand. It's not like it was before the crash. It's all about keeping regular customers happy and the cash flow steady. Then everyone's happy while everyone's happy ... and everyone stays happy,' he said, clearly too hungover to choose his words better. He popped open the can of beer and drank it down in one.

'Don't let the fact that you're pissed off with me ruin a good opportunity, Thorgeir,' Sonja said, using the wheedling tone that had so often worked on Adam.

For a moment she thought that it was having the same effect on Thorgeir, because he sat and stared at her thoughtfully.

'I know you have other carriers as well,' she said, 'and that spreads the risk, which I understand perfectly. But with this opening, using my contact, there's no risk. You can be certain of getting your gear, and everyone wins. I could take some of what the others are carrying for you.'

'You're such a fucking pain in the arse,' Thorgeir retorted. 'Do you really think the others don't have contacts of their own, their own ways of doing things? This customs guy of yours is nothing special. How do you know he isn't squeezing a cut out of every other mule?'

110

'There's one thing I need to ask you,' Sonja said. Bragi switched off the engine and turned to face her. 'Are there other mules you're taking cash from? Or am I the only one?'

'Mules?' he said. 'Is that what you are? A mule?'

Sonja shrugged. 'Mules, workhorses, donkeys. Does it matter what we're called? I'm in these guys' grip. I owe them and this is how I have to pay off my debt.'

'I see.' He took out a comb and ran it through his crew-cut grey hair. 'And no,' he said with a smile.

'No, what?'

'No, I don't have anyone else in this business. You're my one and only.' He grinned broadly.

Sonja could not help cracking a smile in return. 'The thing is,' she said. 'They say I have to pay you out of my cut, so it'll have to be a lot less than the figure you're looking for.'

'No chance,' he said sharply. Then his voice softened again. 'I told you I need the money. It's for my wife. She's very ill.'

'I'm sorry to hear it,' Sonja said, and she meant it. She genuinely felt sorry for him, although she knew that sympathy shouldn't be high on her list of priorities. But there was something about him that made her feel protective towards him.

They stared in silence for a while at the Öskjuhlíð woods beyond the car's windscreen. The frost on the branches had turned to grey, almost silver, in the last of the afternoon's light.

Bragi broke the silence. 'Have you spoken to the guy who makes the decisions?' he asked.

'I've spoken to the one who pays me,' she said. 'I don't know who the top man is.'

'So that's the way it is.' Above them a small Cessna aircraft could be heard coming into land, making its approach to the airport directly over the woods. 'That's Thorgeir Als, isn't it?'

Sonja was speechless for a few seconds. 'How ... How do you know that?' she stammered.

Bragi smiled benignly. 'It wasn't hard to figure out,' he said. 'So who's Thorgeir's boss?'

'I don't know,' Sonja said. It was something she didn't think about. As far as she was concerned, Thorgeir was the beginning and end of all her problems. He had been the one who had called her out of the blue to start with, pretending he could help her. It was him who had caught her in his trap, and now he was the one who called all the shots.

'In this business visibility only works one way, and that's downwards,' said Bragi. 'The man at the top will know who you are, although you don't know him. But you can bet he's someone big; the guy at the top always is when it comes to large amounts like this.' He started the car. 'If it's power you're after, then you need to look upwards.'

111

On her way home Sonja suddenly felt desperately hungry. In her mind she went through a list of everything that she could cook quickly and easily, and decided against every dish; she wasn't in the right frame of mind to buy food and cook it. She was starving and her body was crying out for sustenance, but there was nothing she had an appetite for. She also felt nauseous at the thought of all the fast food the city had to offer. Old-fashioned boiled food was what she really hankered after. Boiled fish with boiled potatoes and butter, the things that had epitomised the monotony of her youth, now appeared to her as symbolic of the kind of security she looked forward to. She turned off Miklabraut and drove back up the slope, into the cloverleaf intersection by the National Hospital and back onto Miklabraut, this time heading west, where she looped down through the narrow streets of the old town towards the harbour.

At the Sægreifinn fish bar she picked a catfish kebab from the chiller and could feel her mouth watering as the snack was grilled in front of her. As soon as it was in her hands, she didn't trouble to pull the chunks off in order to eat them with a fork, but ate them straight off the skewer. The fish was piping hot and the butter dripped from it down her chin. She paused only to wipe it off with the back of her hand as she devoured the fish like a hungry wolf with its prey. Her nerves were of steel, but stress always made her appetite go wild. As she came to the last piece and stood up to leave she began to feel very bloated. And she knew that now she had a momentous decision to make.

Her break for freedom had misfired badly and now she had to accept that the stakes had been raised. What Bragi had said was right, of course: Thorgeir wasn't at the top of the pile, there had to be someone above him. Bragi seemed certain of this, and she reckoned that he must know a good deal about this business. If Thorgeir were knocked out, though, she might find herself in a stronger position to negotiate with whoever his boss was. It had to be similar to the grievance process at any company – it always paid off to go to the top, to where the buck stopped. She had a weapon in her hands to make this a possibility: the kilo she had threatened Thorgeir with was still tucked away in her safety deposit box. She had to acknowledge, however, that there was a very real possibility that whoever was pulling Thorgeir's strings in the Icelandic part of the operation could well be even worse than him. And they might have someone worse than Ríkharður at their beck and call – even worse than José, perhaps, with an equally vicious beast at their disposal. She could find herself with a small army of gangsters on her trail – and on Tómas's too. But right now she could see no other way out. Bragi wanted his share, and with Thorgeir adamant that he wouldn't negotiate, the only option had to be to remove Thorgeir. She'd always thought she'd been caught in a snare; in fact it was a net, whose mesh pulled tighter around her the harder she fought to free herself.

As so often, her thoughts turned to Agla. According to the media speculation, Agla had stolen millions, if not trillions from the bank, siphoning it off to overseas tax havens. She had certainly always been offering Sonja money. Occasionally it had occurred to Sonja to accept it – take some ridiculous amount and then disappear out of the country, taking Tómas with her, leaving everything else behind and starting a new life.

But there were endless obstacles in the way of that plan – ones that she couldn't overcome. How could she tear Tómas away from life here in Iceland? She couldn't take him away from his friends, their language and the environment he knew so well. And there was his father. However much she wanted Adam out of her life, he was still Tómas's father and always would be.

She had taken her decision. It was time to take Thorgeir out and see what happened.

112

'Leave it to me,' he had said, and she had agreed. Now that they were in his car at their Öskjuhlíð meeting place, though, it was a struggle to let the kilo go. It was ridiculous, but Sonja felt that she was saying goodbye to her security. She felt as if the kilo of cocaine, which she had gradually built up by skimming a small amount from each shipment she had carried, was a pressure valve – an insurance policy she could always rely on if the worst were to happen. Every fibre of her being protested at placing it in the hands of a man she hardly knew. For all she knew, he could simply disappear with it and sell it himself, and that would leave her both empty-handed and just as securely trapped as she had ever been. Only this time she would have a furious Ríkharður and Thorgeir on her trail, with no clear escape route.

Sonja held on to the plastic box containing the kilo so tightly that her fingers whitened. 'How does it happen?' she asked.

'Just like I told you,' Bragi said gently. 'I have contacts and I can ensure that Thorgeir Als is raided once I've put this where it needs to be.' He pointed to the box in Sonja's hands. 'And then you'll be rid of him.'

'And Ríkharður?'

'Leave that to me. Ríkharður won't be bothering you for a while.'

His voice was so deep and reassuring, Sonja longed to lean on his shoulder and cry. There was something about the stone-grey hair and this deep voice that made her want to trust him, that gave her the feeling that he wanted to help her, when the reality must be that he was just another abuser, someone else who wanted a slice of her, who wanted her to do his bidding.

'It took a long time to collect all that,' she said. 'It's my insurance policy.'

Bragi nodded. 'I understand,' he said, and put out a hand.

Sonja pulled herself together and handed him the box. 'One more thing,' she said. 'Don't start anything until after three tomorrow. That's when Tómas will be with me. He's my little boy. We'll lock ourselves in over the weekend, so we're safe.'

Bragi nodded again.

As Sonja got out of his car she felt the earth tremble under her feet and for a moment it was as if she was floating on air.

113

'You mentioned that I should let you know if I heard anything about Rich Rikki,' Bragi said, as soon as he had taken a seat in front of Hallgrímur's desk.

'I did, and we both know why Rikki's rich,' Hallgrímur said, without looking up from the computer screen in front of him. This was the way they always did business: straight to the point.

'Let's say I've been in touch with Rikki,' Bragi said, his story well prepared so that even he couldn't tell the difference in his voice as he told the lie. 'Rikki pointed the finger at someone with a stock of merchandise stored away – Thorgeir Als.'

'Much?' Hallgrímur tore his eyes from the screen and sat up in his chair.

'He wasn't sure,' Bragi replied. 'But if the drug squad gets to work today, then there's a jackpot to be won. It might even be a big one.'

'I always thought Thorgeir was just a useful arsehole who got paid in coke for defending mules in court. Are you sure Rikki and his pals aren't just setting Thorgeir up to get rid of him?'

'I can't be sure. It's obvious that it's time Thorgeir was out of the game, but I reckon their quarrels mean you can score a big result if you knock on his door.'

'More than an amount just for personal consumption?' Hallgrímur said. 'It'll have to be if we're going to organise a raid and pull his house apart.'

'I think I can assure you there's more than enough there,' Bragi said. 'If you go in right away. Especially if you concentrate on the garage.' Bragi smiled.

Hallgrímur stared for a moment into the middle distance as he thought. 'Rikki doesn't want the news to get out that he spilled the beans?' he said, framing this as a question.

Bragi leaned forwards and dropped his voice. 'It would be appreciated if it were to be mentioned in the case notes – and for that matter even more widely – that Rikki was the one who grassed,' he said.

'So Rikki wants Thorgeir out, and you want Rikki out.'

'That's one way of putting it.'

'Hmmm.' Hallgrímur looked searchingly at Bragi for a moment and then nodded.

Bragi got to his feet and left without a word.

114

'He's so cute!' Tómas yelled over the pounding salsa music and his mother laughed. She never failed to be filled with joy whenever she had him to herself and every single thing he said or did would make her laugh. 'He's so soft and sweet, he does all sorts of tricks and can walk on his hind legs. And he's called Teddy.'

His mother took a couple of cha-cha-cha turns across the floor, and Tómas scuttled around her, jumped onto the sofa and waved his hands above his head. His mother grabbed him, lifted up his T-shirt and blew raspberries on his tummy as he squealed with laughter. Then he jumped back down onto the floor and took her hands, trying to follow her through a few salsa steps. When the tune ended, they both collapsed onto the sofa, giggling and sweaty.

'You're my favourite thing in the whole world,' she said.

'And you're my favourite,' Tómas laughed. 'You and the dog.'

His mother laughed and kissed his hair. 'You can choose what we have for dinner from the bags and I'm going to fix the door,' she said.

Tómas went to the kitchen and began rooting through the shopping. His mother had said they were going to spend the whole weekend inside and that they should buy everything they would need. So they had filled the shopping trolley with all kinds of food and snacks. There was so much, now Tómas wasn't sure what to choose for dinner. He put a tray of eggs on the worktop. Mum could make an omelette with mushrooms, as they had bought a punnet of those, and maybe they could have some spaghetti as well?

'Mum! Is it really crazy to have omelette and spaghetti together?' he called out to her.

He didn't hear her mumbled reply properly, so he went out into the hall and saw her kneeling by the door with screws between her teeth, fitting a large steel loop to the door.

'What are you doing?' he asked.

She dropped the screws from between her lips to answer him. 'I'm just trying to make the place more secure,' she said, picking up a bar to show him. 'This is the locking bar,' she explained. 'It's a lot more secure than a chain.'

She picked up a drill, plugged it in and began to bore a hole in the wall with a deafening noise. The drill was so big between her hands, and she needed to push with all her strength behind it. The dust flew from the wall and settled in her hair. Tómas felt sorry for his mother. Even though she said that she didn't need a man, one would have come in useful right now.

The moment the drill stopped, there was a knock at the door, taking his mother so much by surprise that she sat back on the floor.

'Hello?' she called through the door. She looked scared and for a moment the fear gripped Tómas as well. Was someone dangerous trying to get in? Maybe that's why Mum was putting this locking bar there.

His fear evaporated when he heard a shrill voice call out something unintelligible from the corridor beyond the door.

'It's the woman next door,' his mother said with obvious relief, opening the door.

The woman was wearing a dressing gown and holding out a plate. 'I just wanted to say thanks for fixing the computer. I really don't know what you did, but that machine is completely different now, so much better!'

'I just put more memory in it,' his mother said.

'Well ... you're so smart,' the woman sighed, and Tómas was filled with pride.

She proffered the plate again and looked at Tómas with a smile. 'I knew the lad would be here with you this weekend, so I thought cake would come in useful.'

'That's a lovely idea,' his mother said, taking the plate. 'Isn't it, Tómas?'

Tómas nodded his agreement and smiled at the woman, who blew him a kiss in return.

'My Tómas will make short work of a cake like this,' his mum said. 'Boys his age have hollow legs.'

'Tell me about it,' the neighbour said.

115

'How did it go?' Sonja whispered into the phone. Tómas was playing in the living room and she had shut the kitchen door behind her when Bragi called.

'Thorgeir has been arrested,' he replied. 'They're still searching his house but they've found enough to keep him in custody for a good while. Whoever is pulling the strings will have to get in touch with you themselves, now.'

'Can we be sure? What if nothing happens?'

'Just you see. Something will happen,' Bragi assured her in the deep, slow voice that she found so reassuring. 'There can't be that many bringing in a few kilos at a time on a regular basis. You're pretty important,' he added.

Important, her? That was a thought that had never crossed Sonja's mind. She had always seen herself as a tiny cog in a huge machine. Considering how Ríkharður and Thorgeir had treated her, she had felt she was just another worthless bitch in their eyes. But now that Bragi said she was important, she would have to trust her own standing. She wondered how long it would be before someone came to her. Probably not until there was a shortage of coke, then someone would tell her to go and get more. But maybe nobody would come calling; she turned the thought over in her mind. Perhaps there really was nobody behind Thorgeir and there would be no order for her to do another trip. That might free her from one snare, only to trap her in another – the customs officer would still want his cut. She could hardly imagine that he would go to extremes to get it, but she had no way of knowing what he knew about her. Maybe he had a recording from the inspection room, from the time when he had found the goods. If he did, though, it would look just as bad for him, so it was far from likely that he would use that against her.

The strange thing was that, when she examined her own feelings, she found she genuinely wanted to help him, because of his sick wife. Or was she kidding herself? Maybe she just wanted to do a different type of trip – one on which she could be sure of coming through customs safely, a trip with a moderate stress level. If she was honest with herself, she wouldn't like no stress at all – she relished the tension; probably more than was healthy.

'I'll let you know when anything happens,' Sonja said, ready to hang up.

'One more thing,' Bragi said. 'If you want to calm your nerves, you might pay a visit to a gentleman who is currently in ward three, section B5 of the National Hospital.'

116

'I want you to wait here for me for a little while. You can get something from the vending machine,' Sonja said to Tómas, handing him her wallet.

He nodded and sat down in one of the chairs in the lobby of the ward, rooting through her wallet.

'How much can I spend?' he called after her.

She turned. 'As much as you need,' she replied.

Tómas had a fascination with vending machines, and Sonja knew it wasn't so much the contents he was interested in as the process of putting in money and getting something in return.

Sonja pushed open the door to the corridor and reached for the dispenser on the wall whose label encouraged her to use its contents to clean her hands before going any further. Working the gel into her hands, she walked along the corridor, looking out for ward numbers. Ward three was opposite the reception desk, and as Sonja couldn't see any staff there, she went on into the ward.

The man was hardly recognisable as Ríkharður. His face was deformed by a swelling that completely hid one eye. A long slash along his chin had been sewn up, the stitches disappearing into the swollen flesh but leaving a distinctive pattern behind them. That would be a mighty new scar to add to the others on his face. Both his arms were in plaster up to the elbows, and it was difficult to make out if the blue of his upper arms was tattoos or bruises. One leg was fixed in a splint and suspended over the bed. Ríkharður emitted a low whine as she entered the room. Sonja was sure there was a look of despair in his one open eye.

'Well,' she said, leaning over him. 'Your mates all think you're a grass.'

He shuddered and said something that Sonja couldn't make out. She lifted the duvet and surveyed the battered body. He gasped as she leaned in close to his face and stared into the open eye.

'Now who's fucking with who?' she whispered.

It was malicious, she knew that. But she couldn't refrain from enjoying the moment, revelling in her power over this man she had once feared so much. The beatings, the pain, the humiliations and the terror he had caused her all came together in one hot pool of fury inside her.

'Now who's fucking with who?' she repeated.

She grinned coldly, long enough for him to see it, then spun on her heel.

In the ward's doorway a nurse gave her a friendly smile as if she was just another visitor. Sonja smiled back and strolled out into the corridor. She had taken herself by surprise. She had expected that the pitiful state of the man in the bed might have tugged at her heartstrings and triggered a touch of sympathy, but she had felt nothing of the sort. It was clear that the last few years hadn't made her a better person.

117

'I'm so sorry,' Agla whispered, her voice almost inaudible as she held onto the door frame for support.

Sonja had promised herself not to open the door to Agla ever again. But when she peered through the peephole and saw her standing there, it was as if that decision had suddenly evaporated. She unhooked the chain and lifted the bar. Tómas came running and a smile spread across his face as he saw her.

'Hi, Agla!' he said, his voice bright. 'Do you want to come and play?'

Agla glanced at Sonja, who looked away and said nothing.

'Not now, little one. I'm not stopping long.'

She reached out and quickly ruffled his hair as he turned and skipped back to the living room. Her awkward clumsiness never failed to soften Sonja's heart. The vulnerable sincerity Agla demonstrated in her relationships with people she was close to was diametrically opposed to the other parts of her personality – the dark plotting, the treachery and the role she had played at the bank, which Sonja could only read about in the papers with surprise. This contradiction was precisely what had sparked her love for Agla to begin with.

Let me be good to you,' she had panted in the toilets at one of the bank's annual parties, one hand deep in Sonja's knickers. They were both drunk, and neither of them had stinted on white powder. A week before, they had kissed, as if by accident. And since that moment Sonja had hardly been able to think of anything else. Agla had been too eager, too heavy-handed, in too much of a hurry to start with, but Sonja found this clumsiness exciting; it made her feel that she had become the most desired person in the world, a perfect goddess worshipped by a trembling and adoring Agla.

But now, as Agla stood leaning against the door frame, apologising, as she had a hundred times before, all Sonja could see was the source of all her misery. The whole chain of events played out in her head. If she and Agla had never met, then there would probably have been no divorce from Adam, so she would never have lost custody of Tómas. And therefore she would never have been caught in the snare. If she traced everything back, all her misfortunes could be laid at Agla's door. Or, to be more correct, it was all down to her own feelings for Agla; all Agla had been really looking for was sex. Sonja's mistake had been to fall in love.

'I can't do this, Agla,' she said, trying to make her voice soft but still determined. 'There are women who can give you what you want. But I'm not one of them.'

Agla stared. Her mouth opened as if she was about to speak, and then she turned and left. Sonja shut the door gently and took deep breaths to calm the turmoil within her. She waited for the feeling of liberation that had engulfed her the last time she had sent Agla away, but this time there was no such thing. Damn Agla, coming here and messing with her emotions, she thought. Damn, damn Agla.

118

'Pack your stuff, Tómas!' Sonja called from the kitchen as she poured yoghurt into a bowl for his breakfast. There was coffee in the pot, and she dropped two slices of bread into the toaster before opening the fridge to get some butter. She was determined to make the most of the last few hours with him before driving him home to Akranes.

It was still dark outside and Sonja shivered, reaching for the radiator and turning up the heating. The radiator hissed comfortingly as the hot water surged through it, and she put a hand on the warm metal to feel it heat up.

Normally Adam wanted Tómas home on a Sunday evening, but this time the boy had begged his father for another night. They had made the most of their extra time together, playing Mastermind and reading a comic in bed until Tómas had started to yawn. Now she wanted to enjoy the additional morning together, sitting by the hot radiator and sipping coffee as she watched Tómas consume his buttermilk, leafing through the paper for the cartoons. She hoped that, as he was going straight to school this time, he wouldn't be so upset to part from her as usual. This time they might be able to manage it without the tears.

'Why is Sponge in your picture and not in mine?' Tómas asked as soon as he appeared in the kitchen, waving a photograph in front of her.

'What do you mean?' Sonja asked, taking the picture from him.

It was the one that had appeared in her mail box one evening – the photo of the Akranes boys team, with Tómas kneeling in the middle of the row of nine-year-olds, Adam behind with the rest of the parents, and on the far left, Ríkharður.

'My picture's almost the same, but without Sponge. Why's Sponge in your picture?'

'Sponge? Who's Sponge?' Sonja felt her heart begin to race until she could hear a pounding in her ears.

'Sponge.' Tómas placed a finger on Ríkharður. 'Dad's friend.'

119

The buzzing in Sonja's ears was so loud, she hardly heard Tómas as he sat in the back of the car, chattering about his dog. It had all come together for her now. It was so obvious, but somehow she had been too close, too involved with everything to see the reality that stared her in the face. It had been there in front of her the whole time. Thorgeir and Adam had been at school together. Why had he called her out of the blue to offer to help her with the divorce? It would have been more logical for him to call Adam. She saw the reason for his lousy handling of the custody issue now.

It wasn't all her fault; it wasn't because she was a bad parent. It had to be because Thorgeir had been working for Adam all along. Sonja gritted her teeth, grinding them together. The tension that surged through her was physically painful. She put her foot to the floor.

'Mum! You're driving too fast!' Tómas called from the back seat as she overtook a fourth car as they passed Kjalarnes. 'It's ninety, remember.'

She relaxed her foot and slowed down, and Tómas became calmer, his chatter turning back to the dog – its smell and the games they played. Sonja nodded and muttered replies, pretending to listen while the storm of fury churned inside her.

And Ríkharður, AKA – the Sponge; Dad's friend, according to Tómas. He often came to visit, he had said. A really cool guy with tattoos and all sorts.

Sonja felt for her pay-as-you-go mobile and switched it on, waiting impatiently for the chime that would tell her it was awake. She scrolled through the messages and found the one that Ríkharður had sent the day Tómas had disappeared – the picture of himself and Tómas treating themselves to ice cream.

She passed the phone back to Tómas. 'Check the picture, will you? Is that Sponge?'

Tómas took the phone and looked at it. 'Yes, that's when we went to fetch Teddy. Dad said it was OK to have ice cream even though it wasn't Saturday.'

The tension in Sonja's body had morphed into exhaustion. Her fury had drained her of energy. Tómas had never been kidnapped, as Adam had led her to believe. The whole thing had been stage-managed to keep her under the thumb after she had threatened Thorgeir; it had been done to manoeuvre her back into the net.

'Mum!' Tómas called from the back seat. 'You just went straight past school!'

Sonja did a smart U-turn and brought the car to a halt outside the school. She got out, opened the rear door and absent-mindedly wrapped her arms around Tómas.

'Mum...' he began, and she saw the sadness that always accompanied a farewell cross his face.

'There, there. Be a big boy. Go to school and think what fun it'll be to see Teddy again this afternoon.' She handed him his schoolbag and pointed him towards the gate.

These agonising parting moments, along with all the pain of the last few years, had all been part of Adam's grand plan.

120

Sonja stood rigid as Adam opened the door. There were emotions churning inside her that she hadn't known she possessed. She opened her mouth to speak but could make no sound. She had been rendered speechless.

Adam glared at her, at first in amazement at seeing her there, then anger flashed across his face like a dark shadow, before his brows untied themselves and his mouth twisted into a smile. Sonja could see that he understood that she knew.

'How could you treat someone you once loved like this?' she said.

Her own tearful tone took her by surprise. She hadn't expected to be docile when facing Adam, so close was she to exploding with anger. But now the exhaustion seemed to have taken hold of her.

'It's horrible how love can turn into pure hatred, don't you think?' Adam grinned. 'How do you like being betrayed?'

'I ... I don't know what to say. I would never have suspected anything like this of you.'

Sonja's mind was in turmoil. Her emotions were in such a chaotic whirl, she could hardly control any of them. It left her feeling faint.

'Survival, my dear Sonja. Survival. I had to do something to keep myself afloat after the crash.'

Adam laughed and Sonja was struck by the thought that she had once found that sound attractive. It never failed to charm everyone nearby when it bubbled up. Now the sound of his laughter was painful and disgusting.

'What a great job you made of it, though. You took me by surprise,' Adam continued. 'It was a shock to find out that you had a talent for anything at all. You know, I was going to let you keep going until you were caught, and then Tómas and I would be free of you.'

The mention of the boy's name was the trigger, turning her exhaustion into sudden fury. She flew at Adam, her hands reaching for his face, but he caught hold of her and held her tight. She fought to escape his grip, and yelled so loud, he flung her away so that she stumbled, lost her footing on the icy ground and fell backwards. She landed in the wet snow, howling with rage, while Adam stood in the doorway and laughed at her.

'The funny part of it is – and it pains me to admit it – but you've become quite important. This pal of yours in customs that Thorgeir told me about looks like he could be really useful.'

'Don't imagine that I'll do a single trip for you, you bastard,' Sonja spat out.

'Yes, you will,' Adam said calmly. 'There are recordings of you taking payments from Thorgeir, and not just one or two, but every single time he's handed you cash. It wouldn't be pretty if Thorgeir were to spill his guts and tell the police just how much gear you've brought into the country.'

'I'm way ahead of you. I'm going straight to the police to tell them the whole story,' she yelled, taking out her phone and waving it as she struggled to her feet.

Adam came calmly down the steps, reached out and plucked the phone from her fingers, replacing it in her pocket.

'Stop this shit,' he said. 'I know you'll do anything for your weekends with the boy, and there are no Mum's weekends in prison. You'll keep doing business in return for one weekend a month.'

'One weekend? Not one weekend, Adam. There are two Mum's weekends every month.'

The tears flowed down her cheeks now.

'One weekend is enough,' Adam retorted. 'It's not good for Tómas to spend too much time with you.'

'Adam, don't do this.'

'We'll see,' he said. 'If you behave, then we might be able to go back to two weekends a month.'

'Behave?'

'Yep. You've shown what you can do. It's a pain to lose Ríkharður for a few weeks, but all the same, a little discipline will do him good. I'll pay your customs guy and you take six kilos on each trip. The next pickup's Copenhagen. I'll text you the address. I want it here at the beginning of February.'

'And if I refuse?'

'You don't have that option,' Adam said, reaching out and wiping a tear from her cheek. 'You'll just do what you're told.'

121

Bragi was up early and was waiting outside the nursing manager's office as she arrived at work on Monday morning. He had waited a long time for this moment and had every reason to do this early in the day.

'Is anything wrong?' the nursing manager asked, concern in her eyes as she shook off her coat and hung it on a hook behind the door.

'No,' Bragi replied. 'Quite the opposite. I bring some excellent news.'

'That's what I like to hear,' the nursing manager said, taking a seat and leaning forwards, elbows on the desk.

'I'm giving notice for Valdís,' Bragi said with a smile.

There was no smile in return. 'What do you mean, giving notice?' she asked. 'You mean you want her moved somewhere else?'

'No,' Bragi said. 'I'm taking her home.'

As he said the words the image he had dreamed of so often flew through his mind; he could almost visualise coming home to find her there. He'd kiss the top of her head and then just look at her. In their own home he'd gaze at her, his happiness.

'How? I don't understand how...' the nursing manager said, shifting awkwardly in her chair as she fumbled for the right words.

'I've arranged twenty-four-hour care. Three shifts to look after her.'

The nursing manager gasped in surprise and leaned back in her seat. 'Can I ask how this came about?'

'This isn't an idea that popped up overnight,' Bragi replied. 'Let's say that it's a while since I lost my faith in help from any direction. You live in the belief that your work is what will come to your rescue when you need it, and then your pension after a lifetime's work is hardly enough to cover your debts. You believe that the welfare system will look after you, but that works in its own sweet ways, which means, for example, that a couple find themselves separated.'

'In a case like this with Valdís—' the nursing manager began to explain.

But Bragi interrupted her. 'On top of that, you live in the belief that your children will be there when you need a helping hand, but when it comes to it you find that they're living on the other side of the world and only come back for a holiday every other year, and that's mainly so they can take their foreign friends around the Golden Circle. So that leaves you on your own. And that's when you realise that you have to do what's needed to sort things out.'

'If this is because of the issue with the bruising—' she began.

Bragi interrupted again. 'That's one reason,' he said.

'When you see to your wife's care yourself, you'll find that she bruises very easily. As I've told you many times, this is because of the blood thinner she has to take.'

'We'll see.'

'Might I ask how you're going to meet the cost of all this?'

'Let's say I've been lucky,' Bragi said. 'I've found a way to boost my income. Necessity is the mother of invention and all that.'

The nursing manager shook her head in disbelief. She leaned forwards and placed her elbows on the table again. 'I would urge you to consider this very carefully,' she said. 'Even when money is no object, it's easier said than done to have a patient with Alzheimer's at this level at home. Maybe some advice from an impartial source...'

'No, thank you,' Bragi said. 'The decision has been taken. Part of the living room is being converted for use as a room for her, and my application for home care has been made. Nursing staff will pay us visits to prescribe her medications and advise the girls I've employed to look after her.'

'Well...' the nursing manager said.

'Yes,' Bragi replied. 'Now I can at last enjoy our own home again.'

He could hardly stop himself from grinning as he left. He knew that he was taking a risk, and shouldn't have been so confident about giving notice for Valdís at the care home; it was still uncertain how soon Sonja would be active bringing in more shipments. But he had waited so long for this moment, he couldn't delay, knowing that she could once again be covered in bruises handed out by some clumsy fool. It wasn't acceptable that she should have to spend the last of her days living that way.

What was more, he had no idea how much longer she had left, so it was time to take a chance on the unknown.

122

By the time Sonja had sat in the car outside Tómas's school for an hour, she had reached a decision. Her thoughts had crystallised and she knew what she had to do; it was simple. Once her priorities had been lined up it wasn't so difficult to take a decision; her priority had to be Tómas. Her own vision of what their lives could become and the mental pictures she had painted for herself had become irrelevances – details, insignificant symbols, dreams that could never come true. The only thing of any importance was to secure Tómas's safety, and she was the only one who could do that.

She was still wet through from sitting in tears in the snow outside Adam's house, and her face was puffy after an hour of weeping in the car outside the school. But when she had finally dried her tears, it was as if the fog of indecision had been lifted. What she had to do now seemed simple.

This had to be an epiphany, she thought, watching her life flash before her eyes as if it was a film. She saw the mistakes, and how her own capabilities had been underestimated. She also saw the fear – the fear that had set the course for her life, not just over the last two years but always, going back as far as she could remember. Her whole life long she had been frightened of something, but now she was going to say goodbye to being fearful for good. It was something that wouldn't control her future.

She would have given anything to have not had to experience life in the snare, but the strange thing was that it had given her strength. She had discovered, having been compelled to do so, that there was more to her than she had ever suspected. Now she knew that she could look after herself.

Tómas still had his overnight bag with him at school, and it contained everything he needed – his passport included. She had reminded him how important it was to have it every time he came for the weekend. In reality she had spent months, probably from the moment she had been trapped, preparing for this day.

123

Tómas noticed right away that his mother seemed somehow absent; there was something peculiar about her when she came to collect him from school. She knocked on the classroom door so that the whole class looked up from their maths books as she peered in, checking that she had the right classroom. She glanced over and saw Tómas.

'I've come to collect Tómas. He has a doctor's appointment that we forgot to mention,' she said to the teacher, smiling, although Tómas noticed that there was something odd about that smile. Nevertheless, he packed his things in his bag and stood up.

'Will he be back today?' the teacher asked. This was a relief teacher who had been taking the class ever since Guðrún, their usual class teacher, had taken a tumble on an icy pavement and broken a leg. Tómas felt as if this teacher was almost a boy; he was so skinny and still had spots on his face.

'I don't expect so,' his mother replied. 'The appointment is in Reykjavík. It's an hour each way from here, so it probably won't be worth coming back afterwards.'

'OK. Bye, Tómas,' the teacher said, as Tómas mumbled his own farewell and followed his mother out into the corridor. He heard the teacher tell the class to get back to their work as the door swung shut behind him.

His mother took his coat and backpack off their hook and nodded towards his shoes.

'Am I sick, Mum?' he asked.

She looked back at him in a daze. 'What?'

'Why do I have to go to the doctor? Am I ill?'

Tómas wasn't happy with this sudden change to the usual routine. His weekend with Mum was over, and today he was supposed to walk home after school. While he was always pleased to see her, there was something weird about this. Maybe he was seriously ill and only his mother knew about it, which was why she was taking him to the doctor? Maybe it was cancer or diabetes, or even measles. That was something serious, the new relief teacher with the spotty face had said.

'Am I really ill, Mum?'

'No, you're not ill at all, my love. I'll explain everything once we're in the car,' she said, taking his hand and almost pulling him along the corridor and out of the side gate. 'Shall we run?' she suggested. 'Race you to the car?'

Tómas didn't need telling twice and took to his heels as fast as he could. There was ice in the schoolyard, snow trodden hard by hundreds of small feet, so he felt his feet slipping under him, and saw his mother was doing the same, sliding on the ice. But he didn't let it worry him and he beat her hands down in the race to the car. He couldn't understand why she had dared him to race, as she knew that he could run so much faster than she could.

Tómas took his seat in the car and his mother had already driven off before he had fastened his seat belt, so there was no doubt that she was in a hurry. Normally she was really strict about the car rules. They had to be late for the doctor.

'Am I going for an injection, Mum?' he asked, noticing that she had shot through an orange light that changed to red as they passed it.

'No, my love,' she said. 'We're going for a trip abroad. You do have your passport in your bag, don't you?'

124

Sonja had thrown a few clothes into a bag, booked the tickets and ordered a taxi. In a daze, Tómas watched her hurry around the flat, picking things up. His eyes were huge and questioning, and when she caught his eye, she was suddenly consumed by doubt and wanted to cancel everything. But this wasn't the moment for hesitancy. The decision had been taken, and she had to stand by it.

'I just thought of it all of a sudden,' she said, trying to inject some cheerfulness into her voice. 'It'll be so good for us to have some extra time together and take a holiday.'

She clicked the case shut, and pushed both the case and the boy out into the corridor, shutting the door behind her. She dropped the keys into her neighbour's mail box. She'd call her and explain; or, more likely, she'd make up some explanation.

Taking a breath so deep that it went all the way to her belly, she tried to appear calm. She was at the bank, and was longing to push the clerk who strolled so casually ahead of her down the stairs that took them to her safety deposit box.

When they finally got there, he unlocked it with the bank's key, and left the room while she opened it with her own key. She pulled out the tray and dropped the gold coins into her handbag, where they rattled to the bottom. Then she split the piles of cash into two – one of foreign currency and the other krónur. The stack of foreign currency was the fatter one; on that score she had made good use of every trip she'd taken overseas. She took five hundred thousand krónur – the maximum she would be able to change since the currency restrictions had been imposed – and would change that into dollars at the airport. She hoped to get close to four thousand dollars for it, but that would depend on the króna's exchange rate, which could fluctuate from day to day. She stuffed the rest of the money into an envelope and dropped it into her bag. She thanked the clerk then jogged up the stairs and out into the car park, back to the car where Tómas was playing a game on her phone.

She pulled up on the pavement next to the house. Even though the drive was empty, it seemed quicker to do it this way. This was one of the little terraced houses in the Smáíbúðir district, with a drive and a flower bed at the front, and a garden at the back.

Sonja took out the envelope full of krónur, fumbled in her bag for a pen and scrawled a message:

'There's not going to be any agreement. I hope this helps.'

She checked the plaque on the door to make sure it was the right place: Bragi Smith's house. She stuffed the envelope through the letterbox.

125

Sonja felt herself breathing more easily once they were through the security check at Keflavík Airport, although she constantly glanced around her. There was still an hour before the school day was over and Adam would realise that Tómas had disappeared. In the light of their conversation that morning, it wouldn't take him long to put two and two together, and figure out that Sonja had taken the boy. She wondered how quickly he would guess that she was taking him abroad. They would make it, she was certain of that. But all the same, her eyes flickered around the terminal and she held tight to Tómas's hand so as not to lose sight of him for a single moment.

The day had been a race run at breakneck speed, but now she was secure in the terminal and soon they would be in another hemisphere.

'Is this going to be a long holiday?' Tómas asked.

Sonja felt tongue-tied. 'A couple of weeks, at least,' she said at last, knowing that if she were honest, then she would have said that there was a good chance they would never come back home.

'Teddy's going to be lonely,' Tómas said.

Sonja gulped. She needed some tranquillity to get her bearings, to think through the last few days' events; some peace to evaluate her situation. Then she would talk to him. She would explain things in a way that he would understand. It was a little too much for a nine-year-old boy to take on board – that they were going to disappear in some foreign country.

'Can I have cake?' Tómas asked, looking up at Sonja, and she nodded.

They went to the counter at the café and Tómas inspected the cakes with care, as if choosing between carrot and chocolate cake was a momentous decision.

They were sitting at a table and Tómas was making inroads into the cake when her phone rang. Sonja checked the screen and saw Libbý's number. She wasn't inclined to take the call but Tómas looked at her questioningly.

'Aren't you going to answer?' he asked through a mouthful of cake.

Deciding it was best to keep things as normal as possible, Sonja thumbed the answer button and put the phone to her ear to hear '*Hi-i*' as only Libbý could say the word.

'*Hæ*, Libbý,' Sonja said, smiling into the phone for Tómas's benefit.

'You didn't show up at the Sewing Circle,' Libbý said, not even trying to hide the accusation in her voice.

'No, I didn't,' Sonja said. 'Something came up at the last moment.'

'Really?'

Libbý was clearly waiting for Sonja to pick up on her question and explain, but instead she kept quiet, leaving Libbý to continue. 'We girls have had a chat about it all, and we reckon that you're depressed.'

This time Sonja's smile was genuine. 'Is that so?'

'Yep,' Libbý said on the in-breath. 'It's typical behaviour for someone suffering depression to cut themselves off from family and friends.'

At one time Sonja would have responded with anger, but now she just laughed. It was clear that she was far more use to the Sewing Circle absent than present. That way they could discuss her to their hearts' content.

'I've even spoken to your mother about it,' Libbý continued. 'She agrees with me completely.'

'Dearest Libbý,' Sonja said warmly. 'I'm touched by your concern, but I'm fine. In fact, I'm feeling a lot happier than I've been for a long time. If anything, better than I've ever felt.'

She ended the call, opened the phone and took out the SIM. She snapped it in two and dropped it into an empty coffee cup on the next table. Then she reached across to Tómas's plate, took a chunk of cake and popped it in her mouth.

As the jet roared into the sky two hours later, Sonja closed her eyes. Tómas sat in the window seat with headphones on, absorbed in a film on the screen in front of him. Between them was an empty seat. She smiled as the wheels left the ground. A moment like this, in an Icelandair jet a few metres above the ground, was the closest she had found to real security for a very long time. She had Tómas with her, nobody knew they were leaving the country, and even if someone managed to figure out that they had taken a flight to Florida, it would still be no easy task to track them down.

She was determined to make as many dog-legs as she could on their journey, in order to throw off any pursuers. She hoped that sooner or later they would find themselves somewhere quiet, somewhere remote where it was cheap to live and where she could eke out her cash as long as possible. And when that was all gone, she could always seek help from Agla.

Agla.

Her heart lurched as Agla's face appeared in her mind. If only things had been different between them. If only Agla's problems hadn't been so overwhelming. She was even facing a possible prison term. Sonja sighed. Fleeing like this was a complete capitulation. All her hopes that things would work out with Agla and her dreams of being able to provide Tómas with something that approached a normal life in Iceland had been destroyed. She had hoped that her war chest would be enough for a down payment on a flat and that eventually she would be able to reach some kind of custody agreement with Adam. But that had been before she had found out how the land really lay, before she had discovered what kind of person Adam really was. Thinking back, she shuddered. All those times that she had consoled herself with the thought that Tómas was at least secure with his father had been a mis-conception. Nobody could be safe living in the house of a big-time drug dealer.

A few times the idea of taking Tómas and disappearing had occurred to her, but she had never been able to reconcile herself with the thought of depriving him of his father. Now that she knew the truth of the matter, though, the decision had been an easy one. Tómas shouldn't be brought up by a dope trafficker. She would disappear with the boy and they could start a new, simpler life for themselves, in a safe place, far from Iceland.

The aircraft shivered and the seat belt signs lit up. This was nothing more than the usual turbulence south of the Greenland ice cap. Once that was behind them, there would be many tranquil hours in the air, after which she would shepherd a sleepy boy and all those cases into a hire car and drive off into the Florida darkness, just as if they were going on an ordinary holiday.

Acknowledgements

For someone who writes in an ancient but dying micro-language the importance of being able to reach more readers cannot be described. There are only 340 thousand Icelanders, so the opportunity to be able to present one's work to a wider audience is rare and precious.

My thanks, therefore, go to all the people who have enabled the English-language publication of *Snare*. First of all, to the clever Quentin Bates, who translated the book; to my extraordinary editor, West Camel; and to my publisher, Karen Sullivan, who took a chance on me.

Last but not least, my thanks go to all the lovely people who have encouraged and supported me along the way. To those generous friends I say, *Takk*.